DELIVERED WITH A KISS

VETERAN MOVERS 4

MARIE HARTE

DELIVERED WITH A KISS
Veteran Movers, Book 4

Smith Ramsey knows all about hard knocks. So, when his newest client gets dumped by her boyfriend, he gets her an apartment in his complex.

Erin thought she'd been in love, but now she realizes what she felt for her ex in no way compares to what she's feeling for the tough ex-Marine who picked her up when she was down.

Actions speak louder than words. Smith's kindness and gentle core lay buried under old hurts. But can he forgive and forget the past to make a future with Erin? And is she making a mistake by trusting in love for the wrong man all over again?

VETERAN MOVERS SERIES

THE WHOLE PACKAGE
SMOOTH MOVES
HANDLE WITH CARE
DELIVERED WITH A KISS

Delivered with a Kiss
978164292-0406
Copyright © November 2019 by Marie Harte
No Box Books
Cover by Angela Waters Art, LLC

NEWSLETTER

Want to be FIRST to find out about new releases, excerpts, and sneak peeks? Get bonus content by signing up for **Marie's newsletter**.
http://bit.ly/MHnewsltr

CHAPTER ONE

"We're having a dinner thing and you said you'd come. Don't be late." The snarled order came loud and clear through Smith Ramsey's cell phone.

Sitting in a moving van parked in front of the client's home, Smith pulled the phone away from his ear and stared at it for a moment, wondering if he'd heard right, before responding. "First of all, I said *maybe* I'd come." If he didn't have anything better to do. Like stare at the walls until his eyes bled.

"We have shit to talk about. You know it, we know it. Don't be a pussy." Cash Griffith was Smith's older, meaner look-alike. They'd learned they shared the same DNA recently.

And a bigger asshole Smith had yet to meet.

"Seriously? That's your invitation?"

Cash swore again, creatively, before adding, "Look, just get your sorry ass to dinner so we can try to get along." He gave a long, drawn-out sigh. "I'll do my best not to bash your brains in when you piss me off."

"Do you even hear yourself talking? I know I'm not the smoothest when it comes to dealing with people—"

"You got that right."

"But even *I* know the difference between asking and telling, dickwad." Smith could all too easily envision steam coming from Cash's ears and smiled, feeling better about life.

"You have to come because I'm apparently annoying when I'm upset. Or so everyone keeps telling me," Cash muttered.

"You're always annoying."

To his surprise, Cash chuckled. "That's what Reid said."

Reid, their other brother. The one Cash had grown up with, the one who'd hired Smith in the first place.

"Oh, and Evan might be there with his girlfriend. Like I said. It's a family thing."

Smith suddenly found himself hip deep in relatives who wanted to get to know him. After a lifetime of not mattering to a mother who hated him and a tough time making friends, he didn't know how to handle this new togetherness. The Marine Corps had been his attempt at forging connections. But now, living in the civilian world, he had to deal with all the extraneous emotional crap that came from having a "family."

Frankly, it gave him a massive headache.

"Look, Smith." Cash sighed. "If you don't come, everyone will blame me. And I don't want to hear it. Seven tomorrow night. Don't be late." Cash disconnected before Smith could answer.

Huh. Now Smith apparently had dinner plans. If he didn't go, he'd end up getting badgered about it; he just knew it.

Smith *liked* being alone. He was good at it, and he enjoyed the fact that his stupid bosses—his brothers—hadn't assigned him a partner for the day's job. With any luck he'd lose himself in work and forget worrying over a dinner that didn't mean anything anyway.

Focus on the now, moron. This you can handle.

Today he'd used one of Vets on the Go!'s shorter moving vans to pick up the client's possessions from a storage facility. Mostly boxes with a few pieces of medium-sized furniture, enough to not quite fill a small apartment. Nothing he couldn't handle by himself. He had just arrived at the assigned address when Cash had called.

Smith sat in front of an older home in Capitol Hill, a decent enough area in Seattle, and waited for the client to meet him. He checked his paperwork and in Finley's barely legible handwriting managed to read *Aaron Briggs, 12:00.*

He tapped the steering wheel to the beat of heavy drums, content to let Fleetwood Mac's "Tusk" fill the confines of the moving van, the windows up to keep out the chilly, early October temperature. A study of the single-level home presented him with two small, wide steps leading up onto the porch to hurdle. Not bad. A glance at his dash showed the time had nearly reached noon, so he figured to head to the door and get this move on.

Before he could reach for the handle, the rumble of a car signaled its approach, and an ancient Jeep rolled to a stop in the home's miniscule driveway. A woman exited the car. On the small side, with long, dark hair that blew in the wind, she looked girl-next-door cute. She glanced his way, smiled, and waved. He automatically waved back, entranced by her happiness he could almost feel.

Those eyes packed a punch, noticeably gold in contrast to her brown-black hair. Hmm. His estimation went from cute to pretty, though he could only speculate on her figure under that long red coat. And totally not his business anyway, he told himself, though he gave the client props for having a hot friend.

Smith left the truck with his clipboard, and the brunette darted over to him.

"Hi. I'm so glad you're here." She took his hand in hers and pumped it like drawing water from a well.

"Ah, o-kay." He cleared his throat when she refused to let go of his hand.

She laughed. "Sorry. I'm just so excited to—oh wait." She hurried back to her car and let herself in to get something.

The front door to the house opened, and a blond guy who looked to be in his early thirties walked toward Smith wearing a frown. "Can I help you?" The guy had his jacket on and a carryall slung over one shoulder, as if he planned to go out. "I'm kind of in a rush." The frown darkened.

This was going to be one of *those* moves—the pain-in-the-ass kind. Smith could feel it. He bit back a sigh. "Aaron Briggs? I'm Smith Ramsey with Vets on the Go! I have your stuff."

The guy blinked. "What?"

The woman returned with a large duffel over her shoulder. "I'm Erin. You have *my* stuff," she told Smith.

He mentally berated Finley for writing down wrong information. Smith hated to be ill-informed. "Oh, right. So E-R-I-N Briggs?" At her nod, he struck the wrong name from the invoice and corrected it.

"Erin?" The man asked in a reedy voice. "What are you doing here?"

She dropped the duffel, squealed, and threw herself in his arms. "Cody, I'm finally here!"

Over her shoulder, the stupefied expression on Cody's face turned to one of horror.

Smith took a step back, anticipating the hot mess to come.

Cody pushed Erin away. "But...why?"

The joy on her face faded, and Smith felt a pang to see such pleasure snuffed. *Not my problem...* He glanced back at the moving van then at her and the immovable Cody. *Not my problem yet.*

Hell.

Erin frowned. "When we talked Friday night, you told me either I committed to you or we were done. I told you that I'd pack up right away and be here this week before I hung up. So, I'm here."

"Seriously?" Cody gaped. "I thought you were being sarcastic. That it was a joke."

"A joke? Cody, I packed up everything and had it shipped here over the weekend. I told you I was coming." She studied him. "You changed your hair since the last time I saw you. I like it." She looked so earnest as she leaned forward and took the guy's limp hand in hers. "I chose *you*, Cody. I left Kansas for good. I'm here now. Ready to move in." She glanced uncertainly at Smith and the moving van, then back at Cody. "Like you said. We either move in together and live happily ever after, or we need to go our separate ways, because being apart is too hard."

Cody pulled his hand from hers and ran it through his hair. The stylish cut looked as if it had been done at an expensive salon.

And the nice khaki's and pricey sweater he wore said he had an upscale kind of taste. Smith could see him and the woman together. Apparently, Cody couldn't.

"Well, yes, I did say you'd need to move out here. But I didn't think you'd actually do it."

A dark blue SUV pulled up behind the moving van, and a pretty blond woman stepped out, leaving the vehicle running. "Cody?" She took a good look at Erin, narrowed her eyes, then smiled back at Cody. "Honey, if you don't hurry, we'll be late for the meeting. And make sure you have your things for our dinner date this evening."

Erin's face lost all color. "Cody, who is she?" Erin faced the woman. "Who are you?"

"I'm his girlfriend. You must be the Kansas mouse."

Erin gaped, her eyes huge as she turned back to Cody.

Smith had to hand it to the guy. A smart man would have cut and run, but Cody stood there, looking like a dumbass, caught between his girlfriend and a woman who'd uprooted her entire life to be with him.

"Erin, I don't have time to go into this right now. I—"

"A girlfriend?" Erin's eyes welled. "You told me just *five days ago* that we could make our relationship work if I moved out here. But how can that happen if you already have a g-girlfriend?"

The woman sighed. "Cody, we don't have time for you and this... person." She sniffed and said in a loud voice, "Talk about trading up when you found me." She cleared her throat. "We have to go. Now."

Cody reached out to caress Erin's face. "Damn. Bad timing. We'll talk about this when I get back, okay? I'm sorry, Erin. You should have said you were serious about coming." He walked around her, ignored Smith as if he wasn't standing there, got in the SUV, and left.

Erin stared in shock, tears spilling down her cheeks.

Smith stood rooted in place, not sure what to do. He had a job to finish, but asking the woman what she wanted him to do with her things after she'd been shot in the heart didn't seem right. Fuck, but he *hated* emotional drama. A bunch of the guys at work—including Cash—were into reality TV where this stuff happened all the time. Not him, though. He'd rather have a root canal.

Just looking at Erin's misery twisted his stomach in knots.

She cried harder, her silent sobbing cascading into a waterfall of denial, confusion, and (deservedly) loud-ass grief. She seemed so small to be so loud. But he understood pain, knew all too well how it felt when life kicked you in the teeth.

"Ah, Erin? I, um—"

She crumpled to the ground before he could catch her, but to his relief, she remained conscious, seated on her knees on the lawn, a weeping mess.

He had no idea what to do. His inclination was to pick her up and carry her someplace warm and settle her down. But being so much larger than the woman, and a stranger at that, he didn't want to intimidate her in any way.

He crouched by her and set the clipboard down, then gently tapped her shoulder. "Erin? Are you okay?" Clearly, she wasn't, but damned if he knew what to say at a time like this.

She sniffed and stared up at him. Her eyes shimmered like gold, her expression painful to see. "Why? Why would he tell me we could make things work? Why say that if he didn't want me to come out here?" She blinked, and fat tears rolled down her cheeks. "I gave up everything for him."

Smith couldn't take it any longer. She looked so pathetic and uncomfortable on the ground.

He sighed, drew her close, and stood with her in his arms, her light weight negligible. Erin clutched his neck and sobbed into his chest. Smith wanted to find Cody and pound him into human hamburger.

He held Erin close and lied that everything would be okay as he took her to the truck and placed her in the passenger seat. Then he took a step back, not wanting to crowd her.

After a few shuddering breaths, Erin took a packet of tissues from her jacket pocket and blew. She sounded like a foghorn.

Smith looked away. Her sadness wasn't funny, but damn, for someone so tiny, she could make some noise.

He cleared his throat and glanced back at her, watching her try to compose herself. "You okay?"

"I-I don't kn-know." She clutched the tissue in her hand and, between the hitches in her breathing, asked, "Did I r-really give up my apartment and friends and m-move all the way out here for my boyfriend, who already has a girlfriend?"

"Seems so."

She looked down, her misery tangible. "I mean, w-we just talked about our relationship this past Friday. He…" She paused and seemed to catch her breath, because her next words were more even. "He told me we needed to commit or break it off. He's been upset that I refused to move out here. So, he gave me an ultimatum. And I took it." She blew her nose again. "I don't know how he can possibly be confused. I told him I loved him enough to move out here. And I wasn't being nasty or anything. I don't think I sounded sarcastic. I'm not a sarcastic person, honestly."

"He sounds like a dick."

She blinked up at him.

"I mean, he didn't once apologize at all for your trouble. Just left for some stupid meeting while you're standing there, all the way from freakin' Kansas." Yeah, total dick move any way Smith looked at it. "And he sure as hell didn't try to explain away his girlfriend. Look, I just met the guy. But it's obvious he and that blond are tight. How come he never mentioned her when he was begging you to move out here?" *And none of this is even remotely your business. Shut up, Smith!*

"Yeah, that's right." To his relief, she started to look angry instead of sad. Maybe he'd been right to chime in. "He didn't think I'd come out here. So probably that ultimatum about rooming together was a lie. He wanted to blame me for us breaking up so he could cover the fact he had a girlfriend."

"Seems so." Pleased she seemed to be done with the crying jag, Smith took another step back. "So where do you want me to take your stuff? You're not staying here, are you?"

"No way." She glared at Cody's house, and he wondered what she envisioned. Her ex's head mounted to a wall? Maybe her foot up his ass? She didn't speak, and he figured she probably needed a moment to herself.

Considering he was never this friendly with customers, he blamed his chattiness on the sight of a woman in need. Though Smith thought of himself as enlightened, old habits were hard to shake. The one good thing his so-called mother had taught him was to always respect women. But maybe he should respect the fact that Erin could take care of her own mess, and he should finally shut his fat mouth about her business.

Deciding to do that very thing, he was about to ask for new directions when she started talking. And talking. And crying again.

"I broke my lease. I left Kansas behind. I ignored my parents, my sister, my friends. They all told me I was foolish to come here. That he'd break my heart." She wiped fresh tears away and met his gaze. "That I'd never make it on my own."

Wow. Hadn't he heard *that* his whole life. "So, prove them wrong."

"How?" She sniffled. "I spent nearly everything I had to get that express moving service. Everything I own is here. I can't afford to move it back, let alone find a place to live. You know they all demand security deposits up front. And it's expensive here. I googled the cost of living in Seattle."

"There are cheaper apartments outside the city. And some even in the city if you know where to look." He paid dirt cheap for his place. But then, he also served as the building handyman for his crotchety landlady.

"That I can find today?" She blinked rapidly and wiped her cheeks. "I have a truckload of things I need to put somewhere. And storage takes money. Hotels take money. New apartments take money." She stared crying again. "Food takes money."

He wrestled with an idea, driven by the need to help her. And not just because she was a pretty young thing who looked vulnerable. Hell, she didn't just look it. She *was* vulnerable. All alone in a new city? Christ, had she said she was from Kansas? "Wait here." He walked away, taking his phone out. He made the call and had to promise to throw in changing the oil on Tilly's car. But…just maybe…he had a solution for the poor woman.

Smith returned to see a bunch of crumpled tissues on her lap. Then he remembered how much he hated people, didn't trust women, and how much nonsense he had coming his way on account of his recently acknowledged siblings.

He hesitated, not sure he should offer Erin anything but a compassionate "you're better off without him" and a good-luck handshake.

"I'm so sorry for all this," she apologized, her cheeks flushed. "None of this is your fault, and you had to watch me make a fool of myself. I know you have a schedule to keep and a job to do, and I'm in the way." She let out a sad sigh. "Boy, did I mess up royally."

"No shit, attaching yourself to that loser," he muttered then froze, not having intended to say that out loud.

Her lips parted, and he had the insane notion he'd never seen a more perfect mouth in his life. "I…oh." Her slow smile told him he hadn't hurt her feelings. "Cody is a loser, isn't he?"

"Totally." He ignored the odd racing of his heart.

She blew her nose again. Her mascara had run, her eyes looked puffy, her nose red, and wisps of her hair now framed her face in a frizzy kind of halo. She might be cute, but she was an ugly crier. So why did he find that even more attractive? Man, he was an imbecile for sure.

Smith shrugged, ignoring his weird, inappropriate feelings. "So what now? Do you have someplace you want me to take your things? Any friends in town? Relatives?"

She shook her head. "Nope. I'm all alone out here. I thought Cody and I would make friends together. That he'd be my f-family." She cleared her throat, took a deep breath and let it out. Her tone evened. "But I guess that's over. I'll have to max a few credit cards and put my things back in storage before I can make enough to ship everything back home."

"Or you could move into a rental that's recently become available."

Erin stared at the scowling giant, not sure she'd heard him correctly. "Huh?"

He flushed, but the scowl didn't disappear. For the entire time she'd known him, roughly forty minutes, he'd done nothing but frown, glare, or look expressionless. Exceedingly handsome under the bluster, her tall, dark, and sexy moving man was seriously built.

He stood a solid head and a half taller than her own tiny stature. He had a rough edge of handsome going on, that short dark hair contrasting with his jade green eyes. A tan skin tone told her he spent time outdoors, as did the rough hands that had held her close to that warm body. Smith Ramsey was tall and muscled. Solid. And a lot menacing, if she told herself the truth.

That glare he wore would have scared her if she hadn't witnessed how gentle he'd been moments ago. How he'd taken care to make her more comfortable and tried to bolster her spirits. The poor guy likely wanted nothing more than to put this entire experience in his rearview mirror.

She sure the heck wanted to.

"I said there's a rental that recently became available. I know because it's in my building—Emerald Estates." His scowl seemed to deepen, were that possible. "I'm serious. It's a decent enough place. Not super fancy, and the unit is an efficiency. It's a steal, but it comes with conditions."

Here it comes. She might be a little naïve when it came to living independently. But she'd had to deal with unscrupulous men before. Not counting Cody. She sniffed to hold back more hurt, angry tears.

Disappointment rose, that this stranger might try to take advantage of her, especially having seen her boyfriend dump her. Could her day get any worse?

"The only reason I get a cheap rent is because I do all the handyman stuff in the building," Smith said. "The landlord is a pain in the ass old lady who likes bossing people around. But she's more than fair. I fix everything that needs fixing, she cuts my rent in half. We just had one of the tenants move away to be with family. Mrs. Fine was ninety-four and left because she needed live-in care. So, it's my job to clean out her unit. If you wanted, you could have it, but you'd have to clean it up first."

Erin blinked. "Really?" This was the answer to her current dilemma. "What kind of rent are we talking?"

"I think Mrs. Fine paid near to what I did. She didn't have much money. You need to talk the rent over with Tilly. Like I said, it's an efficiency."

It wasn't as if Erin had much to move, and she didn't plan on staying in the city, she didn't think. Just long enough to make enough money to leave again with her feet under her. "Where is it? Is it in a safe neighborhood?"

"Surprisingly, yes. It's in Greenwood. And to be honest, you can't touch a place in Greenwood for even half that kind of rent. Not unless you know somebody."

"It seems too good to be true." She looked at Smith, feeling hope for the first time since arriving at this mess in her life.

"Well, it is." He rubbed the back of his head. "There's always a catch. Tilly—the landlady—she's a ball buster. And she needs help. Her cook just quit. So, if you want the place, you have to clean it out first. And you have to work for free as Tilly's cook and housekeeper."

To offset the rent, that seemed more than fair. "But what if I can't cook?"

"I'd suggest learning fast if you want the place." He paused. "I like the old lady, but she's gone through a lot of helpers in the past six months. She's hard to get along with, I won't lie."

"But you work for her."

"I like my place, and I've dealt with a hell of a lot worse." He frowned. "But she might be too much to handle. You seem kind of nice."

"I am. *Too* nice." She shook her head. "But I need a place to live. Do you think she'll want a deposit up front? I can't afford that right now."

Smith shrugged. "No idea. But she can tell you what she wants. If you're interested, we'll drive over right now and see what's what.

I've got your things, and you have nothing to lose. You in or out?"

She glanced at Cody's home—it was not now and never would be hers—and turned back to Smith. "Let's go."

She wouldn't look back. No matter how much it hurt.

CHAPTER TWO

*S*mith sat on an ugly couch in the living room of his oldest brother's house and did his best to pretend it wasn't crushing him second by second to be anywhere near reminders of the woman who'd given birth to him. Angela Griffith had died a few months ago and left her house to Cash, not Reid. A situation that nagged him with curiosity, but one that he had no right to ask about unless he wanted to open up to the two of them.

The discomfort of grief he had no business feeling weighed heavily, so he did his best to focus on anything else. And the one subject that continued to come back to him made him hide a small smile.

Erin Briggs.

He'd introduced her to Tilly yesterday. The old lady had told him to wait outside her apartment and slammed her door in his face. Twenty long minutes later, Erin had stepped out of Tilly's apartment looking shell-shocked. But she'd accepted Tilly's terms and asked him to move her things into Mrs. Fine's living room. He'd left it stacked with boxes and a few dressers, sparingly little to fill up the place.

Overwhelmed and annoyed with Erin's effusive gratitude, he'd hustled away before she teared up again or worse, made him want to offer comfort, which still baffled him. Smith didn't take to strangers and generally didn't like people. What the hell had he been thinking to help Erin into anything but a plane trip back to Kansas?

He burned to know what Tilly had said to convince Erin to stay and planned to take it up with the crank pot later, when he wasn't so glutted with "family."

"So, you're more quiet and morose than usual." Jordan Fleming, Cash's girlfriend and Smith's coworker, plunked down in the chair near him and guzzled from her beer bottle.

Smith liked her. Jordan was real. An ex-Army MP who didn't tolerate anyone's shit, she'd taken him down once for talking smack. He respected her for it. At one time he'd considered asking her out. She was cute in a rough-and-tumble kind of way. But even then he'd seen something sparking between her and Cash. Though it would have amused him to fuck with the guy, he didn't want to hurt Jordan.

He snorted. "Do you get bonus points for using a word like 'morose'? I didn't think you Army types knew how to read."

She smiled through her teeth at him. He bit back a grin; it wouldn't help his cred to look amused or happy being anywhere near his brothers and their girlfriends.

"You're really giving me crap about being stupid? You're a Marine. I thought you guys walked around grunting and dragging your knuckles on the ground."

He glanced up as Cash entered the room. "Well, some of us fit that stereotype, sure."

Cash grunted.

"See?"

Jordan coughed. "Um, well, ah, what's up, Cash?"

He glared at Smith, who glared right back, before answering, "Something's beeping in there, and you told me to keep my hands off your food."

"I didn't hear anything."

"Well, maybe because I accidentally knocked the timer into the sink."

She frowned then jumped up from the chair. "Oh, the chicken." She rushed past him, shoving Cash in Smith's direction on the way. "Be nice," she growled and disappeared into the kitchen.

Smith just sat, staring at his brother.

His *brother*.

He'd grown up thinking he was an only child, the product of a questionable accidental pregnancy, according to his ex-mom, Margaret Ramsey. Good old Meg had never liked him, and up until eight months ago, he'd never understood why. A petite blond with ice blue eyes, she didn't look much like Smith. Brittle and angry all the time, she loved nothing more than to tell him he'd never measure up. Never be as good as his amazing, successful, hard-working cousins.

No matter how hard he worked or how he tried to make her love him, he failed. With his father supposedly dead, he'd had no one but his mother in his life. And yeah, he did blame her for his fucked up inability to make friends.

Then to learn she wasn't his biological mother? That his "real mother" had raised his perfect brothers—not cousins—the good sons she'd loved and adored? The ones she'd *kept*?

Was it any wonder he'd hated Cash and Reid on sight?

"It's so weird how much we look alike," Cash muttered and took a seat farther from Smith than the one Jordan had occupied.

"Yeah, I don't like it either." Smith and Cash might as well have been imprinted from the same genetic cookie cutter. Same dark hair, same green eyes, similar facial features and brawn. "But I'm taller than you."

"You are not." Cash frowned. "I'm six-four."

"I'm six-five." Smith smirked.

Cash's frown grew darker. "I can bench more than you."

"Yeah?" The need to prove himself returned full force, a lifetime habit of always having to be the best and never managing it thanks to the Griffith brothers. "Let's see."

"I don't have any weights here." Cash took a swig of his beer then lit up with pleasure. "But I bet I can out-arm wrestle you."

"Bring it."

They cleared the coffee table and knelt over it, facing each other. Smith didn't want to but gripped his brother's hand as he rested his elbow on the table.

God, even their hands were about the same size.

Cash didn't seem so pleased by the contact, which made him feel a little better.

The big douche looked him in the eye. "When I say go."

"Hey, watch your elbow. No cheating."

"Fuck you. I don't need to cheat to win."

Smith raised an eyebrow but said nothing, and Cash swore at him some more before counting down. "In three, two, one…"

They had four matches, all of which proved difficult to win. Smith was sweating when someone entered the room, but focused on the battle, he spared them no attention.

With the matches evenly won, two for Smith and two for Cash, this one would decide the ultimate victor.

"Oh my God. Are you two serious?" Reid asked as he stepped forward. Next to him, Naomi, his girlfriend, whistled.

"Wow. Two sexy, muscled men battling it out. Reid, you didn't say we'd have live entertainment."

Smith strained, annoyed Cash seemed to be as strong as he was. Reid's arrival in no way hampered their bout. Both men continued to press for the win.

"I will end you," Cash warned. "I am the ultimate champion."

"You sound like a bad movie," Smith growled.

Cash, the bastard, laughed. "Been watching *Gladiator* and *300* with Jordan. She has a thing for sweaty men who kill each other."

"Cash Griffith," Jordan barked. "What the hell are you doing?"

Cash winced, and his moment of inattention was all Smith

needed. Smith used extra effort and pushed. Hard. Cash went down.

The room grew silent.

Cash stood and glared down at Smith. "You cheated."

"What?" Smith stood as well and took a healthy drink from his bottle. "Not my fault you couldn't keep up." Man, the guy had power behind all those muscles. Smith wanted to flex his cramping hand but didn't want to show any sign of weakness.

"Bull. You—"

Jordan said his name again, and Cash stilled.

Smith watched with appreciation. Jordan had the guy on a tight leash. He liked it. He smirked at her. "Does he sit on command too?"

The old Cash would have lunged for him, but this Cash smiled through his teeth. "I do whatever she wants. And if, by the grace of God, she asks me to rip off your head, I'll do it with pleasure."

Reid chuckled. "That's some kind of power you have, Jordan."

"And some kind of ability with food." Naomi took an appreciative whiff. "What is that wonderful dish I smell?"

Jordan smiled. "Garlic chicken. I have mashed potatoes and carrot souffle too."

Naomi sighed. "I'm starved, and that sounds fantastic."

Smith watched her, keeping his distance. Unlike Jordan, whom he understood, Reid's girlfriend remained a puzzle. Naomi Starr had looks, class, and a brain. She seemed kind of distant, as if too pretty and better than everyone else. She fit Reid in that way.

Reid had an elegance about him. The guy was upper management all the way. Sophisticated and brainy, he wore khakis and button-down shirts all the time and looked right at home in them. While Cash and Smith did manual labor and liked it, Reid seemed to prefer sitting behind a desk.

The Griffith brothers shared the same dark hair and height, but Reid had gray eyes and a more streamlined build. Not so broad in the chest or packed with muscle. And of the two of them, Reid was by far the more laid back, easier to get along with.

Yet Reid and Cash had grown up together, tight brothers who loved and respected each other.

Something Smith had never, and would never, have.

"Oh, and I brought dessert," Naomi claimed and held out a covered pan to Jordan. "Chocolate cake."

"Yum."

"I hate chocolate." Smith's confession had everyone turning to him. Probably shouldn't have mentioned that out loud. Yet everyone acting all schmoozy and as if his being present didn't bother them annoyed the shit out of him.

"That's not humanly possible." Naomi looked dumbfounded. "It's chocolate."

Reid gave him a look and said to Naomi, "Everyone has their own taste, honey. But I'm sure he'll try a piece just to be polite."

The subtle warning made an impact, and Smith flushed, feeling like a bratty kid told to behave.

Smith shot Reid a look. "I'll shove a piece of your—" *ass through the wall, you dick*, went unsaid as Evan's timely interruption saved the gathering.

"Hey, we're here. Sorry we're late." Evan and Kenzie breezed into the living room with wide smiles. "We had to drop Daniel off at a friend's and got caught in traffic."

Smith liked Daniel, Kenzie's younger brother. The kid was scary smart, obnoxious, and funny. They'd met back when Evan had started dating Kenzie, because Evan had been working alongside Smith and the others while Cash healed from a broken arm.

Hmm. Should have arm-wrestled the other arm. He glanced at Cash's weak hand and saw Cash staring at him.

"Bring it," Cash mouthed.

"Anytime," Smith mouthed back and grinned. Cash grinned with him, and at that moment something clicked. A feeling of camaraderie. Smith immediately backed away from it and scowled at the guy.

Kenzie stepped into his line of sight, smiling and exchanging hugs with everyone while Evan greeted the gang. Smith had a soft spot for Evan. Technically, they weren't related by blood. Evan's dad and Reid's dad were brothers. Yet Evan was the cousin everyone liked and wanted around. He did Vets on the Go!'s financials, was a CPA, and filled in when anyone needed a hand. It was tough not to like the guy. He seemed to charm everyone, including Smith.

To the extent Smith had been bamboozled into calling Evan's mom Aunt Jane and sharing a dinner with Evan's family. The experience had been eye-opening, because even knowing who Smith really was, everyone had been accepting and fun to be around. Kenzie and Daniel in particular had talked to him, while Aunt Jane mothered him with Evan watching on in kind amusement.

MARIE HARTE

So strange that they'd taken to him and that he'd…liked it.

"Hey, Smith." Kenzie hugged him, and he couldn't help smiling down at her. Man, was she pretty, especially glowing with happiness. In a way, she reminded him of Erin.

Once again, the thought of Erin made him want to smile.

She took a step back, and he gave her a gentle pat on the shoulder. "I see you're still pretending to be Evan's girlfriend. That pity date really spiraled out of your control, huh?"

She laughed, and Evan rolled his eyes.

Smith smirked. "When you get tired of him, you know my number."

"Yes, you're on my speed dial."

Evan chuckled. "For when we need someone to watch Daniel. He's still in awe and fear of you. It's the fear we need to keep him in line."

"I like Daniel." He paused to note Reid and Cash staring at him in surprise. "What?" he barked.

"Just didn't realize you could do more than growl and snarl at everyone," Cash offered.

Smith shot him the finger, and Reid grinned. "See, now that's the Smith we know."

"And love," Jordan added with a wink his way.

That shut Cash up fast.

The evening progressed as they ate a delicious meal. Wisely, they'd put Smith next to Evan at the end of the table. He mostly kept his mouth shut, eating his second helping with pleasure. He

24

could see what Cash saw in Jordan. Besides kicking ass and looking fine, the woman could cook.

Evan elbowed him in the side. "You awake?" he asked in a low voice. The others were laughing about something Reid had said.

"Yeah. Why?"

"You haven't said much."

Smith shrugged. "Not much to say."

As if he'd asked for the attention, a laughing Reid turned from Naomi to regard him with a hint of caution. "So, Smith. What do you think of the company and where we're headed?"

Uncomfortable with being in the spotlight but not allowing it to show, Smith thought about his answer. "Aside from Cash being an ass and you catering to his immature behavior, I'd say the company is doing all right. People seem to like us, and Evan has filled in as best he could."

"Thanks so much," Evan said drily.

"Could you be more specific?" Reid asked. "Not about Cash being an ass, but about the daily workings of the company. I like to know how things are going from another perspective."

"From an outsider's perspective, you mean." Finally. It was almost a relief to have them come out and speak the truth. All this togetherness crap had been wearing.

Cash frowned. "If that's what he'd meant to say, he'd have said it."

Reid put a hand on Cash's shoulder. "I *meant* from someone newer to the company. Evan's been good about letting me know how he thinks we can improve. But his ideas always revolve around our bottom line. You're more of an operational kind of guy."

"So's Cash. So's Jordan, though she's probably brainwashed to say whatever Cash thinks."

Reid spoke before Jordan or Cash could argue. "I've already talked to them. Now I'm asking you what you think. Don't be afraid to tell me the truth."

Smith bristled at any notion he might be scared. "Fine. The crew does a good job of getting organized. Sometimes we get confusing info on the clients though. Finley and Dan occasionally get details wrong. And I don't like that. You should let the moving crew call the client to confirm the details before we go on a job."

"Noted. What else?"

Smith wanted to have something else to complain about. But honestly, Reid had a good company staffed with excellent veterans. Despite most of them being from services other than the Marine Corps, Smith found himself respecting if not liking them. Even Funny Rob, an Air Force dweeb who wasn't all that funny.

"Well," Smith added, "Cash could probably work a little harder. I know he's nursing that healing arm, but he seems to pair himself with the harder workers so he can slack some."

"Asshole," Cash snarled. "That's totally not true."

"Well, it's a little true." Jordan shrugged. "Hey, you always end up with either Lafayette, Hector, me, or Heidi."

"See?" Smith sat back and let the fur fly.

"But that's because you guys annoy me the least of the team."

Cash glanced at Smith and sneered. "I work with him, I spend most of my day trying not to put his head through a wall."

Smith snorted. "As if you could. Though with Little Army, you might have half a shot."

Jordan tried to hide her smile. They all called her Little Army because she was small but tough. The chick had a set of guns on her too, as she liked to point out when trying to out-flex Cash. Yeah, Smith had to admit there were worse people to work alongside than the gang at Vets on the Go! They'd all served their country, knew the sacrifices that came with military service, and still worked hard, pulling their weight.

If he didn't necessarily get along with all of them, well, that was more his fault than theirs. And he knew it. But damn if he would admit it to anyone other than himself.

"Your people get the job done," he said to Reid, ignoring Cash. "What more do you want to know?"

Out of the corner of his eye, Smith saw Cash frown. Whatever. He didn't like the guy, never would, and didn't see the point of continuing trying to get close.

Maybe this was a good time to leave. "You know, it's time for me to—"

"Cake," Naomi cut in. "Who's ready for dessert?"

Before he could blink, the table was cleared and the cake set in the middle, served up on smaller plates. Jordan and Cash left and reappeared with coffee and cups.

Smith did his duty and took a plate of dessert. He ignored Naomi watching him as he took a small forkful. As expected, the cake wasn't to his taste. But to keep the peace, he pretended to like it.

She beamed at him. "I knew if you gave it a chance, you'd like it."

He pushed it around on his plate, hoping the mushed part made it look as if he'd eaten more than that one bite. Thankfully, that seemed to make Reid happy as well, and talk returned to people they knew and funny stories from Naomi's latest public relations client. He continued to push around the chocolate mess on his plate, wondering when he could leave without hearing a ration of shit about it.

"Uh oh. It's time." Naomi stood and pulled Kenzie and Jordan with her. "Let's go, girls." They grabbed coats and purses and left before Smith knew what the hell was going on.

When he saw the others watching him, he stood. "Time for me to go too."

Evan sighed. "Smith, stop avoiding the elephant in the room."

"Cash? I've talked to him tonight."

"Such a dick." Cash shook his head.

Reid spoke up. "I know this can't be easy. But we'd like to talk to you about Angela. About…our mother."

There it was. The truth finally out in the open. What Smith had been wanting to talk about since he'd first learned his mother wasn't his mother, and that he had brothers she'd loved better than him.

Yet now, the words wouldn't come. Like a big pussy, he felt hot and cold, nervous yet furious because he didn't know how to comport his feelings.

"You first," he managed and leaned up against the wall so he had room to breathe.

The others remained seated around the dining table, probably in the same room Angela had once fed her boys and her nephew, Evan. Comfortable family time where everyone shared stories and laughter, then got sent off to bed with kisses and hugs.

Oh, Evan had tried telling him that his brothers hadn't had an easy time of it growing up, but it couldn't all have been bad. He'd dare any of them to compare their childhoods to his.

Reid looked at Cash, who nodded, and Reid said, "Our father—my father—Charles Griffith, died six years ago. He passed while we were still in the Marine Corps. To be frank, he wasn't the nicest man."

"He was a fucking bastard, and I'm glad he's gone," Cash said, his voice flat.

Evan cringed. "I hate to speak ill of the dead, but he wasn't a pleasant person. He hated Cash."

Normally Smith would pipe in with a sarcastic comment like, "We all hate Cash." But the raw emotion floating in the room kept him quiet.

"Angela seemed to have had no one," Reid said. "No relatives other than her sister-in-law. But she never really got along with Aunt Jane. So, she spent her life pretty much alone."

"Well, as alone as she could ever be." Cash snorted. "The woman lived with her head in the fucking clouds, buried in soap operas and books. She lived in a fantasy world where her kids didn't matter, but two fictional strangers falling in love was everything. Total bullshit."

Smith wanted him to say it. "You're telling me she was a bad mother." Not exactly what Meg had told him.

"Mother?" Cash scoffed. "The woman gave birth to us, but that was about it."

"That's not true, Cash." Reid shook his head and met Smith's gaze. "She tried, but something in her snapped. We were young, and one day she just wasn't there anymore. I mean, physically she was. But mentally she was gone. Angela lived in a world of make-believe up until the day she died.

"We didn't know about her having any friends, but some woman named Margaret took care of her final resting place. And apparently Margaret visited her at the assisted living home Mom was in. She was a mystery to us, but maybe not to you."

They waited.

Smith didn't want to talk about himself and his life. Not yet. "So why did Angela leave the house to Cash and not you?" he asked Reid.

Reid glanced away, and Smith saw Cash dart a concerned look at his younger brother, who answered, "I don't know. We think maybe it was because she missed Cash's dad so much, and Cash apparently looks just like him. Allen something."

Cash snored. "She used to call me her 'All-in.' But I think she meant to say Allen. She never saw me at all."

Smith saw the wounds Cash couldn't hide, and it confused the hell out of him. Angela had kept them while she'd thrown him away. But even an absent mom had to be better than a bitter, hateful woman who spouted venom with every breath.

He cleared his throat. "The woman who called herself my mother was her sister. Margaret Ramsey raised me as her own." *And she hated me more than anything in this life.*

"That would match what she said in the journal we found, where she mentioned Meg a few times." Reid shared a glance with Cash.

Evan asked, "Did Margaret ever mention Reid or Cash?"

"Meg didn't tell me she wasn't my mother until I left the Corps eight months ago." And he still didn't know how to feel about the revelation. Relief or sorrow that he couldn't even claim the one tie he had to family? "She'd mentioned my perfect cousins all my life, but that's it. I only knew you guys were amazing and could do no wrong." *But she did say that my real mother hadn't wanted me. She apparently had an ideal family and didn't need me to ruin things.*

"Perfect? That's a load of crap," Cash said. "Angela's perfect family only existed in her mind. None of us mattered. Hell, I moved out at sixteen. I don't think she ever noticed."

Reid nodded. "I still wonder if she had some mental illness that was never diagnosed. Her journal is a little off."

Smith wanted to read it but knew better than to ask.

Cash stood and stuffed his hands in his pockets. "You should read it. To see what we're talking about."

Reid left and returned with it in hand. "Here." He handed it to Smith.

Smith didn't want to touch it, but he took the book. "I'll get it back to you."

"Take your time. We've read the thing." Reid grimaced. "It's… You'll see." He paused. "In it she mentioned having a son. Riley."

Smith blinked. "Riley's my middle name."

Cash studied him. "Did you come to us for a job to check out us?

'Cause no way in hell I'm believing a coincidence brought you to us."

"Since I'd just left the Corps, I was at loose ends. Seemed a good time to meet you."

Reid nodded.

Evan watched him a little too intently. "So, what was Meg—your aunt, I guess—like?"

Smith had mistakenly shared a few details with Evan not so long ago, but he'd be damned if he'd share his pathetic life with Reid and Cash. Not now, maybe not ever. At least they'd had each other. He'd had no one. Rage that he'd lived a lie never quite left him, and it reared its head again. "Look, all this catching up was just swell." They couldn't miss that sarcasm. "But I have work in the morning. I'll see you guys later."

He left, not looking back, and heard Reid tell Cash to let him go.

Yeah. They had each other and Evan for support.

Smith didn't have anyone. And he told himself he liked it that way. Because what was the point in wishing for something that would never change?

CHAPTER THREE

*E*ight days after first moving into her new efficiency apartment, Erin continued to wonder about her new part-time employer. She had no idea how a person who looked so sweet could be so cantankerous, ornery, and downright bitchy. And Erin hated the B-word.

"I said I don't like onions," Matilda Cartwright, her seventy-nine-year-old employer and landlord, griped for the fifth time that afternoon.

"Yes, I know, Tilly. That's why I didn't put onions in the casserole." As she'd mentioned the previous four times.

Erin had understood Smith's warnings from the get-go. Her twenty-minute interview with Tilly had warned her the woman would be a challenge. She stood an inch or two shorter than Erin. And if Tilly weighed a hundred pounds, it would be a miracle. Yet she ate as if she was the size of Smith.

Thoughts of Erin's "savior" had stayed with her throughout the week. Smith Ramsey left a lingering impression. Granted, he'd been bigger than any man she'd ever dated. Harder, stronger.

Meaner too. And distant. Since last Wednesday, she'd seen him only in passing even though he lived right next to her.

Fortunately, the walls in the old building were thick; she only ever heard him if he slammed out his front door.

"Girl, I'm talking to you." The older woman pointed a cane in Erin's direction.

"Go sit down while I get your plate, Tilly. I swear, you'll love it."

The woman gave a loud harrumph before scuttling to her table, which was big enough to fit four in the small dining area of her two-bedroom apartment.

Honestly, dealing with Tilly was like dealing with her grandmother all over again. Erin had loved Grandma Freddy, though the woman had alienated most of her family with her crabbiness and old-fashioned ways. But it was Grandma Freddy who'd taught her to bake, to sew, and to prepare to be a good wife to some lucky man someday. Just as her grandma wanted girls to act like ladies, she'd also taught her grandsons and nephews to act like gentlemen.

She would have been appalled at how terribly Cody had treated her granddaughter.

Much like Tilly had been when she'd heard the full story. Except Tilly hadn't offered sympathy, only a "dogs will be dogs" before hiring her on the spot. For two cooked meals a day plus a bit of cleaning once a week, Tilly had knocked off three hundred dollars from Erin's already cheap rent. Tilly had also agreed to a month-to-month term, as Erin didn't know how long it might take her to get back to Kansas.

If she even wanted to go.

It had only been a week, but she'd started to enjoy her time on the west coast. She felt independent, so pleased not to have to tuck tail and return home that she even forgave Smith for ignoring her attempts to be friendly.

Still burned from Cody, she wasn't looking for a new man in her life. But it wouldn't kill Smith to stop and chat for a few minutes once in a while. Besides Tilly, he was the only person Erin knew. Yet he treated her as if she had the plague, darting away anytime they happened to leave their apartments at the same time.

Erin sighed and grabbed the chicken pot pie she'd fixed for lunch. A good thing Erin could cook, because Tilly had finicky tastes and only liked homecooked meals. "McDonalds and Subway bedamned," she liked to say. Which always caused Erin to grin because who the heck said "bedamned" anymore?

She cut two slices of the pot pie, one for Tilly and one for her. Tilly had insisted on them sharing lunch for the past week, and Erin had no problem enjoying at least one meal a day she didn't have to pay for. Plus, Tilly kept the loneliness at bay.

Using Tilly's fine china, she prepared for lunch. Everything looked lovely. A lace tablecloth covered the old oak table. Delicate plates and crystal glasses filled with ice cold water were accompanied by cloth napkins and actual silver silverware. She lit the candelabra centerpiece and sat down to share a meal.

Tilly studied the table, sniffed her approval, then started to eat. Taking her cue, Erin dug into her pot pie. It was delicious, though it could have used a touch of onion.

"Passable," Tilly said after she'd cleaned her plate.

"There's a lot more left. May I get you another helping?"

"I suppose."

Erin bit back a grin at the older woman's patronizing air, recognizing the look of humor in her sharp blue eyes. It was as if Tilly played the part in a play, the grand lady to Erin's peasant worker. Yet instead of being insulted, Erin played along, charmed, because as Smith had said, Tilly had a good heart.

Erin had watched her landlady interact with the tenants a few times. Saw the warmth when she dealt with the children, or the compassion she hid behind her bluster when she allowed one hardworking family to slide a few days on their rent. The woman loved to talk about "her people" because she felt responsible for them.

In a city this size, it would be easy to get swallowed up in the vast population, everyone too busy to notice anyone else. But with Tilly in charge, no one got lost. And Erin needed that right now. A lot.

"So, did that nutter call again?" Tilly asked when Erin returned with her second helping.

"He did." Cody the Jerk had called twice more since her disastrous arrival last week. Not to apologize, but to talk. "I haven't answered."

Tilly slapped the tabletop. "Good for you. What a fuck-knuckle."

Erin had been taking a sip of water when Tilly let that slip. She choked it down, her eyes watering, and blinked at her employer. "Wh-what did you say?"

"He's a fuck-knuckle." Tilly grinned. "I overheard Smith saying it the other day. I think it applies. What kind of man breaks a girl's heart then doesn't offer one apology for it?"

"You know, I've gone over and over that conversation in my head. The one Cody and I had before I moved out here. And Tilly,

I just don't remember being anything but honest with him. I swear, I wasn't sarcastic when I said I was moving out here. I was nothing but sincere."

"I believe you. You're a little too wide-eyed-innocent to be lying."

Erin frowned. "Is that a compliment?"

"Well, honey, let's face it. You're no slammin' seductress. You're pretty in a wholesome way. A good girl kind of way."

"Do you think that's why he got another girlfriend? Because he wanted a slammin' seductress?" Had Cody been upset because she wasn't sexy enough? The few times they'd made love, she'd thought it meant something. He'd been so nice and tender. And, well, a little on the boring side. She'd wanted hotter, naughtier sex, and more frequent sex at that. But she'd kept that to herself, because as Grandma Freddy always said, a lady was only a lady if she acted as such at all times. And no one wanted to be the town slut.

Yeah, Grandma Freddy had been full of advice, but at least she'd been honest, someone Erin could talk to. Erin had tried to show Cody she cared. They'd dated for well over a year and exchanged the L-word before ever becoming intimate. She'd done her best to be a woman with a sterling reputation who respected him enough to take his lead in bedroom matters.

Who knew Cody had been getting his freak on with the blond lady in the SUV? Just thinking about how smug the other woman had been, how disgusted Cody had seemed that Erin might want to live with him, made her want to hit something. Then cry all over again.

"You stop that right now." Tilly smacked Erin's foot with her cane.

"Ow." Erin glared and rubbed her foot.

"Good. You be mad, not sad. That fool doesn't deserve one more tear." Tilly shoved a forkful of pot pie in her mouth and with her mouth full said, "Did you ever cook for him?"

"All the time when he came to visit. I told you we met when I was taking care of my sister in Pennsylvania." Back when Joy had been recovering from breast cancer, Erin had stayed with her, Tim, and their two children for six months. She'd cooked, cleaned, and carted her niece and nephew around while Joy went to chemo and Tim did his best to provide for his family.

Erin had loved being needed, included in their tight-knit clan. She adored her niece and nephew and still missed them.

"Technically, you can blame your sister for meeting Cody. She owes you."

"No, Tilly. She doesn't." Erin let out an exasperated sigh. "As I told you before, Cody is no one's fault but mine."

"Good, you remember that." Tilly pointed her cane at Erin, then put it against the wall to dig into her food once more. "Girl, you're a wizard in the kitchen. You'll have no problem finding a man worth keeping if you take it nice and slow. Don't feed him any cookies until the third date at least, and don't give him a piece of your *honey pie*, if you know what I mean, until you know him well enough not to blush when he takes off your bra. That always worked for me."

"Honey pie? What... Oh!" It was like Grandma Freddy lived and breathed in Tilly. "Geez." The woman had no filter. No one but Erin's grandmother had ever been so frank with her. Heck, Erin's mom couldn't even say S-E-X without either spelling it or blushing fire-engine red. Not that they discussed more than recipes or family when Erin called home. Erin had learned about the birds and the bees from her grandmother and books. Period.

"Your problem is you've been sheltered," Tilly said, as if reading her mind. "You need to live a little. Have some fun with a real man, but don't feel the need to jump into bed or anything. I mean, you should if you want to. I'm all for sexual freedom. But that just doesn't seem like your style."

"Uh, no. It's not." God. Erin could feel her cheeks overheating. "More water?"

"Water? Oh, sure."

Erin escaped from the table and took a moment to gather her composure. When she felt reasonably settled, she returned to find Tilly's empty plate. She handed Tilly the water then sat to share the rest of the meal.

"What about Smith?"

Erin blinked. "What?"

"Smith Ramsey. My handyman. What do you think of him?"

Erin did her best not to blush. "He's nice. He helped me move and didn't make fun of me when I looked stupid with Cody."

Tilly nodded. "That's my boy. Smith is a good man. He's a bit crass and obnoxious on occasion, but he's kind at heart. And he can fix about anything." Tilly gave her a knowing onceover Erin wanted to ignore but couldn't.

"What?"

"He could help you get over Cody."

"Really? Because I can't even get a hello out of him," she said, annoyed now that she thought about it. Then realizing Tilly might take that comment out of context, she explained, "I've tried to say hello when we pass each other in the hall, but he runs away or ignores me. I think he grunted at me once. And when I tried to bake him cookies as a thank you—not flirting, *just* as a thank you —I couldn't find him to give them to him. Either he was out for two days or he ignored me knocking at the door."

Tilly cackled. "That boy. You know, I don't think he's ever brought a woman home in the whole time he's lived here. And my single lady tenants haven't gotten anywhere with him, though I've seen him wave and be polite when occasion demands it."

"Maybe he's gay." And wouldn't that be a crime for single women everywhere.

"Could be. Though he sure seemed to like the look of Jill and Mallory Keen in their bikinis a few months ago at our summer picnic."

Erin frowned.

"You know, that married lesbian couple in 5A? The real pretty ladies who strut around in shorts and yoga pants all the time?"

Ah, the personal trainer couple down the hall. If so, she couldn't fault Smith his taste. They were beautiful and fit and made Erin feel like an out of shape frump.

Tilly continued, "Funny thing about Smith. He can be a right asshole to the men around here, but he's always polite to the ladies. Well, to everyone but you, apparently. Interesting." The calculating expression that crossed her face gave Erin the shivers.

"Tilly, no. I don't want any help with my social life. I've got enough to do for you and my job."

"Writing about nuts?"

"Editing about nuts. And crops and agriculture." The agricultural magazines she edited for didn't appeal to her creative side, but they paid well enough that she didn't starve.

"Magazines are dying." Tilly shook her head. "It's all about cell phones and computers anymore. Sadly. Bah. I don't know how you can afford to live anywhere editing for no-name magazines."

Thanks for that, Tilly. "It's not a bad way to make money, you know." And it allowed Erin to live anywhere so long as she had access to the Internet.

"Get me a cup of tea and we'll call lunch quits. And don't forget, you're coming for dinner tonight."

Which meant the conversation had ended. Thank God.

"I'm looking forward to it." She prayed Tilly would drop the whole matchmaking with Smith idea. Erin had enough problems trying not to think about her sexy, taciturn neighbor. She hadn't been enough to hold Cody's interest. What made her think she could nab Smith's? If she'd been in the market for a man, which she *so* wasn't.

After fixing Tilly a pot of her favorite jasmine green tea, Erin poured her a cup then left the pot for her on her side table, next to the recliner which faced her television. Tilly had an addiction to daytime TV.

Erin would have liked to have so much downtime, but in order to make ends meet, she had to get busy. She went home, ignored the depressing sight of her nearly-empty apartment, and went to work on the laptop she'd propped on the $20 table purchased at a garage sale the past weekend.

She now had a table and two chairs, an uncomfortable, inflatable single bed, and a beautiful cherry antique armoire and matching dresser she'd brought from home. She had no television, but she didn't need one with a laptop. And she had a cheap set of cookware, dishes and cups, and silverware she'd acquired from Walmart, so she could at least cook and eat.

"I have my health, two great jobs, and a place to live. What more could I want?" she asked herself in her empty apartment covered in tacky mango-orange painted walls. The vinyl floor passed as functional, if not pretty. No one would ever mistake the fake-wood flooring for real hardwood.

The kitchen, while not large, had a decent gas stove, microwave, and small refrigerator. A wall of counters gave her enough space to prepare food for one, but she needed a small island or butcher block to give her more room to prepare. Ideally, she might be able to use Tilly's kitchen to continue her home cooking show. That's once she made herself indispensable to the woman and bribed her with treats.

Erin stopped dithering and buckled down to work. She edited four articles, posted on two magazine blogs, and checked over a few agricultural social media sites.

But her dream job lay just out of reach, sharing her recipes on a profitable home-baking vlog. Back in Colby, she'd had a weekly series that had garnered her thousands of followers, and she had to continue to serve up sweets. She'd accounted for her move to Seattle, promising to come off her hiatus as soon as she settled in.

Since the move, she hadn't filmed anything new, though she continued to answer questions and comments on her vlog. She was giving herself another two weeks of time off. After that, she'd have to start posting again, which created a whole new host of problems. But the added income from a few vendors on her site helped. And she needed the money now more than ever, living in Seattle.

Heck, the other day she'd bought a bag of ground coffee for ten dollars! And that was apparently on the low end. She groaned, turned back to work, and didn't look up until her timer went off at six.

Fortunately, Tilly didn't insist on eating supper at an early hour, like many of the seniors at home. *Not home. Colby,* Erin told herself. *Seattle is my home now.* She felt more grown-up living on her own, so far away from family. At twenty-five, she had no call to be tied to her parents. Even if she did sometimes feel so alone here.

Erin stood with a sigh, stretched, and left her apartment to head down the hall to Tilly's. Only to bump into Smith on her way. "Oh, sorry."

He didn't move, though she rebounded a step back. He grunted at her and walked away.

Erin had had enough. "Hey." She grabbed his arm and froze him in his tracks. "Could you at least smile or say hello? I swear, I'm not asking for anything other than a polite greeting. It's called being neighborly."

Smith turned around, and his presence had an impact, as usual. The man dwarfed her in size, but it was that aura of power that overwhelmed. Smith seemed to be burning with fettered rage just under the surface. She swore she could see it in his eyes before they crinkled, and he smiled at her.

And that smile knocked her off her axis.

Man, he was hot. Handsome, sexy, *realllly* good looking. Her mind kept going in circles, trying to provide a better description.

"Sorry. Hello, Erin. How are you?"

"Uh, um. Good. I'm good. How are you?"

"Great. You all settled in?" He was speaking slowly, making eye contact, acting friendly.

"Are you making fun of me?" She planted her hands on her hips, calling him on what sure the heck seemed like a patronizing attitude. After Cody, she was done playing nice just because a woman "should ignore rudeness and be kind because men don't know any better." Geez, were her mom and grandma wrong on so many counts.

His grin widened. "Maybe." He brushed a lock of hair out of her eyes as he studied her, and her heart did jumping jacks. "You are so little."

She fumed, angry and wanting to provoke a similar response. Not at all the way she normally behaved with people. Erin was nice. Usually quiet until she grew to know someone. Polite, well-mannered. "Look, buddy. I can't help that God made me the perfect size, and that you're too jealous to deal well. I have been *trying* to thank you for being nice when I needed it. I don't care for your platitudes. Now excuse me while I have things to do. I won't bother you again."

She moved to pass him when Smith grabbed her arm.

She froze.

He quickly let go. "I'm sorry, okay? I'm not great with people," he rumbled.

She saw him looking at her oddly. "What?"

"I don't know. You're pretty."

She blinked, confused. "Thanks?"

"I'll say hello from now on, okay?"

Her insides felt fluttery, and she couldn't look away from his deep green eyes. Such beauty on a man so rugged. He had the thickest eyelashes, and when he smiled, his eyes seemed to shine. "Sure."

He nodded and moved aside, his hand outstretched to let her pass. She walked in front of him toward the end of the hall, expecting him to take the stairs. But he followed her to Tilly's apartment at the end of the corridor.

She glanced over her shoulder in suspicion as she knocked.

"Come in," Tilly yelled from behind the door.

Erin pushed inside, but she couldn't close the door because Smith followed her.

She narrowed her gaze, and he grinned wider, stealing her ability to think.

"Hello."

"Hello," she repeated, waiting for an explanation to replace the smug look on his face. Instead, he bypassed her to Tilly.

"Well?" Tilly snapped. "Get the grub going, Erin. And you, boy, give me the rundown. What's going on with unit 6B? The truth."

He sighed. "Yes, ma'am." He glanced over at Erin and rolled his eyes, which startled her into an involuntary grin.

Not sure what to do with his sudden sense of humor, she turned on her heel and went straight to the kitchen, wondering what the heck to cook for herself and two people who ate like four.

. . .

S MITH HADN'T REALIZED E RIN WOULD BE THERE WHEN T ILLY HAD invited him for dinner. A glance at Tilly's table showed three table settings instead of two. He took a moment to think about how that made him feel and wasn't surprised that the idea of spending time with his cute neighbor didn't bother him at all.

He'd been thinking about her all week, wondering how she was handling a ball-buster like Tilly. He liked the old woman, but hell, she was an acquired taste, and she knew it. Yet Tilly had apparently invited Erin to join them, and she hadn't done that with any of her prior cooks.

To be honest, he had gone out of his way to avoid Erin, torn between wanting to check on her and feeling a little too attached to Ms. Sweetness and Light. But she hadn't seemed so nice earlier, riding his ass to be polite.

He grinned.

Tilly cleared her throat. "Ahem. Unit 6B?"

He took a seat across from her, settling on her antique blue couch and taking up nearly the entire sofa. They sure made people smaller back in the day. Hell, only someone the size of Erin would consider this thing big enough for two. "The unit's hot water is shot in the sinks and shower. I'm thinking it might have a control valve blocked or unplugged. I had to google that, by the way. I'm no expert, but I think the hot water heater might be the problem. You need to call in a plumber."

"Oh, hell, no."

"Look, I know you hate to part with a single penny, but you can afford it. And didn't you tell me it's been fifteen years since the heater was installed? Gas heaters normally only last ten to twelve years."

She frowned something fierce. Smith did his best not to laugh at her. Tilly's rage looked cartoony comical, her lined face pinched in anger, her eyes bulging as she stared daggers through him.

He held up his hands in surrender. "Hey. Don't shoot the messenger. You do what you want. But I'm not taking the blame when people complain about their hot water not working. I'll just point the finger your way."

"I'll give you a finger." She flipped him off.

He grinned. "You're welcome."

She sighed. "Oh hell. I know you're right. But before I spend what little money I have left…"

He knew for a fact Tilly was loaded. A friend of Meg's back in the day, Tilly had given him the job because she knew him. Fortunately, Tilly had a strength of character and kindness inside her Meg never had. She also had a small fortune left to her from her deceased husband.

"Eh. I suppose it's not all bad." Tilly shrugged. "I'll be sure to write it off."

"Plus, you can buy something from this century that will be energy efficient and save you money in the long run."

"There's that." She hobbled to her feet, waved him away when he stood to help, then told him to wait for her.

Smith stood in place, overly conscious of the sounds from the kitchen. Would Erin wear an apron? He'd been having the strangest dreams lately, of her offering him cookies wearing an apron with nothing beneath.

Yeah, his nights had turned into a sweet hell he needed to fix. Soon. Time to find a woman before he ended up asking out his neighbor. A poor thing like Erin wouldn't be able to handle a monster like Smith. He'd hurt her feelings or prove too much in the sack. And she'd been through enough with dickbag Cody.

Not to mention a smart guy didn't fuck around at home. If things went south with Erin, as they no doubt would, he'd have to deal with a pouty, crying woman who lived right next door. Uncomfortable, to say the least. Smith might not be great when it came to social situations, but he had a brain he used on occasion.

No, he'd steer clear of Erin Briggs except for the sporadic, uber polite hello.

"Use these guys," Tilly said as she returned, handing him a scrap of paper. "Call 'em and see what they have to say." She continued past him toward the kitchen.

He glanced at the paper. "McSons Plumbing?" He followed her and found Erin putting something into the oven. A sauce cooking on the stove smelled of tomatoes and garlic. His mouth watered.

Tilly smiled at him. "I hear they're good looking and reasonable. They did some work for a friend of mine, and she recommended them."

"So, which is more important?" he asked drily. "That they're good looking, reasonable, or good at their jobs?"

"Good looking," Tilly answered without missing a beat.

Erin snickered.

Smith sighed. "Fine. But they'll have to work around my schedule if you want me to handle them and the tenants." He ignored the way his pulse raced seeing Erin's smile.

"No problem. Now what are you cooking for us, Erin? Isn't she great? An amazing cook and so smart. She has her own business, you know." Tilly was less than subtle, staring from Smith to Erin and practically chortling with glee.

But he had no intention of falling into whatever scheme the old woman had planned. No way in hell he'd do more than eat and be as pleasant as he could be for a guy who hated chitchat.

So, an hour and a half later, he could do nothing but stare at Erin in consternation, wondering how in the hell he found himself sitting with her at Ringo's Bar. On a date.

CHAPTER FOUR

*E*rin smiled at Smith. She'd been wrong about him. He did have a mode other than standoffish jerk. "Thanks again for bringing me along. I know this isn't a date, that you were just trying to get Tilly off your case," she said in a hurry, still embarrassed at the way Tilly had been throwing them together during dinner.

"Uh-huh." He frowned down at his beer.

She took a sip of the concoction the waitress had suggested. Just Say Yes! —a mix of cranberry syrup, vodka, and two other alcohols that combined to make the potent drink both sweet and tasty. Erin didn't drink much, but she felt entitled after that dinner. "I mean, I really like Tilly. She means well, but it was beyond obvious she wanted us to go out together." She laughed at the thought.

"What's so funny?"

She drank some more, then nibbled at the pretzels on the table. Between Smith and Tilly, they'd consumed most of the meal.

They hadn't seemed too bothered at her excuse she wasn't hungry, finishing off what should have been leftovers while she'd picked at her small plate of noodles. Between Smith's brooding presence and Tilly's obvious and poorly thought out matchmaking skills, Erin had been too on edge to eat. Now she was hungry and thirsty. Pretzels and a cocktail. The meal of champions.

"Funny?" she said to answer Smith, who sat studying her. "The thought of you and me." She laughed again.

"Explain."

"Well, for one, you're a giant. I'm—"

"The perfect size. I remember." He smirked.

"Plus, I'm nice. You don't like people."

He nodded. "True."

"And I'm done with men. You're definitely a man."

"Again, true." He drank and watched her. "So, you going to try chicks or are you just saying you're not dating guys for a while?"

"Chicks?" She blinked, feeling a little muzzy. She hadn't eaten anything besides the pot pie at lunch and a few noodles at dinner. And now the pretzels. The alcohol might just be hitting her harder than she'd expected. "Wait. Are you asking if I'm attracted to women?"

"Are you?"

"That's kind of personal, isn't it? Wouldn't the answer be no? I mean, I just broke up with Cody."

He watched her carefully. "You can be into guys and girls, you know."

"Are you?"

He choked on his beer. "Ah, no. I'm straight. I like women."

"Me too." At his surprised expression, she amended, "I mean, I just like guys. Not women. I'm just not dating."

"Gotcha."

"What about you? Are you not dating too?"

"Why would you ask that?"

"Well, you are out with me."

"But you said this wasn't a date." The grin he shot her devastated her brain into frying on the spot. "You interested?"

"I just said I wasn't dating anymore."

He laughed. "Honey, there's dating and there's the rest of the way the world works. You don't have to date to have sex."

She sat up straighter, gaping. "Are you telling me you want to have sex with me?" came out louder than she'd intended.

A few guys near their table laughed. "If you don't want her, I'm game."

"Pick me, pick me!"

"Oh man. She's so cute."

Smith turned and glared at the table, who toasted him then turned back to one another.

Erin's face felt hot enough to leave burns. She finished off her drink and waved down the waitress for another.

Smith ordered another beer for himself as well. "You're a light-weight. Better lay off the booze."

"You're not my father," she snapped, not liking how she continued to come across as pathetic or weak in front of him.

"Christ, no. Fine. You want to drink and get stupid, go ahead."

"I'm not drunk, Smith," she said primly. "I had one glass. I'm old enough to know my limits." She really shouldn't get another, but now she had to drink it to prove herself. She'd just eat more pretzels to counter the emptiness in her belly. Right.

"So how old are you anyway?" he asked.

"Twenty-five. You?"

"Thirty-two."

"Ah, an old man." She sneered at him.

He only laughed. "An old man who can hold his drink." He took the bottle the waitress dropped off. "Thanks, Lisa. You're the best."

Lisa smiled, a little too friendly, Erin thought, as she set a new cocktail in front of Erin before strutting away. She muttered under her breath, "Nice that he flirts with her and not me."

"Huh?"

Gah. He had ears like a bat. She took the drink Lisa had left her and sipped. So fruity. Yum. "I said I bet you get in fights a lot." She studied him. "You're big. What are you? Six-two or some-thing?" Anything over five ten was a blur to her.

He leaned back in his chair, king of the bar. "Six-five. Two-twenty. All muscle. What about you?"

"That's none of your business." She frowned at him.

"You know, you really are cute."

She blushed.

He grinned. "So how are you doing since moving in?"

"Okay, I guess." She sighed.

"What?"

"You'll make fun of me." Man, he'd been right. She was a light-weight. One drink and she felt wobbly, talking like Tilly with no filter. Erin never had been one for keeping secrets, and she was even worse when drinking.

"I won't." Smith leaned in closer, his expression serious. So handsome.

"I'm lonely." She drank more, focused on feeling good. "But it's natural. I'm new to the city, and the only people I know are Tilly and you. And you've been ignoring me."

He looked uncomfortable. "I, ah, sorry. I've been busy at work."

"Please. You were avoiding me. But it's okay." She smiled at him, knowing exactly how to get under his skin. "I probably scare you."

As predicted, the arrogant lunkhead scowled. "You don't scare me."

"I do too." She sipped again and giggled. Oh boy. Erin never giggled. "You're afraid you'll get to like me too much." A total reach, but what the heck, Erin had a right to be obnoxious after dealing with both Tilly and Smith in the same night.

"Yeah, right. I just don't want *you* falling for *me* when I'd only break your heart."

She stared, wondering if he'd said that or her slightly inebriated self had heard wrong. "I'm sorry. Did you just say you're worried you'll break *my* heart?"

"Yeah."

"Man, you have some kind of colossal ego."

"That's not all that's colossal." He wiggled his brows.

Torn between laughter and disgust, she blurted, "You're so conceited. I mean, sure you're handsome. It's obvious you're tall and have muscles. But you're an antisocial jerk."

"I am not." Now he looked insulted when earlier he'd agreed he didn't like people.

"You are too." She finished off her drink, needing to use the restroom.

"I'm honest."

"Well, you can be honest and be nice about it."

"Hey, I didn't tell Tilly to shut up at dinner when she went on and on about how great you are."

"I am great at cooking. I could cook everyone at this bar under the table."

He frowned. "What does that mean?"

"It means I'm a great cook. And someday when my YouTube channel has a bazillion followers and I have a cookbook and a show on TV, you'll regret you never tried to get sexy with me."

He just stared at her. Then he sighed. "Yeah, you're done. Wait here." He left and returned moments later.

She'd been stacking pretzels on the plate, no longer hungry. She felt a little sleepy, a little loopy, and dang it all, happy. For once she hadn't been wallowing alone in her apartment watching reruns of *The Great British Baking Show*.

Smith loomed over her like a thundercloud.

"Man, are your eyes pretty." A hiccup came out of nowhere and made her want to laugh again. "Whoops. Not sure where that came from." She paused. "I need to pee."

"Time to go." He gently helped her to her feet, not hauling her around, as she'd expected. He marched her toward the restroom and waited outside while she did what she needed to. Afterward, he walked her to his truck. He had to lift her into the thing since she had a tough time getting in herself.

"Do they make these for giants or what?"

"Good thing I drove," he muttered.

The drive back to the apartment building didn't take long, but it was enough to even her out. "I'm not drunk, Smith. I'm happy and enjoying myself, for once. It's been a while since I went out."

"I didn't know that. So, you're not a barfly?"

"No." She grinned at the thought. "I'm pretty much what I look like. A homebody. I like my family. I like to cook. I like reading and finding new things to try. I had a bunch of friends at home, you know."

"So why did you leave?"

"I was bored. Cody and I were never together much. I did think I loved him." She blinked back useless tears as he parked the truck.

But she must have missed one because Smith wiped her cheek with a finger. "Aw, don't cry."

"I'm not sad. Well, I am a little. But I'm more angry I let him get to me. When I think about how much I tried to be good and let him be the all-important part of our relationship, it just makes me mad."

He helped her out of the truck and walked with her into the building toward their apartments. But he paused in front of his unit, glanced at her, and frowned.

"Well, thanks for—" She stopped when he opened his door.

"Still game for some conversation?" He nodded for her to enter.

Curious about his place, she preceded him inside. He shut and locked the door behind them, but he didn't worry her. She trusted Smith on a level she'd have to consider later, when she wasn't so affected by him.

To her shock, his apartment looked homey. He had laminate floors that looked like hardwood, not crappy tile, she noted with envy. A big brown sectional couch and chaise sat over an area rug and faced a large television mounted to the wall. Two bookcases flanked the TV, filled with books. She walked up to one and touched it, stunned to find it a real book and not a place holder. Fiction and nonfiction lined the shelves.

"Wow. You read?"

He glared. "Yeah, I read. And I can count on more than my fingers and toes too."

She chuckled. "Who would have guessed?" She walked past him, studying her surroundings.

"Make yourself at home," he said with no small amount of sarcasm.

"Thanks."

The apartment had a lot more space than hers. She noted a bathroom off the hall that led back into his bedroom. Knowing she'd probably never be allowed back in after annoying him tonight, she peeked inside to find the small space dominated by a queen-size bed, which must be tough for such a large man to sleep in. But she didn't think a king would fit. He had one dresser and a closet. Everything looked neat, dusted, and the bed had been perfectly made, not one wrinkle on the comforter.

The bathroom had towels hung perfectly straight, no messy toothpaste all over the counter, nothing but a cup and toothbrush holder with one toothbrush standing straight in it. A picture of a comic book hero had been framed and set on one wall of the small area. He had a full tub and shower, as opposed to her tiny standing corner shower. The toilet had a fuzzy blue cover to match the blue floor mat and blue towels.

"Huh." She never would have expected Smith to be so neat. Or so color coordinated.

She walked back to the kitchen to find him standing, arms akimbo, waiting. "Seen enough?"

"Not yet." She stared in awe at his kitchen. It had an L shape, plenty of counter space, and a glorious kitchen island that he probably used as a table, because in the open space where a dining table might have been sat a bunch of free weights and a weight bench instead.

The kitchen didn't look high end. No granite counters or stainless-steel appliances, not that she would have expected those in Emerald Estates. But everything looked exceedingly clean and organized. It even smelled lemony fresh.

"Wow. You're a clean freak."

"I like things neat. Sue me."

"I might." She sighed, running a hand over his countertop. "I miss this."

"This?"

"My kitchen. My home cooking channel is a real thing, you know. I teach people how to cook and vendors pay me—not much, I admit—to advertise on my channel. Plus, I'm creating a cookbook at some point. I hope."

"Well, you killed the spaghetti tonight. Tilly loves bragging about your skill in the kitchen."

They stared at each other as a sudden silence settled over them. She thought he looked to kick her out of his apartment. And Erin didn't think she could bear the quiet, being alone and lonely tonight after being in Smith and Tilly's company. Going out with Smith had been fun and exciting, even if he did sometimes get on her nerves.

"So, ah," he said. "Do you," she started at the same time.

They broke off. "You first," he offered.

A glance at the microwave showed the hour had reached eight thirty. Did he need to get to bed early?

"Do you want to watch TV together or something? Or do you need to get to bed? I'm not keeping you up, am I?" she asked.

. . .

SHE'D HAD HIM "UP" SINCE HE'D BEEN FORCED TO WATCH HER full lips nurse those drinks at the bar. God, the woman had no business looking so innocent and putting such carnal thoughts in his brain. He didn't know what it was about her that had him thinking about sexing her up so damn much.

"Bed?" he repeated weakly, having homed in on that one word. Sure, he'd be happy to make use of his bed. If she'd join him in it.

Unfortunately, not only was she his neighbor, a naïve sweetheart from a small town in Kansas and just getting over a broken heart, she was also buzzed. He had no doubt she'd tied one on. In just two cocktails.

He bit back the smile that threatened. Tonight she'd worn jeans and a pale blue short sleeved shirt that hugged her curves just right. Erin might be small, but she was definitely all woman. So fucking pretty, was all he could think as he stared into those bright eyes, now shadowed with uncertainty.

What had she asked him? "Oh, I don't go to bed until closer to eleven. Um, sure. You can hang out. We could watch TV." Or something, like Netflix and chill like fucking bunnies until dawn. *Man, this is hell. Send her home and go take a cold shower.*

Yet her admission that she was lonely hit him hard. He felt that way all the time. He'd just gotten better about sitting with it until the feeling passed. Although… Since working at Vets on the Go!, he had Ringo's Bar to call a second home, the same place the gang liked to hang out on the weekends. And then there was Evan and Aunt Jane, who kept insisting he come to Sunday brunch to join her and her new beau in Bainbridge Island.

He hadn't taken her up on that yet, but knowing he had people to spend time with, who wanted his company, filled that emptiness he'd learned to live with. Erin didn't have anyone. While a big part of him—and growing bigger—wanted to have sex with her in the worst way, the better part of him insisted he give her a friend.

"What kind of TV do you watch?" she asked. "Military shows? You were in the Marine Corps, right?" She'd seen his last promotion framed on the wall, apparently. One of the proudest days in his life had been making Staff Sergeant in the Corps.

"Yeah, I like military shows. But I'm into all sorts of things." Action, fantasy, porn... He cleared his throat, grateful for the constrictive jeans and long tee-shirt hiding his enthusiasm. "You pick."

He waited for her to sit down then grabbed them both glasses of water to drink. Though two beers didn't do much but soothe a parched throat for him, the water would help. He needed a clear head around Erin.

He handed her a glass then sat on the couch, keeping a few throw pillows between them. He liked the sectional, typically making use of the long chaise, where he liked to relax. Erin could sit on the couch. No way he could get into any trouble if he lay away from her, facing the TV. Two friendly neighbors watching mindless entertainment...

Erin watched him as she sipped, and he wanted nothing more than to be a glass of water. She put the glass down, and he stifled a groan. "No, you pick what we watch since it's your apartment. Something fun though. No romcoms or dramas."

"Like you have to tell me that." He snorted. He settled on a Marvel movie on Netflix, content to watch superheroes kick ass. Considering he'd spent his youth buried in comics, living on fantasies of superpowers and being anywhere but with his "mother," his addiction to superhero movies was a no-brainer.

She turned to him. "Can I ask you a question?"

"Sure."

He felt himself relaxing for the first time since being in her presence.

"Do all men want slammin' seductress types? Is it always about sex with guys?"

The hardon from hell returned with a vengeance.

He refused to look her way. She sounded sad, and he wanted to jump her. Yep, two people living in completely separate worlds. "Well, I can't speak for all guys."

"Yeah, but you're a man. I need a man's perspective."

"Fine." He gave a loud exhale. "No, it's not always about sex. I mean, sure, the initial attraction is physical. You like what a chick looks like, you want to talk to her. Get in bed with her. But if you're talking about a relationship" —*of which I am in no way an expert*— "then I think the sex, though important, is less important than how two people get along." He paused, and when she didn't say anything, he continued. "I mean, I haven't dated all that much. And yeah, I like sex with a woman I'm attracted to. But to be a couple, I'd have to want to get to know her. To want her to get to know me. I'm not just a fuck machine. I'm a man with likes and dislikes, and it would be nice if she learned some of them because she wanted to."

How many times had he wished someone liked him for more than his brawn? Or because he had a brain and not because he looked or acted like the proverbial bad boy? So pathetic that he'd had only two major girlfriends in his entire life, and neither had stuck around for longer than a few months. Fuck, now *he* was feeling down. He straightened his back against the cushions, still sitting up, the rest of him sprawled out on the chaise.

"Huh." That was all she said.

After a moment, he'd calmed down enough that he could glance over at her without wanting to jump her. She seemed engrossed in the superhero movie, no more mention of sex or what men wanted. He didn't know whether to be disappointed or amused.

They watched the movie in companionable silence, which should have been weird but wasn't. Erin's presence didn't feel intrusive. She didn't make any noise, just sat there, near him but not next to him. And he liked having her there, oddly enough.

He kept taking subtle note of her expression. She laughed at the funny parts of the movie and looked enthralled at the action sequences he liked to watch over and over again. He wouldn't have thought Erin the type to like the action, but she looked entertained.

Fortunately, she said no more about kisses or seducing men. Because his cock couldn't handle the pressure. His jeans had been too tight all night long, his erection coming and going with her soft breath, her smiles, her laughter.

It didn't help that her smile lit up her face, and her eyes dominated her features, the light color so striking, it was all he could do not to stare at her. He didn't want to give off creepy vibes though, so he did his best to pretend to watch the movie.

At the end, he stretched, wondering if he ought to tell her to go or ask her to stay longer. It had passed ten, and he normally hit the rack around this time when he had an early morning ahead of him. "So, you want to—" He cut off abruptly when Erin settled over him, straddling his hips.

"Smith?" She gently placed her hands on his shoulders.

His entire body turned to stone. "What are you doing?"

"Can I ask you something?"

"You can't ask me something from over there?" He nodded to her previous spot on the couch, his arms along the edges of the couch. He gripped the cushions for dear life.

"No. I can't." She leaned closer and pressed a soft kiss to his mouth. It was there and gone in seconds, but he felt it to his bones.

"Look." He had to clear his throat to speak. "You had a little too much to drink tonight. I get it. Maybe it's time you went home and—"

"Don't you want to kiss me back?"

Was she on crack? Hell, yes! "You want the truth? I want to *fuck* you back, until you're bowlegged and praying my name. But no way in hell am I touching you." Tonight at least. To prove it, he gripped the cushions even harder, his fingers bloodless. "You need to get off me and go home before you do something you'll regret. You'll feel pretty stupid about this in the morning, but you'll thank me for it." He gave her a strained smile, the best he could do considering his cock threatened to break off.

Unfortunately, she smiled back at him. "You were so sweet when I broke down at Cody's. And you're sweet now, being all noble since you think I'm drunk."

"I'm not noble."

"I'm not drunk." She leaned closer to whisper, "And I'm not in any way under the influence. I just want to feel..." She paused and licked her lips.

He groaned, wanting that mouth to move lower, to lick slower, and maybe to open wide and suck. "Feel what?" he asked hoarsely, even knowing it to be foolish to encourage her.

"To feel like I matter," she answered, her vulnerability too fucking honest, too real.

He knew he'd regret this. Knew it to be a huge-ass mistake, but he couldn't deny her. "I don't think you know what you want. And I'm not all that sure you aren't a little tipsy."

"I had two drinks hours ago, not to mention a lot of water since."

"Well I'm not moving from this spot. You want to prove something to yourself, go head. But don't expect me to do anything about it." There. That should send her home.

Instead, she stroked his shoulders, her hands so damn warm, and smiled at him. "Perfect. You stay right there and don't move. I promise I'll go when I'm done."

"Done?" What did *done* mean?

To his shock, Erin lowered herself, so that she straddled his groin, sitting over an arousal he couldn't mask. She gasped as she ground against him.

"Oh. That is nice." She leaned forward and kissed him again, forceful yet still sweet and soft.

She made everything worse as she rocked against him, riding him while she kissed his cheeks, his throat, then sucked on his neck.

Smith was close to coming in his pants. He nearly shot off the couch and clenched the cushions, deserving a medal for keeping mostly still. If only his damn hips would listen. "Erin…"

"Just a few seconds more," she moaned.

Jesus, she was getting herself off while she rubbed all over him. Her mouth returned to his, and he kissed her, fucking her with his tongue the way he wanted to with the rest of his body. She sucked him deeper, and that made everything worse.

She kissed her way to his ear, whispering words that made no sense. And her little pants and groans made their fondling so fucking hot. She ran her hands over his chest and abdomen, the heat bleeding through his thin tee-shirt.

"Oh, yes, yes," she moaned as she ground harder and sucked his throat, coming and shuddering and pushing him way over the edge.

"Fuck, yes," he hissed and threw his head back as he came in his pants, the orgasm shattering. He shuddered and arched into her, the contact as stimulating as her scent, her taste.

After a moment, he came back to himself to find her forehead tucked against the crook in his neck, her hands stroking his chest and arms, petting him as he came back down.

She lifted her head to look down at him, and her smile lit up the entire room.

"Thanks for tonight. You're fun, Smith." She rose to her feet, steady as a rock, then turned and headed for her purse on the counter. At the door, she paused and winked at him. "What's your favorite kind of cookie?"

Too confused to do anything but answer, he said, "Molasses."

"Good to know." She waved and left.

He stared at the back of his front door in stunned silence, realized he continued to breathe hard, then swore at the mess the girl next door had made in his pants.

"What the hell did she do to me?"

And how could he get her to do it again?

CHAPTER FIVE

*E*rin hadn't seen Smith in three days. She'd been so busy with her editing and work for Tilly that she hadn't spared him much thought. What a crock. She thought about him every five seconds. But she'd been *trying* not to think about him.

Not an easy feat considering she'd ridden the man to orgasm after knowing him for only a week.

How strange to feel so proud of that fact. She grinned to herself as she finished preparing Tilly's meal for the evening and readied to drop it off. There. Now she deserved to think about the best sex with a man she'd ever had. Clothed or unclothed.

For the first time ever, Erin had been the aggressor. She laughed to think of the poor man, not sure what to do with her. Smith had looked a little wild around the eyes when she'd straddled him. No matter that she'd tried to convince him of her sobriety, he wouldn't make a move on her. So she'd made hers on him.

He hadn't complained. If he'd said no or told her to leave, she would have. She wondered how many of Smith's past girlfriends —or lovers—had ever seduced him. Not that Erin had, exactly.

She'd had an orgasm from some kisses and that large bulge between Smith's legs. She thought he'd had an orgasm as well, but she couldn't be sure. He'd squeezed the heck out of the couch though.

She laughed again. How liberating to sexually indulge and not feel badly afterward. Then again, she hadn't had real sex. No touching or penetrating, no fondling body parts if she didn't count touching his firm, muscular chest. And land alive, that man had *huge* biceps. Just thinking about them made her fingers curl.

The room started to grow warm, and Erin fanned herself. So okay, she was superficial for liking Smith for his looks. But she also liked him for being so mindful of her state of mind, for trying to take care of what he'd considered a vulnerable woman.

She sighed. Smith. So handsome and sexy.

And so unavailable.

Had it been an accident or on purpose that they hadn't crossed paths since the bar on Thursday night? The old Erin would have been heartbroken and full of self-doubt. But the new Erin loved that she didn't mind him being absent. It didn't bother her in the slightest. And she hadn't been listening for him for the past few days. Nope. She'd been way too busy to care what he thought and did. And so what if it was already Sunday and he still hadn't stopped by? She didn't care at all. Not when she had a life to lead.

All the energy she'd been putting into work had paid off. She had several of Tilly's meals prepared well in advance of next week and already delivered. She also had next week's edits done through Wednesday.

So, what to do with the rest of her weekend? At four o'clock on a Sunday in Seattle, a woman could do just about anything. Erin had decided to bake Smith cookies. *Oh yeah, I'm a rabble rouser, all right.*

She swallowed a sigh, allowing herself to become the new Erin by increments. Still a lady, but one who intended to own her sexuality, Erin planned on having sex if it felt comfortable, whether or not she planned on dating her partner. It would be safe but fun, and she refused to feel guilt afterwards.

Considering the only man in the city she knew of—not counting despicable Cody—was Smith, she wondered if she ought to go out and expand her horizons. But who could she ask to introduce her around? The question bothered her while she worked, so she turned toward other avenues of change.

Social life—working on it.

The job—time to get a few more editing clients.

Cooking show—request to use Tilly's kitchen and hope she says yes.

Family—answer the phone.

"Hello?" she answered as she finished placing the baked cookies on a tray to cool.

"Erin? It's Mom."

"Hi, Mom." *I will be patient. I will. And I will get her to treat me like an adult.* "How are you?"

"Oh fine, honey. I just thought I'd check in." As she'd checked in the day before. And the day before that.

"Mom, we talked less when I lived down the street from you."

Her mother laughed. "I know. I just miss my baby."

Erin rolled her eyes. "What's new in Colby?"

Twenty minutes of small-town gossip from the dentist's office, where her mother worked as a hygienist, followed by another fifteen minutes of her father's antics at the hardware store he managed, had given the cookies enough time to cool.

Erin tested one and moaned.

"What did you say?" her mother asked.

"Just tasting one of the cookies I baked for my neighbor." And kind-of-not-really lover.

Hmm. Should she ask Smith to volunteer his time and body for her sexuality self-help project? Or should she ask him to introduce her to friends? He hadn't said anything to her since their mutual kissing on the couch. She took that as a sign of disinterest.

Just as she started to feel a tinge of embarrassment for her behavior, she knocked the shame away. She hadn't done anything wrong. Instead, she'd taken charge of her life and had fun for once.

"Erin? Erin, are you there?"

She realized she hadn't heard anything her mother had been saying. "Oh, sorry. I think I lost you for a minute." *Due to my girl power fantasy.* "What did you say, Mom?"

"I asked about your neighbor. Are you making friends? Have you talked to Cody since you broke it off with him?"

"No." She'd given her mother a brief explanation about Cody, mostly stating she'd made a mistake, not that Cody had been two-timing her. Bad enough her mother now knew she'd been right about Cody not being the man for her daughter. Erin didn't want to compound her mother's I-told-you-so moment by letting her know she'd been correct about his loose character too. "Cody and I are done, I think. It's for the best."

"The best. Right." A large pause. "When are you coming home?"

"Mom, we talked about this. Seattle is my new home. I want to see what it's like to live in the big city, away from family for a while. I need to be independent."

"But you can still be independent here. You could move to cousin Edna's apartment, the one over her garage? She's on the other side of town." A whole fifteen minutes away. "Bob? Bob, come here. It's Erin on the phone."

Erin sighed. Great. Now she had to talk to her father again. She loved her parents, but they acted as if she was still in high school. Her father refused to believe his youngest daughter could live on her own. At least her mom trusted her to be able to balance a checkbook and fend for herself.

"Erin," her father said as he took the phone from her mother. "How are you, honey? We miss you. When are you coming home?"

"I'm not, Dad. I'm good here."

"In Seattle?" He huffed. "Bunch of hipsters and rich people drinking coffee all day. What do they have out there we don't have in Colby?"

Smith Ramsey, for one. She cleared her throat and her dirty mind. "I need to be on my own, Dad. Trust me, I'm fine out here. I have friends."

A friend. Two if she counted Tilly.

"Who are these friends?" he asked with suspicion.

"In fact, I'm making my neighbor cookies. He helped me move my things when it didn't work out with Cody. He's a really nice man."

"Nice man, eh?" Her father groaned. "Men aren't nice. They're dogs. Don't trust him. And did you get those locks for your door I told you about?"

Having parents who worked for a hardware store and dentist had ensured Erin knew how to fix things around the house and to have clean teeth. She knew he meant well, so she answered in a chipper tone. "I'm all set. The building is safe with great neighbors on either side of me." Not a lie. She had the stairwell on one side of her and Smith on the other. But try telling her father she lived right next to an accessible entry point and he'd imagine her at the mercy of criminals hanging around stairwells. "I have a chain lock and a deadbolt. No sliding backdoor for a balcony or anything. I told you. The windows all lock too. The place is solid, and my landlady looks after everyone. They're all so nice. It's like a family here." The half-truths continued to pile on.

"Well, good. I like you being looked after."

"How's Joy doing? Has she called lately?"

He launched into stories about Joy and Tim and the grandkids, giving her a break about living so far away.

By the time she disconnected, her parents felt better about her living in the city, and she considered her one-way trip to hell for all the lying she'd been doing. Yes, she wanted her parents to feel fine with her being away, but she should have been able to tell them the truth. How could they respect her if they didn't know the real Erin, the one capable of so much more than living in their shadow?

But she was still finding her way, she thought, and gave herself a break. It took guts to live alone, away from everything she knew. And it took even more guts to get back out in the social scene after living for someone else for so long. Screw Cody Williams. Erin didn't need a man to make her feel complete. A husband and kids? Who needed that?

"I do." She hated herself for wanting what she'd been raised to believe awaited a woman set on the right path. "I can do whatever I want to and be a 'good girl' because it's my life. I don't owe anyone any apologies," she said to the delectable molasses cookies she placed into a plastic container.

She continued to reaffirm herself as she tidied up her small kitchen.

Once finished, she took a good hard look at her apartment and wondered how Tilly would feel if she repainted it a better color. Anything but orange.

Someone banged on the door, startling her.

She set the cookies on the counter and moved to look through her peephole. She opened the door with a smile. "Hello, Smith."

He glared down at her, and her smile widened. She didn't know why the sight of him in a foul mood should amuse her, but it did.

"Erin." He just waited.

"Oh. Would you like to come in?" She stepped back so he wouldn't run her over.

"Shut the door. I have some things to say to you."

She sighed. Great. First a lecture from her parents, then one from Smith. She shut the door behind him. "Are you hungry?" He wore a pair of jeans and a short-sleeved navy-blue polo with a logo on it. Vets on the Go! His work shirt? "Did you just come from a job?" *God, look at those massive arms.*

"Yes and yes."

She grabbed him a cookie from the tray. "I baked you some molasses cookies."

He blinked at it, and his frown disappeared. "Huh?"

"For being so nice and taking me out to Ringo's Bar on Thursday. These are for you." She motioned to the plastic container on the counter.

He shoved half the cookie she'd handed him into his mouth and groaned. "Fuck, this is good."

She colored at his word choice but basked in his praise.

He tucked the rest of the cookie in his mouth and chewed with concentration. She handed him another one, and he took it without having to be asked.

"Have you eaten dinner yet?"

"No. I just got home." He chewed with ferocity, his glare returning.

"Would you like me to make you something to eat?"

"What are you making?" He swore. "No, damn it. I came over here to talk."

She refused to make this awkward. Thursday night had been a monumental step for Erin into becoming the independent woman she wanted to be. "What did you want to talk about?" She smiled, deliberately throwing a hint of innocence into her voice.

Smith's gaze dropped to her mouth. His lids lowered, and she remembered how sexy he'd looked after she'd kissed him. Aroused so easily by the man, her nipples grew hard, and she hoped he didn't notice.

"Oh, no. No, you are not distracting me." He stalked her until he had her backed against the wall. "What the hell was the other night about?"

"Excuse me?"

His eyes widened. "Are you gonna try to tell me you were so drunk you don't remember grinding all over me on my couch?"

"What? No, not at all. I kissed you. It felt good. You were lovely."

He blinked, and she had the odd notion she'd thrown him for a loop. How delightful.

"I—you—" He blew out a breath. "You used me."

She cocked her head. "In what way?" His green eyes looked so dark, so deep. "Wow, you have pretty eyes."

"You said that already," he snapped. "At Ringo's, when you were drunk, you—"

"I was never drunk. A little buzzed maybe, but that wore off at the beginning of the movie."

"A-ha. So you *do* remember kissing me."

"Yes." She was confused. "Am I not supposed to remember you?"

"No. I mean yes. I just… Why the hell did you kiss me? You came hard, Erin." He stared down into her eyes. "And I wasn't ready for you."

"I don't understand. Ready for me?"

He startled her by lifting her off her feet, holding her against him and the wall, his face so close she could count individual eyelashes. "You aren't drinking now."

"No. I made cookies." Drily, she added, "I like to be sober when working around a hot stove."

"Good. Then there's no excuse for me not to do this." He leaned in for a kiss, one that was so light, so soft, he seduced her into a shivery mess in seconds. A hand came up to cup her breast, and the feel of his palm against her nipple shot her libido into overdrive.

"That's it," he crooned and kissed his way to her ear. He whispered, "If you ask me nicely, I'll show you how good it feels when I take charge. Would you like that, baby?"

Not sure what to say when her body refused to stop reaching for his, she braced her hands on his shoulders to get some space. But that meant looking into eyes that seduced her into a quivering *yes.* She nodded, caught in the spell of his mean grin.

Sexy, independent Erin wanted to see what a man could do for her that she couldn't. At least, that was what Erin tried telling herself. Because honestly, he'd stolen her ability to reason the moment he'd become so domineering.

Smith kissed her, his tongue invading, his hand more insistent over her breast. He tugged and pulled on her nipple, making her writhe in his grip. He wrapped her legs around his waist, and she happily complied, finding that happy place where his body rubbed hers at the perfect spot.

"Oh, no. Not this time," he whispered and sucked at her throat.

She tangled her fingers in his hair, lost to his touch, so needy it hurt.

He slowly lowered her to her feet and knelt before her.

"What are you doing?" she rasped, stroking his soft hair.

"Getting you ready," he whispered as he removed her shoes then parted her jeans. He tugged then down and off and shoved his face against her underwear.

His hot breath seared her, and she moaned, pulling his head closer.

He chuckled, then tugged her underwear to the side and slid a finger through the wet heat there.

Shocked, she could only stand there and feel.

"Fuck. You're so wet." He looked up, catching her blush. "And tasty, I'll bet. Let's see." He wouldn't remove her panties though, the material pulled to the side as he shoved his face close and *licked her.* Right there, lapping her up like a hungry tiger.

She froze, her body locked up tight as desire rushed past her defenses.

He groaned and licked, shoved his tongue deeper, inside her, then replaced it with his finger as he nibbled at her clit.

"Smith, oh, yes." She was so close, ready to come, standing against the wall, while Smith licked her to orgasm.

But he stopped and stood. "Oh hell no. Not this time." He watched her as he unbuttoned his jeans and pushed them and his underwear down, exposing a huge erection. "Slide those panties off."

She stared at him, enrapt, and did as he ordered. When he gripped himself and started pumping that large cock, she couldn't look away.

"Yeah, you got me so hard the other night I came in my pants. Not very comfortable. Not very nice, Erin," he said, his expression fierce. He continued to jerk off while he stared at her, and she found it the naughtiest, dirtiest thing. "I like that pussy. All nice and trimmed. And wet. So wet." He licked his lips, his hand moving faster. "Touch yourself. Let's see who can come first."

She had never done this before, not in front of anyone. Smith was like a sorcerer, weaving a spell she couldn't resist. She tentatively put her hand between her legs, and his gaze leapt to her nimble fingers.

"Yeah, that's it. Get yourself off." He knelt again, so she couldn't see him. "Now part your lips for me. That's a girl."

She did, and he put his mouth there, sucking her into a mighty climax that had her crying out his name.

Dazed and lost in the throbbing pleasure, she was barely aware of when he stood and drew closer, taking her hand to wrap it around his dick. He put his hand over hers as he kissed her, the desperate duel of lips and tongue in time to the hard pulls of his shaft.

And then he groaned and kissed her hard, and she felt wet warmth over her hand and against her skin. He pulled his mouth away and swore while he made her finish him.

She finally glanced down as he started to soften in her hand, and she saw his seed over their entwined hands. "Spread your legs for me," he said, his voice low.

She did, still entranced by the warm flesh in her hands. He shocked her by inserting a finger between her swollen folds, the intrusion enough to revive her desire. He pulled his finger out and sucked it clean. "You taste good, Erin." He kissed her, and she tasted herself on his lips. "Don't you think?"

Then he took her hand from him and raised her fingers to her mouth. "What do I taste like?"

She met his dare and licked a drop of his seed from her finger, pleased when his gaze darkened. "You taste good too," she whispered, trapped in a confusing and powerful emotion she couldn't quite name. Gratitude? Affection? Or was it just intense lust?

He let out a loud breath and stepped back. Grabbing a paper towel, he wet it to clean himself. Then he righted his clothes while she watched, still half naked. His gaze softened as he stared at her. Smith grabbed another towel and dampened it, then returned to clean her hands and gently between her legs. He had her step into her panties and jeans, then zipped them up.

He grabbed the container of cookies from the counter and approached once more. With a devilish grin, he put a finger under her chin and closed her gaping mouth before giving her a quick kiss. "Thanks for the cookies, neighbor."

The arrogant giant left. Pretty as you please.

Now what did she do about that?

SMITH RETURNED HOME, TOSSED THE COOKIES ON THE COFFEE table, and collapsed full-out onto the couch. Motherfucking night and day, what the hell had he just done?

So much for not getting involved with the crazy sexy neighbor. After that baffling sexcapade Thursday night that hadn't been enough, he'd intended to keep his distance. Girl-Next-Door-Pretty would not get his panties in a knot. No way. He'd been seduced by better and had come out unscathed.

He'd been too busy to see her again anyway, with one guy out and a double-booked job over the weekend since Cash had been manning the phones to cover their admin guy. But though Smith had done his best to forget the incident with Erin, he woke up hard and angry, and only jerking off in the shower seemed to help. Or jerking off before bed. Or during the day if he had a break.

Fuck. He hadn't been this horny since his teenage years. Somehow Erin had wormed her way into his brain with her innocent-as-fuck touching and kissing and grinding. And the worst thing? She hadn't come after him for more. Hadn't tried to seduce him into dating or buying her stuff. Or even helping her with anything. What the hell?

So, he'd decided to get even. To get in her loop the way she seemed stuck in his.

And boy, had that backfired.

Now he knew what she tasted like. How she looked when she came standing up. His dick started to spike again, and he swore the thing had a mind of its own. He wanted inside that hot beauty next door. So much that he considered offering her a thanks with more pleasure than she could stand.

He might not be so experienced when it came to dating and relationships, but he knew what to do in bed. Or on a couch. Or against a wall.

He grinned at that. With any luck she'd be as confused as he was about their nonexistent relationship and come on over to discuss it. Then he'd offer her some no-strings-attached orgasms.

He groaned, remembering how good she'd tasted, how sleek and pretty she was between her legs.

Yeah. He'd set the bait. Now he had only to sit back and wait for the siren next door to take it.

MARIE HARTE

But damned if the woman would do things the easy way.

By Wednesday afternoon, Smith had had enough. For once he had a day off, so at ten in the morning, he pounded on Erin's door.

No one answered.

He left and stomped down the hall to knock at Tilly's.

She answered in a huff. "What?"

"Is Erin here?"

Tilly blinked. "Erin? She lives right next to you, dumbass."

Smith gritted his teeth. "I know that. I want to talk to her, but she's not home. I thought she might be here taking care of you, Mrs. McMouth."

Tilly laughed. "Ah, to be young and stupid again. Come on in, numbnuts. I have cookies."

Since he'd given himself a stomachache by eating all of his molasses cookies Monday evening while waiting for Erin to come over, he had no problem eating more of Tilly's. Erin had apparently made her some kind of lemon bar, and Smith devoured three of them before Tilly smacked his hands and hid them away.

"Jesus, boy. When's the last time you ate?"

"Last night. I don't know." Agitated, his appetite either nonexistent or off the charts, and fretting about stupid shit, Smith had been at odds to explain his disturbing fascination with Erin. She was just a woman, after all. A nice young woman from Kansas who was new to town. He hadn't thought she had a treacherous bone in her body. Now he wasn't so sure. "Tilly, what do you know about Erin?"

Tilly would tell him the truth. They had an honest relationship

82

built on trust and hating people. They liked each other, would never admit it, and mostly loathed everyone else.

"What do you want to know?"

"Quit playing dumb. Is she dating a bunch of guys or what? Was Cody her only boyfriend?" Because the woman being a player would make so much more sense than that Smith had fallen for a woman too innocent to know she was driving him insane.

"'Fraid she is what she looks like, Smith. Erin's a nice girl, too nice, if you ask me." She paused, her eyes narrowed, no doubt waiting for an obnoxious comment. He waited her out, and she huffed in disappointment before adding, "Her family's all in Kansas, I think. Except for a sister in New Jersey. Or Pennsylvania. Some place in the northeast. Erin came out here for that idiot boyfriend who was cheating on her. She's all alone here but for me and you." Tilly gave a pregnant pause. "So I introduced her to my nephew, Rupert. He's showing her the town, if you know what I mean." She wiggled her eyebrows, and Smith saw red.

Then common sense prevailed. Tilly was nearly eighty. Her nephew had to be in his fifties or sixties. He shook his head. "Oh, I know what you mean."

She grinned at him. "What do you want with the girl, anyway?"

"Never mind. I'll talk to her when I see her again."

"That's if she doesn't see you and run the other way." She slapped her leg and laughed. And laughed some more at his sour expression.

"Whatever." He left Tilly in a great mood and spent his morning lifting weights to work out his aggression. Then a run in the cool October air helped clear his mind. After he returned home and showered, he cleaned his apartment, not a fan of dust or clutter.

Enough time had passed that Erin should have returned. He made himself lunch and waited around, just in case she decided to come over.

Minutes passed.

He knocked on her door again. Nothing. Fuming, he returned to his apartment, then paused. It wasn't exactly protocol, but he had her cell phone number from the contact sheet at work. After a quick hassle dealing with Finley, a wacky ex-Navy guy obsessed with magic, he managed to secure Erin's number.

The question then became, did he have the stones to use it?

CHAPTER SIX

*E*rin knew she'd done the right thing accepting Tilly's offer to show her around town, even if it had come from Tilly's oddball nephew, Rupert. Sixty years young, Rupert had a perpetual spark in his big brown eyes and a devilish grin. He had a lewd sense of humor that had turned her face red more than once. And his aged Oldsmobile could only be called a monstrosity, but she did feel safe in it. The man drove slower than a sloth.

Her silver fox companion had parked near a playground in Queen Anne, a nicer area in Seattle just south of Greenwood, where she currently resided. The northern part of Queen Anne Avenue boasted amazing shops, and she and Rupert did their share of window shopping. Though he walked with a cane and slight limp, his impairment hadn't slowed him down much.

He told her his favorite places to eat, pointed out a few idiots and numbskulls to steer clear of (he had a beef with a pet supply store owner for some reason he refused to elaborate about,) and treated her to lunch at 5 Spot, an American eatery that made the best Val Verde Scramble. She'd ordered breakfast in the afternoon while Rupert had gobbled down sweet potato pancakes.

As they sat drinking coffee to wash down brunch, she tried again to pay for their food.

"Nonsense." Rupert slurped his coffee. "You're new to town. It's my treat." He leaned closer and winked. "Besides, I'm hoping rumors will circulate that I'm dining with a beautiful younger woman. Make my girl, Willie, jealous. It's good for her to know I'm still quite a catch."

"But you are. Handsome, charming, and you know everything about everyone." She smiled, enjoying herself.

He nodded. "I've lived in Queen Anne going on fifty years. The town has changed a lot, but it's still home."

He called it a town. She thought of it as just one nicer area in a grand city. "Is this your favorite neighborhood in Seattle?"

"I'm biased, but yes. Green Lake is nice. Magnolia too. The Downtown area is pretty busy. Have you been to Pike Place Market yet? You know, the farmer's market? Where they throw the fish around? It's right on the water."

"Not yet. It's on my to-do list."

"I'd take you down there, but I promised Willie I'd help with a new cat we found."

"Oh?"

He nodded. "Willie started a hometown rescue for strays over a year ago. We've been taking them in, fostering them, then helping the animals find places to live. I don't suppose you want a cat or dog?" Before she could remind him she'd just moved into her apartment, he shook his head. "Ah, never mind. Aunt Tilly has a no pets policy. Too bad. You look like a dog person."

"My mom has a dog. Vanilla. He's a mutt with a lot of border collie in him. A sweetie and a great guard dog." The thought of her Vanilla gave her a touch of homesickness. "I miss him." She surprised herself.

"Pets bring out the best in us. And the worst, sometimes." He sounded sad. "But you know, we're not here to talk about animals. What brings you to Seattle, Erin?"

So Tilly hadn't mentioned Cody, apparently. "I came because of a man." She shook her head and confided, "It didn't work out. The problem is, everyone back home told me he was no good. I spent a lot of money and time to get to here. Now if I go back, they'll all know they were right."

"Can't do that."

"No. Plus, I'm learning to like it out here. It's more expensive, but it's all so alive. And I like being on my own." She paused. "Though I won't lie. I'd like to make some friends and start getting out more. Except I work for Tilly and from home, so making friends isn't as easy."

"Now don't you worry about that. I know just the person you need to talk to." He smiled. "In fact, I know everyone around here." He laughed. "You want to make friends, I'm just the person you need. So, we talking gal pals or finding you a man? Because if you're looking for a man, my girl Willie is the one you want to talk to. She's got connections."

Erin blinked. "Connections?"

"Oh, not with strippers or escorts or anything. She's done with all that."

"Not what I'd meant." *Done with all that?*

"But she's a woman who knows all about matchmaking and

making it stick. She can read people." He studied Erin. "Come on. You need to meet her."

WHICH WAS HOW ERIN FOUND HERSELF IN A VERY STRANGE situation with no one to blame but herself. She should have said no the moment Rupert had mentioned strippers in conjunction with Willie. But he'd been so nice, and he was Tilly's nephew. Besides, she'd had nothing better to do all day. It had been good for her to get out and see new things.

At least the current nuttiness kept her mind from Smith. Every time she thought about him and what he'd done to her on Sunday, she grew lightheaded. God. How did the man *do* that to her? They barely knew each other, yet he brought her to orgasm so easily. She'd been with Cody for months and it took forever for her to climax, and usually she had to make that happen herself.

"So, what do you think?" Willie asked.

Erin brought herself back to the present, aware she needed to find some kind of excuse to leave. Soon. Before she broke down in hysterical laughter and offended her hosts. Willie fit Rupert. She seemed small and delicate, but then she opened her mouth and swore like a sailor, truck driver, and New York taxi driver combined. She had tanned skin, wrinkled with age, and striking hazel eyes. Yet she wasn't exactly pretty. Memorable for sure. She wore a shawl over a housedress that looked as if it had been in style in the 70s.

She matched her house for sure. The décor could only be called eclectic. Besides the motley group of cats and dogs lying around, most with battle wounds—torn ears, a missing eye, a stump of a tail—she had a bunch of collectibles. Erin noticed a few Hummels and a Lladro along with some strange looking figurines all set on doilies in a hutch. Upon closer inspection, she blanched. Some of those figurines looked to be…er…engaging in sex.

"Like my Sixty-Niner? That's a favorite of mine," Willie said, seeing Erin's attention.

Erin blushed and heard Rupert chuckle. "It's very…interesting."

"Sure is." Willie winked at Rupert. "My honey tells me you want a man."

"*What?* No, I'm just looking to make new friends. I'm new to the city and—"

"And you have no man. No problem, girl. I can help."

Lord. "No, really. I'm kind of seeing this guy in my apartment complex." *Sorry, Smith.* "But I just thought it would be nice to get out and see the city and meet new people. Tilly's been a big help."

"Rupert's aunt is nice enough, I suppose." Only someone like Willie would call Tilly nice. "But she's out of touch."

Someone banged on the front door, which sent the animals into a frenzy. "Sic 'em, Mathmos," Willie ordered, and a long-haired Chihuahua joined an elderly shepherd as they raced to the door, barking as if the devil himself had come calling. The white Persian cat that had earlier been eyeing Erin jumped up onto a plush, puke-green La-Z-Boy covered in a pattern of yellow flowers. The cat stared at her with hostility bordering on boredom.

"We're always busy around here, aren't we, Barbarella?" Willie asked as she stroked the cat's fur.

The cat continued to watch Erin, and she suddenly knew how a helpless mouse must feel.

"I'll see who it is," Rupert said.

He and the animals returned with a large hunk of a man, one who looked surprisingly familiar. Tall, though not as tall as Smith, he had a muscular torso under a Pets Fur Life Tee-shirt.

"Hey, Willie. Hi," he said to Erin and smiled. "You look familiar."

"I was just thinking the same thing."

He stared a moment more then snapped his fingers. "You live in Emerald Estates, don't you?"

She nodded. "Oh, yes. I've seen you around."

He held out a hand. "Brad Battle."

She took his hand, rough with calluses, noting how it dwarfed hers. "Erin Briggs. I just moved in two weeks ago."

He held on a moment longer than she would have before letting go. His eyes warmed. "Welcome to the neighborhood, Erin. How'd you hook up with these two?"

Willie hooted—there was no other word for it. Rupert laughed.

"Tilly introduced me to Rupert to show me around."

"I'm her nephew," Rupert said.

Brad's brows rose. "Small world." He had sandy colored hair and green eyes lighter than Smith's. Handsome, almost pretty.

"What are you doing here?" she asked.

"I help out at Pets Fur Life, a local animal shelter. Willie and Rupert help us out a lot."

"He's a fireman too." Willie nudged her in the ribs. "And single."

Brad grinned. "Yep. And *so* in demand." He rolled his eyes. "From Willie, Rupert, my boss, my team."

"Not to mention all the ladies." Rupert gave a low laugh. "I know what that's like."

Willie frowned.

Erin had about reached her limit on new experiences. She liked everyone, but the cat had yet to stop watching her. She didn't think it had blinked the entire time she'd been standing there. And now the hairy Chihuahua had joined the cat on the chair, also watching her with suspicion.

Brad stared past her at the hutch of figurines, his brows drawn in thought. Then astonishment.

"You know, it was great hanging with you today, Rupert. But I'd better be getting back." Erin gave him a peck him on the cheek. "Thanks so much for showing me Queen Anne." She turned to offer Willie a hug and saw a scowl on the woman's face. "Uh, er, great to meet you, Willie."

"Yeah. You too. But mind, he's taken." She nodded to Rupert.

Did the old woman really think Erin had made a move on Rupert? How embarrassing. She refused to look at Brad.

The shepherd glanced from Willie to Erin and growled.

"Right. Taken. Got it." She stepped toward the door.

"Hold on. I'll drive you back," Rupert offered.

"You know what? I can take her back," Brad said. He handed Willie a stack of papers Erin only now noticed. "We both live in Tilly's apartments. Only makes sense." He turned to Erin. "If you're okay with that."

"That would be great. Thanks."

Rupert glanced from Brad to Erin and smiled wide. "Sure, sure.

Okay. Anytime you want to see the sights, you call me, Erin." He waved goodbye and put an arm around Willie's shoulders, which seemed to satisfy the older woman.

Erin turned and left before Willie could command her strange assortment of animals to attack.

Brad joined her and opened the door of his Mustang.

"Thank you," she told him. "I mean that."

He grinned. Oh wow. He had a dimple. And a manly chin and kind eyes. And that body… Okay, she needed a moment to process. Except instead of feeling enamored, she just liked looking at him. Her mind returned to Smith, comparing the two, and she had no idea why thoughts of her mean neighbor turned her on when this perfectly lovely man did nothing for her.

She got in the car and buckled in.

Brad joined her and did the same. "Anytime. I've known Willie and Rupert for a few months. They're great people, and they really care about the animals. But they're a little…different." He paused. "You know, this is the first time I've been in their living room. Um, was it my imagination, or were some of her figurines X-rated?"

She laughed in relief. "No. I saw that too. Oh my God." She laughed some more.

"So, you and Rupert aren't a thing, are you?" he teased. "I did my best not to lose it when Willie warned you off. Although, hey, maybe you're into older guys."

"Stop. Please." She shook her head. "Rupert was so sweet today. Tilly asked him to show me around."

Brad drove with competence, making her feel safe. She glanced subtly over at him. Were his arms larger than Smith's? She didn't think so.

"You know," Brad said after a moment. "I'd be happy to show you around town. I grew up here, but I was away for a while when I served in the military. When I came home, things had changed. It took a while to meet new people. I know that's not easy."

"No. It's not. And I work from home. I edit for some online magazines. When I'm not doing that, I fix Tilly's meals and clean for her."

"Nice." He smiled, his green eyes flashing with approval. "She's a tough old lady. I like her."

"Me too." Brad had that going for him. He could see beyond the surface, and he was nice. So why did she find him too much like Cody for comfort? She wanted to tell him she'd be happy to go out. And she should. But strangely, she felt as if she were being disloyal to Smith. A man she'd twice had almost-sex with but had yet to talk to her since their last outing. Why was that, anyway? "I'd like to go out, but I don't want to give you the wrong impression." She found it difficult to say but forced herself to. "I moved out here to be with my boyfriend. But it didn't work out. I'm kind of on my own and not really into dating right now."

"No problem." Brad didn't shift his expression, nor did she feel anything but his sincerity when he said, "It's good to have friends. So, if you want to go out or meet people, as friends, let me know. I'll give you my number." She plugged his cell number into her phone and saw a number of texts she'd missed. "And hey, if you change your mind and want to date, let me know that too." He gave her a flirty smile that made her blush.

She tucked her phone away to look at later, not wanting to be rude. They talked about his job for the Seattle Fire Department and her life in Colby compared to Seattle.

He parked behind the building near her car.

"Thanks again, Brad." He was sweet and charming. And someone she'd like to call a friend. "You know, once I get myself more settled, I'd love to go out sometime."

He flashed her a grin. "Great. You have my number. Oh, and I'm in 6B if you ever need anything." A unit upstairs.

She nodded. "I'm in 1A."

They walked inside together. He waved and continued up the stairs. She walked to her apartment and heard a beep from her phone. She hadn't realized she'd had it muted earlier. A glance showed another text. From Smith.

Text me when you get back.

Her heart raced. Instead of texting him, she knocked on his door.

After a moment, he opened it and glared at her. "Well it's about time." He dragged her into his apartment. It looked the same as it had last time, neat as a pin.

"Hi. What's up?" She studied him, wondering what it was about the man that sent her senses reeling. Brad seemed like the calm in a storm. Smith would be the rampaging tornado, knocking everything down.

"Where have you been? It's four o'clock. I wanted to talk to you." His frown deepened. He fidgeted as she watched him, and he barked, "What?"

Someone not familiar with Smith would be intimidated. Man or woman, a person would have to be crazy not to be a little taken aback by his powerful frame and dark moods. But Erin felt it comforting. *I am so weird.*

She swallowed back a sigh. "Smith, are you okay?"

He looked murderous. She was so turned on she blushed.

"Am I okay? I don't know. My next-door neighbor keeps sexing me up then ignoring me. I'm not sure if that's a good or bad thing."

"Oh." Wait. He'd noticed her absence? That meant he wanted her to be around him more, then. Didn't it? Excitement made her breathy, and she hated that she loved he'd missed her. She wasn't trying to play games. "I didn't think you wanted me around."

"What?" His eyes grew comically wide. "Are you kidding?"

"Well, you never called or texted until now."

"I…" He opened and closed his mouth, giving her an odd look. "You didn't either."

"I didn't want to be presumptuous. We had fun together, and I like you. But I'm not pushing you for anything, Smith."

"I know." He sounded subdued. "So, ah, what… What have you been up to today?"

She didn't think that's what he'd started to say, but she didn't want to fight with him. She'd much rather make love with him.

The thought struck her mute.

"You okay?" He stepped closer.

Her awareness skyrocketed. He smelled amazing, as if he'd recently showered. Like sandalwood over his typical, manly scent. She couldn't describe it, except to say he smelled good, clean. Sexy.

She cleared her throat. "I'm fine. Just a tickle in my throat. Today I went out with Rupert, Tilly's nephew. He showed me around Queen Anne."

"Huh. Did you have fun?"

He stood close, and she had to look up at him to make eye contact. Smith made her feel small, both protected and exposed at the same time. She didn't think he'd hurt her, not physically at least. But emotionally he affected her in a way she didn't yet understand. She felt electrified near him, attuned to his expressions, the things he did and didn't say.

He raised a brow at her silence, and she blurted, "Um, fun. Yes, we had fun. It got a little weird at Rupert's girlfriend's house, though. She has strange pets and even stranger collectibles." Sixty-niner. Geez. She eyed Smith, wondering if their size difference would make that act harder or easier.

She blushed at the thought.

"Rupert's got a girlfriend?"

"Yes. I gave him a kiss on the cheek to thank him for taking me around, and she warned me away." Erin could laugh about it now. "I thought she was going to sic her evil pets on me."

Smith grinned. "That would have been something to see."

"Lucky for me, Brad Battle knows them too. He arrived in time to bring me home, so I didn't have to share the car with Rupert again."

Smith's smile vanished.

"Brad lives in 6B. Upstairs." She pointed up. "Do you know him?"

"He's a decent enough guy." He sounded as if that pained him to say. "Did he ask you out?" She felt weird about answering but needn't have bothered. "Of course he did." Smith watched her like a hawk. "What did you say?"

"Is this really your business?"

He shrugged. "Maybe not. Humor me."

"I, well, I just… I told him I had just broken off with my boyfriend and wasn't ready for a relationship." What would Smith make of that, since she'd done sexy things with him in the short time she'd been away from Cody?

Smith seemed to relax. "Well, that's true. Probably a good answer. Brad's a good guy, but he's a fireman. And they're like pus—ah, they seem to attract a lot of women."

"What were you going to say?" To her amused astonishment, he seemed to be blushing.

"Erin."

"Tell me."

"I was going to say pussy-magnets. Happy now?" He stroked her cheek and slowly leaned close.

She waited, trembling.

The kiss barely landed, a feather of touch, and it shook her balance. Literally. She teetered in her haste to get closer and fell into him.

"Oh."

He didn't move, not at all fazed by her weight. She gripped his arms, in lust all over again. The humor and desire in his gaze made her breathless. "You're strong."

"Uh huh." He kissed her again, teasing with the brush of his mouth. "And you're a lightweight. Thank God." He nibbled his way across her cheek to her ear and took her earlobe in his teeth.

She clutched his arms, aroused, confused, and feeling more for him than mere physical attraction.

"How about having dinner with me tonight?" He blew in her ear, and she gasped. He pulled her closer, rubbing that huge, hard body against her. "Yeah. Just you and me and a pizza. Maybe we can watch a movie again...or something."

She blinked when he moved back, putting distance between them. "A m-movie?" *Get it together, Erin!* She didn't like his smug satisfaction. But the sight of his obvious erection helped soothe her ego. "And pizza. I can do that."

"But only if you bring some of those lemon things you gave Tilly. I think they might be even better than the molasses cookies."

It took her a moment to understand what he was talking about. "You liked my cookies?"

"I love your...cookies." The look he shot her breasts and the rest of her body told her what he really meant.

"Smith."

"Erin." He smiled, and the unguarded happiness on his face stunned her to silence. He sighed. "What now?"

"I just realized what a huge pain you're turning out to be. Now I need to make more lemon meltaways."

He huffed. "I'm a pain? Baby, look in the mirror. You've got me hurting from sunup to sundown." He grabbed her hand and held it against his impressive arousal.

She wanted badly to squeeze, to watch him come this time instead of feeling it in her hands. And then she wondered how she'd become such a sexual creature when for years she'd never had the courage to do the things she'd done with Smith.

"But I won't hold it against you." He squeezed her hand on him and groaned, then deliberately tugged her away. "This thing between us, it's strong. I don't know what it is, but we're gonna find out together. And no more ignoring me."

"You were ignoring me," she said in a small voice, thrilled and scared that he felt the same connection she did, so soon after her mistake with Cody.

"Whatever. Point is, it's confusing."

"I know." She sighed.

Which seemed to please him. He hugged her, then pushed her toward the door. "Yeah, yeah. No skimping on the lemon things. See you at six, okay?"

"If I can get them done by then." She frowned. "How come this dinner comes with strings attached?"

"Because I said so." He smiled and shut the door in her face.

"Huh." *I must be insane to spend more time with a man who makes me lose all control.* But then, she'd never felt this way before. Free and uncertain and attracted to a man who clearly wanted her.

"I could do worse." She had—Cody.

But Smith was nothing like her ex. He didn't lie. He said what he thought, maybe a little too much. And he hadn't liked her avoiding him.

She smiled as she went back into her apartment and brought out the ingredients for her lemon meltaways. He liked her. She liked him.

Now what to do about that?

CHAPTER SEVEN

*S*mith didn't know what had come over him. He didn't cater to women much. He was pleasant, polite. And he was an unselfish lover. Why should he care so damn much that Erin had ignored him? She seemed embarrassed to admit she'd thought he was avoiding her. Had he been? He'd been waiting for her to come to him, and perhaps she'd done the same.

She had a point. But Smith wasn't used to having to pursue women. They came to him. At his size, he was difficult to miss. His muscles and looks were enough to lure potential bedmates. Yet he'd been the one chasing a lover this time. *Hell.* Every time he saw her, he wanted her a little bit more.

Erin's smile made her entire face light up, and he could stare at her for hours and not grow bored. He wanted to do something for her, anything, to hear her laugh again.

Knowing Brad had had her all to himself annoyed the shit out of Smith, and that bothered him too. Because he felt...jealous.

Fuck. What the hell was the matter with him?

It didn't help that his new brothers seemed way too happy with the women in their lives. And now even Hector and Lafayette, twin coworkers, had also paired up. Every damn body he knew seemed to have found love and come out the better for it. Which showed him how jacked up his life was that he had no one and never had.

But things were different now. He knew Meg wasn't his mom. Angela had died. He had brothers. A cousin. Hell, even Aunt Jane. He had only to accept them and let them in.

A familiar tension gripped him. He hated being afraid, worried that he'd open himself up and get stepped on all over again. No matter how many times he tried, the results had always been the same.

"You're my penance, boy." Momma *frowned at him. Slight, blond, and blue-eyed, his beautiful mother looked nothing like him.*

Five-year-old Smith asked, "What's penance, Momma?"

"Atonement. A need to do right. I'm being punished because of you."

He started to cry, not wanting to get her in trouble. "I'm sorry."

"You can't even stop from pissing in your pants."

Shame filled him. But he hated the dark, and being shoved in the closet for hours on end scared him so much.

"I won't do it again if you put a light on."

"You'll do it again because you hate me." She sighed and straightened his shirt. "God hates me too. Because she *can do nothing wrong, and* I *can do nothing right."*

"Momma?" He tugged her arm, already tall and spindly, and constantly hungry. "I love you."

"I know you do." She seemed to soften. The doorbell rang, and her expression turned glacial. "But you don't matter." She answered the door, and Uncle Allen entered, all smiles as he saw Smith standing there.

The visit went as it always did. Uncle Allen asked him questions. They played blocks and cars together. Then he went into the back to talk to Momma. Smith watched TV, away from Momma's room. But he heard the moans and grunts and things banging anyway, things he was supposed to ignore.

Allen would appear, ruffle Smith's hair and smile, then leave with promises to return the next month.

For a long time he did. Until he didn't. And Momma grew angrier and meaner, because she deserved so much more out of life than him. She wanted good little boys like his cousins who didn't wet their pants or their bed and weren't hungry or scared or needy.

But poor Momma had nothing else but a waste of a child. So, he'd do his best to make it up to her. He tried so hard, but he never could measure up.

"And now I know why. She wasn't my mother, and I'm not her son." But good old Uncle Allen must have known. And he hadn't cared enough to stay.

The memories left a bad taste in his mouth, as they always did. Smith wondered what he thought he was doing with Erin, a decent woman too sweet for her own good. Then he told himself to stop being a drama queen. Hell, it was just pizza and lemon bars. And if he were lucky, some quality sack time with the beauty next door.

Why make a big deal of it?

He scrolled through his phone, clearing out old messages and emails, and realized he had tomorrow off thanks to Cash making up for the weekend.

Smith hadn't talked to his brothers in more than one-word sentences since that dinner almost two weeks ago. They tiptoed around his growls and brusque attitude. But he didn't care, still so angry about things beyond everyone's control. He knew he shouldn't blame them for growing up with their mother. They hadn't had an easy time of it either.

But fuck, at least Angela hadn't raised them to believe they had nothing going for them. Meg still fucked with his head, hearing her in his dreams and at times like this, when he should have been stoked about sharing a meal with Erin. Smith instead wondered why Erin wanted to be with him. For what she might get out of him? Money? Favors? Sex? That seemed to be her only interest. Yet she'd had time to hang with perfect Brad Battle, a fucking fireman no less. Pussy magnets, those firefighters.

But Erin had told him no. Or so she'd said.

What if she'd been lying?

He ordered their pizza and tried to control his thoughts, ignoring the notion he'd never be good enough for anyone or anything, wrestling familiar demons a constant trial. He tried to distract himself with a book and finally lost himself in a wizarding world far away, where evil wore black and the white knights won in the end.

If only life were that simple.

Someone knocked at the door.

His palms felt damp. Smith wiped them on his jeans, conscious he wore a form-fitting Tee-shirt on purpose. Hell, if Erin only wanted him for his body, he could handle that. As long as they could be honest with each other, he could deal with all his emotional bullshit, shoving it behind simple pleasure.

Feeling better about things and knowing he could please a woman, no question, he took back some well-deserved arrogance and opened the door.

The pizza guy stood there with two pies. Disappointed it wasn't Erin, Smith paid the guy and stepped back inside.

Fifteen minutes later, she still hadn't shown up.

When she finally knocked, he opened the door and snarled, "You're late."

She shoved the plate of goodies at him and snarled back, "You're welcome."

His ire faded, the sight of Erin in a mad was nothing compared to the sight of her bare legs. She wore shorts and a sweatshirt with butterflies on it.

"It's October, and you're wearing shorts?" Not that he was complaining. Though he'd seen her bare legs before, he'd been focused on other parts of her. But now, seeing those toned thighs and calves, her smooth skin so close, he wanted to touch her.

She blew out a breath, and her hair flipped up. "Something's wrong with the heat in my apartment. It feels like a sauna in there. And my oven was acting weird. This is the second batch. The first one burned."

"I'll take a look at it." He started to move past her, but she stopped him with a hand on his arm.

"Can we please just relax? I'm frazzled."

He took a good look at her and nodded, now feeling bad about needling her. "Sure. Come on." He led her to the kitchen island where two plates sat. "Extra cheese or the works?"

"One of each." She smiled.

His surly mood vanished as if it had never been. Funny how her happiness seemed contagious, especially to a guy who didn't usually have much to smile about. He served up the pie, giving himself the same. "Beer? Soda? Water?"

"Beer would be good. And don't even think of calling me a light-weight," she growled.

He held his hands up in surrender, trying not to smile at her. "No problem. You want an ale or a lager?"

"Something light."

He handed her a pale ale and took a lager for himself. Then he stood across from her and watched her gobble down her pizza. He ate with her, and for a time, they didn't talk, too full of cheese and dough.

"Sorry if I was crabby," Erin apologized first.

"Me too."

"What? You're sorry I was crabby?" She grinned. "Or you're sorry you answered the door like a jerk?"

"Both." He chuckled. Something about Erin brought out laughter. "What's up with your apartment?"

"No idea. I haven't fiddled with the thermostat at all, but suddenly it got super-hot inside. Then my oven went on the fritz."

"Since the heat and the gas oven aren't related, you have an unhappy coincidence."

"Great," she groaned. "Now how am I going to prep Tilly's meals?"

"You can use my place if you need to," popped out before he could catch it. Her smile of thanks erased any hint of unease.

"Thanks. I can make them in her house too. I just like to make her food ahead of time, so I know if I need to buy groceries or to plan around her tastes. Tilly's a little picky."

"Who would have guessed?"

He ate more pizza before he realized Erin was watching him with wide eyes. "What?"

"You really put a lot away." Her gaze wandered the breadth of his chest, and it was all he could do not to perk up and flex for her. "Where does it go? Not to fat, that's for sure." She sighed and looked down at her stomach. "You're so lucky."

"What are you talking about?" He drained the rest of his beer and got another, then grabbed her a water when she asked for it. "You're tiny."

"I could lose five pounds."

He rolled his eyes. "From your feet? Gimme a break."

She frowned. "Guys have no idea how hard it is to be a girl. Everyone expects you to be so skinny."

"Yeah? Well you have no idea how tough it is to keep a girl interested without muscle."

"What are *you* talking about?"

He flushed. "I don't mean me. I've been into lifting since I first tried it in high school. It helped with my aggression problems."

"Aggressive? You?" she teased. "No way."

"I know. What a shock." He glanced at his weight bench, and his smile faded as he remembered trying so hard to be strong to impress Meg. When that had failed, he'd stuck with it because it made him feel better. "Sometimes you think the only thing you have going for you is on the outside, because the inside sucks. But then you get big, and it still doesn't matter."

He saw her watching him with keen eyes and flushed. "I mean, that's what I heard. A few friends in the Corps use to share stories. It's not easy when you're naturally small as a guy. Women can be just as superficial, you know."

"I believe you." She sighed. "But men only care about boobs and butts. Cody liked me thinner."

"Cody is a horse's ass. I thought we established that."

She smiled. "We did."

"Besides, where the hell could you lose five pounds from? Not your ass, which is perfect. Or your belly, which I happen to know is nice and firm." He drank more beer, staring at her perfect breasts. To his satisfaction, her nipples beaded through the material. He decided to make his move. He put the beer down and rounded the island to stand directly in front of her. "And not those pretty breasts. They're perfect." He watched her and raised a hand, seeing her eyes wide, her breath coming faster. She made no move to stop him. He put a hand on her breast and cupped the mound.

"Oh, that feels good."

"Yeah?" He molded her flesh, then teased her nipple, loving how she responded to him. "You want more?"

"I, I… I don't know." She clearly wanted him, but now she played hard to get? She pushed his hand from her. "We need to talk."

He was so stupid. Why had he been teasing her when he could have kissed her into saying yes from the get-go? He'd lost his moment, and now she wanted "to talk." He groaned, crossed his arms over his chest, and leaned against the island. "Fine. So talk."

ERIN FELT THREE KINDS OF FOOLISH AS SHE TRIED TO CALM HER raging body. She had no idea how to act with Smith, confused at her feelings and at a loss as to how to control her body around the man. She also wasn't very good at playing games and never had been.

"Look, I'm just going to be honest with you." She noted the narrowing of his gaze, but he only nodded. "You confuse me."

"*I* confuse *you?*" He barked out a laugh. "I think it's the other way around."

"Would you hush up?" she snapped. "I'm trying to explain."

His lips tightened, but she thought she saw amusement in his eyes.

"Are you laughing at me?"

He coughed. "Wouldn't dream of it."

"Okay. Look. I'm not good at this." She pointed to him and her. "At relationships. I obviously misread signals. Look at Cody. Before him, I had two boyfriends in college. Neither lasted long, but that might have been my fault because I just grew bored with trying to make them happy. I'm done pleasing other people. This is the new me. It's my life, and I plan on living it the way I want to."

She felt emboldened confessing her need to be strong. "I don't owe anyone anything. I'm doing it all on my own. No help from Mom or Dad or Joy—my sister," she explained, reassured that he seemed to hang on every word. "I could have dated Brad, but I don't want to. And I don't feel guilty about that. Just because he asked doesn't mean I had to say yes."

Smith stiffened. "Is he giving you a hard time?"

She blinked. "What? Oh, no. He was super nice. When I told him I just wanted to be friends, he was fine with it."

Smith relaxed. "Good."

"But you confuse me," she continued. "I feel different with you. And I don't know why."

His intense stare made her want to squirm. Smith listened to her with his entire being.

"I'm not playing games with you," she told him. "Heck, if you want the truth, I've never done stuff with a guy the way I did with you. Especially not after just meeting you." She hated that her cheeks heated.

He nodded. "I believe you."

She blew out a breath. "I don't care if you believe me. I'm just saying you make me do things I don't do with other people. Oh, stop frowning. I don't mean you made me do something against my will. I mean you make me forget myself. When you touch me I…"

He stepped closer and tilted her chin up. His voice soft, he said,

"You what? You lose control? You want to touch and be touched? You want to feel closer?"

"Yes, all that." She gripped his beltloop and tugged on it, frustrated he seemed so far away. Afraid he was growing too close too fast. And she didn't really know him that well. "I want to be the new me, but I'm afraid I'm falling into an old pattern. I like you, Smith. A lot. But I don't really know you. And I…"

His face grew guarded. "And you what?"

"And I want to get to know you," she whispered, unable to look away from him. "I love your body, okay? You're sexy. You know it, so don't act surprised. But I like when you laugh, and I have no idea what you like to eat or drink or do."

He looked confused for a moment then pleasantly surprised. "Oh, well." He leaned down and planted a kiss on her cheek. When he straightened, he looked…happy. Which for Smith was saying a lot. The man always wore such an intense look—of frustration, annoyance, even desire. But happiness appeared rarely, in Erin's experience.

His eyes looked soft, his mouth curled up in a half smile. "I actually have tomorrow off since I worked all day yesterday. Would you, I don't know, like to go out?" He shrugged, his movements stiff. "I could show you parts of the city you haven't seen yet. Some cool stuff around here that you could walk to if you wanted."

She couldn't look away from this vulnerable side of Smith. Good Lord, he seemed almost shy as he asked her out, and she couldn't have said why that charmed her.

Erin smiled. "I'd love that. Do you think we could go downtown to Pike Place Market too? I've seen it on TV and want to see if they really do throw fish around."

"Sure." He took a step back. "I should probably be honest with you as well."

"If this is the part where you have a girlfriend, I'm going to brain you with your own beer bottle."

He didn't seem to know how to handle her laughing at herself. "Um, no. I'm not the cheating kind."

That's what they all say.

"I like you, and I want to fuck you. So much, in a whole lot of different ways."

She gaped, not sure she'd heard him right. But he was still talking, his cheeks pink, and she wanted him to have his say.

"The choice to be with me or not is yours. I'm just being honest. I like you telling it to me straight. I want that. From you. Honesty, I mean. I want you. I think you're hot, and you're cute. I still dream about going down on you." He blew out a breath. "But I'd like to know more than your body. And that's weird to me."

"It is?"

He nodded. "Being with you is…different. You make me laugh. I don't laugh a lot. My life hasn't always been great. I'm good now. But I'm messed up when it comes to people." His expression turned flat, and she hated that he seemed down on himself

"I don't think you're messed up."

"You don't?"

"Well, you're a little tactless. And you say what you feel. But that's not such a bad thing. I'd much rather be with someone who's honest than a charming liar." Then she blushed. "Not that we're together. I just meant—"

"I know what you meant." He smiled. "So, if you're okay with us being honest with each other, and the fact I want you like crazy doesn't bother you, maybe we could slow down and get to know each other before I bang your brains out."

She grew tingly just thinking about it. "You know I'm going to be thinking about that all the time now. The banging, I mean."

"Good. I shouldn't be the only one suffering."

She gazed down at his erection and swallowed. "Oh."

"Tell you what. While I'm suffering from blue balls every night, and you're all hot and bothered over in your apartment, we can take our time getting to know each other. Then, when you feel like you can handle me, you tell me when."

"When?"

"When I can fuck you."

She felt so warm. "Or make love to me?"

"Erin, call it anything you want, and I'll do it. But you have to decide. I'm already there. I'll bend you over the couch right now if you say the word."

She wanted to, so badly. But the old Erin remained, wanting a connection with the person she gave her body to. And she refused to feel badly about that either. Her life was her own. And not her parents or Grandma Freddy or anyone could tell her that her decisions were wrong.

"Okay."

He gaped. "Okay?"

Realizing how he'd interpreted that, she stammered, "S-sorry. Not about the couch, I meant about letting you know when. And there will be a when. I just need to know you." She blushed. "I'm naïve and small town, aren't I?"

"I think you're sweet."

"Ugh. And nice. And the girl next door." She crossed her eyes. "I've heard it all before."

"Well, girl next door, unless you want me to remind you how sweet I find you, with my head between your legs, I'd suggest we change the subject. How do you feel about making out? Is that okay to do before you say when?"

She felt excited, happy and ready for the next step. With Smith, who hadn't called her a throwback or old fashioned because she wanted to wait. "I think that's doable."

He groaned. "Don't say doable. You're doable. Fuck. Let's watch TV or something before I forget I'm only allowed to stay above the neck."

She grinned. "Well, now. I didn't say that. Maybe just above the waist."

His eyes brightened. Dessert happened on the couch. And the lemon meltaways came much, much later.

CHAPTER EIGHT

*S*mith hadn't felt so good in ages. Hell, maybe in forever.

His date with Erin had been amazing so far. They'd been together for two hours, and he couldn't remember the last time he'd had so much nonsexual, nonviolent fun with anyone. Better than fucking, fighting, or tossing live grenades, Erin's laughter invited him to partake in her joy.

He saw the city through her eyes. The dirt of the streets and sidewalks, the beauty of the many cultures and varied people, the scents of homemade pierogies and seafood chowder. Men throwing fish around while customers ordered. Her amber-eyed gaze took in everything. He'd offered to buy her something to eat, a pair of earrings she'd stared at a little too long in the market, and even a cool hair band she seemed to like, but she'd refused.

She just liked to look and take everything in, she'd said. Personally, he thought she counted all her pennies before she made a purchase and had no plans on being without. A frugal woman, and one he'd come to respect more and more. She didn't make fun of him for loathing chocolate, though she did say she felt sorry for him.

"Do you hate all sweets? You can't, because you ate my cookies."

"And I'm dying to eat them again," he said with a wiggle of his brows. The memories of last night refused to leave his mind's eye. He'd sucked on her pretty nipples and cupped her, bringing her to orgasm despite herself. That she responded to him so prettily made him feel ten feet tall. And when she'd offered to soothe him as well, he'd forced himself to decline. Being there for her was what he'd intended in the first place, not to seduce her into saying yes too soon.

She flushed. "Oh, stop it." Then something caught her eye, and she gasped. "Look, Smith. Flowers." He followed her to the bouquets, not surprised when she bought a tiny bundle for two bucks. She might not be a spendthrift, but she liked beauty. He tucked that away for future reference.

They continued through the marketplace, and he wondered why he hadn't been down here since he'd returned from Camp Pendleton back in January. But why would he? He wasn't a shopper and hated crowds. Being here with Erin made all the difference.

"Do you like soccer?" he asked as she looked over a clothing vendor's wares.

"I like soccer players' legs," she admitted with a grin.

He felt a little funny, looking at her and seeing someone who was so much more than a neighbor, friend, or lover. But what, he didn't know.

"What's wrong?" she asked him. "I shouldn't have said that, should I?"

He forced a laugh, wondering why he had to make such a big deal about liking her. She was cool and sexy. So what? "I like you being honest. I was just going to say we should go to a Sounders game. That's the Seattle soccer team. I love soccer. American football, not so much."

"Oh, come on. Men in tights and shoulder pads? Yum." She smirked.

He shook his head, and they left the market to walk around downtown.

Erin tended to gawk at shoes and handbags, lingering by windows that had assortments of feminine things. She also loved going in and pawing through girlie doodads, soaps and candles, jewelry, notecards. A lot of crap that took up a lot of space in the already tight confines of those tiny boutiques. He felt claustrophobic just looking from the outside in.

"I'll wait for you on the sidewalk out there," he said while in one such place with her. "Where I can breathe."

She laughed at him. "I'll be right out. I saw something I think my sister would like, and her birthday's coming up."

He nodded and tried to walk out but found his way hampered by a super helpful saleswoman.

"Excuse me." She tapped his arm. "Were you looking for something in particular? For your girlfriend, maybe?" She smiled back at Erin, now talking to the other sales person.

"Nah, she's the one looking. I'm here with her."

"Well, if you need help, ask for me. Caitlyn." She ran a hand over his arm and squeezed, her come-on obvious. He should call her on it, but he didn't want to make a scene for Erin.

Instead, he left, stewing. This was what he hated about people. The backstabbing, loose-morals way of looking at the world. No one cared about loyalty. And it wasn't limited to women. He'd seen so many fellow male Marines who thought it was okay to screw around as long as the spouse at home didn't know.

Granted, not everyone had been so thoughtless. But many had, and on top of what he already knew about love, the idea of being in a committed, monogamous relationship seemed out of reach.

And why the fuck am I blowing this so out of proportion? He felt like a moron. Some stupid chick had hit on him. So what? It happened a lot and he dealt with it. Yet he felt offended on Erin's behalf. They had appeared to be together, after all. Should he mention it to her? Nah. She didn't need to know, and they weren't really a couple or anything. Though *he* imagined breaking the jaw of any guy who looked at her wrong, he had no right to do so.

"All good? I wasn't too long, was I?" she asked as she joined him outside. She held up a small bag. "I got a pair of earrings and a matching bracelet for my sister."

"I'm good." He forced a smile. "I was worried about you never coming out. I don't know if I'd be able to survive that place if I had to go in looking for you."

She laughed and put her hand in the crook of his arm as they walked toward one of his favorite stops—a store that sold used books and comics.

"Smith?"

The voice stopped him in his tracks, and Erin halted next to him.

Damn it.

He glanced up to see Reid approaching with a shit-eating grin, his gaze moving from Erin to Smith and warming.

Erin watched them both, waiting.

Reid waited as well, his gaze expectant.

"Hell," Smith muttered. "Erin, this is Reid, my boss. Reid, Erin."

"Hi." Erin smiled at him.

Reid smiled back. "I'm Reid Griffin, Smith's boss and *brother.*" He shook her hand, looking like a poster ad for good teeth and good hair. He wore khaki trousers and a gray sweater under a dark jacket. Erin would probably find him good-looking.

And that annoyed Smith to no end.

Erin compared them both. "His brother? How nice to meet you." Reid released her hand, and they continued to smile at each other.

"How do you know Smith?" Reid asked.

Smith glared. "You don't have to give her the third degree."

"Smith, be nice." Erin squeezed his arm, and that mollified him a little, because she had no problem showing slick Reid they were together. "Smith and I are neighbors and friends."

"Friends," Reid repeated, staring at them both.

"Yeah. Got a problem with that?" He would have stepped forward to press his point, but Erin held him back, tugging him by the arm.

Reid shrugged. "Not at all. In fact, this is perfect. Naomi and I wanted to invite you to dinner, Smith. But I didn't know if Naomi being there would be weird, just the three of us. Now you can bring Erin, and it'll be the four of us. How about it?"

"Well, I'm kind of busy and—"

"This Saturday night at seven o'clock. Dinner at our place. I'll text you the directions." Reid took Erin by the hand again and squeezed. "I hope I didn't put you on the spot or anything. But Naomi and I would love for you to come."

The bastard was using all that Griffith charm, and Erin was falling for it! Smith saw her stare back at the idiot.

"Oh, I bet Smith would love to come. I know I would." Erin looked up at him, and Smith was nodding before he could think about it. Anything to make her happy.

"Awesome. We'll see you guys Saturday night. Don't bring anything, either. I mean it," Reid said to Smith. Then he left them standing there, staring after him.

"Why did he think I might bring something?" Smith mumbled. "I don't even want to go."

Erin tugged him forward. "Sure you do. He's your brother. Wow, Smith. I'm learning all about you. You hate chocolate, girl shops scare you, and you have a brother."

"I have two." He sighed. "There's more to the story. I think we need another coffee break."

ERIN WATCHED SMITH, AWARE HE HADN'T LIKED REID MUCH. THE man had seemed so nice and polite to Erin, but what did she know? Appearances could be deceiving.

They sat at a local coffee shop and had the place mostly to themselves. She sipped at a latte while he tore pieces off a pastry and pushed them around his plate. He hadn't touched his coffee yet.

"Okay, tell me. Quit moping. You look like a teenage girl dithering over how to break up with her boyfriend."

That shook him out of his funky mood. "Excuse me?" His deep voice still had the ability to make her shiver.

She didn't miss his effect on most everyone they made contact with. People either stared at him, in awe of his looks and size, or they gave him a wide berth. She preferred the latter, weirded out to find herself jealous over the big guy. Especially when they were, for all intents and purposes, *almost* friends with benefits.

"Tell me about Reid. I'm not going to judge you, you know." She took hold of his hand resting on the table, and he stared down at their entwined fingers.

"Fine. It's a shitty story. You sure you want to hear it? We're having a nice day."

They were until he'd started brooding. "Lay it on me."

He gave her faint grin, then sighed and pulled his hand away. "Short version: the woman who raised me wasn't my mom. I found this out months ago. Apparently, my real mom was her sister, who gave me up because she didn't want me. Meg—my aunt—hated me forever. And I recently learned I have two brothers. Reid and I share the same birth mom. Cash—he's a huge asshole, by the way—and I share the same mom *and* dad. They were raised together and didn't know they had different dads until their mom passed away. Our mom," he corrected, not used to the dynamic. "I went to work for the guys because I wanted to check them out. Then they learned about me. So now they keep trying to make us into this big happy family, and that doesn't work for me."

She kept track of what he did and didn't say, and she didn't miss the slight waver in his voice when he mentioned a big happy family. Something he wanted even if he acted like he didn't. Growing up with a mother who hated him explained a lot about his gruff nature. "Why doesn't the big happy family work for you?"

"Because it's all fake," he growled. "They don't want me. They feel sorry for me because Angela lied to everyone and screwed me over. I guess she screwed them over too. I don't know. She had a diary they gave me to read, but I haven't read it yet."

"Why not?"

"Because I hate her and it hurts to bring up the past," he said bluntly.

She nodded, feeling for him. Her family smothered her sometimes, but they loved her. And she knew she always had a home to go to should she need it. Smith had no one but a few biological ties to strangers he felt uncomfortable around. "Reid seemed nice. Was that a front?"

He sighed and ate a piece of pastry. "He's okay. I guess."

"And Cash? The not-so-nice guy?"

"He's loud and obnoxious." Smith glared at his coffee. "And it's weird that he looks like me." He paused. "They have a cousin, Evan. I worked alongside him for a while. He's not bad. He's pretty smart, actually. He and his girlfriend invite me to stuff, and his mom keeps insisting I call her Aunt Jane." He got a funny look on his face, one of disbelief and amusement. "She keeps inviting me to her new place in Bainbridge."

She frowned, not familiar with that neighborhood. "Bainbridge? Is that close?"

"Bainbridge Island. It's a ferry ride away."

"Oh. Right." She sipped her coffee, watching the emotions cross his face. She wondered if he realized how confused he looked. "That sounds nice, your aunt and cousin including you."

He shrugged. "It was weird. But nice, I guess. I like Evan's girl-friend." He gave her a faint smile. "She has a teenage brother who's really smart. The kid is also a smartass. I like him."

"A smartass. No wonder you like him. It's like looking at your-self, am I right?"

"Maybe."

"So, this thing at Reid's. You don't want to go?"

He sighed. "Not really. Reid's nice, but we have nothing in common. And Naomi is this fiery redhead who owns her own business and dresses in heels and shit. Like, she and Reid are on a totally different level than me."

"What level would that be?"

He shrugged, and a hint of pink colored his cheeks. "I don't know. I'm smart enough. But I'm not the executive type. Reid is. Evan is too. He's a big shot CPA. He, Reid, and Cash own the company. I just work there."

She nodded and remained quiet while he continued.

"I was fresh out of the Corps when I came home. I knew it was stupid, but my first stop was to Meg."

She took a moment. "Your mom. I mean, your aunt."

"Yeah." He sighed. "I thought she might be glad to see me. I used to send money home, you know? Thought that might soften her up. But she was just as spiteful as ever." He drank his coffee and continued to tear at his pastry. "Now I know why. She raised her sister's kid. And she was secretly in love with my father—Cash's dad."

"You know, you really need to write a book about all this. Or maybe a Lifetime movie script."

His tension eased as he laughed. "No shit."

She smiled at him, feeling a lot of empathy for a man who hadn't had much softness in his life, but who still managed to help her in need. He could have turned into a giant jerk after being raised by such a mean-hearted person. Instead he buried his kindness behind gruff words and that huge frame.

"Would getting to know your brothers be so bad?" she asked. "What if you let them in then learn they're asses? You never talk to them again. Although you do work for them. That could be awkward."

"I only took the job when Meg told me their names. I was curious. She used to talk about my amazing cousins all the time when I was a kid. I could never measure up." He frowned. "I used to hate the fuck out of them."

"I would too," she admitted, "if my parents constantly talked about them being so great and treated me badly."

"Yeah. I can't let go of that. And it makes it tough when Reid or Cash try to be nice. I just want to smash their faces in."

"Maybe you should. You said Cash is like you."

"Unfortunately."

"Then he probably likes to fight too. You should go at it, let the anger out, and go from there."

He perked up. "That's not a bad idea. I'd love to rearrange his face."

"I was thinking more like some kind of therapeutic counseling with pugil sticks or padded boxing gloves. Tilly was watching that on TV the other day during a *Dr. Phil* show." She shook her head at him. "What about Reid? Do you want to hit him too?"

"I do, but I'm afraid I'd break him. He's a little weak."

"It's obvious you could clobber him. Why not go to dinner and feel him out? A free meal is never something you turn down, you know," she teased.

He speared her with his stare. "Would you go with me?"

"Did you not just hear me? Free dinner? Of course."

The relief he tried to hide brought tears to her eyes, so she pretended to choke on her coffee to hide her compassion. Man, she hadn't figured on today being so emotional. Learning about each other's likes and dislikes had seemed a simple enough thing. Smith hated chocolate but liked fruity treats. He loved soccer, hated football, and wasn't into shopping. At all. But he'd walked and talked with her, held her hand a few times, and glared at anyone who walked too close.

And he kept trying to buy her stuff, which freaked her out. So used to being the one to cater to others, she didn't know how to handle someone being there for her. God, he had to stop being so darned sweet. He was making her fall for him, something she swore she wouldn't do so soon after being dumped by Cody.

Looking back, she had trouble understanding how she could have thought herself in love with him. He'd been slick and handsome but nowhere near as attentive and kind as Smith.

Erin sipped her coffee and pondered her dilemma. "Tell me about Cash," she said to Smith. And as he described a man very much like himself, she wondered how she could help Smith deal with his family problems. Or if she should. None of this was her business. Heck. She could barely deal with her own messy life.

An apartment on the fritz. An argumentative landlord she needed to please to keep her rent affordable—or what passed for affordable in Seattle—and an ex-boyfriend she hadn't gotten the nerve to deal with. Cody continued to leave her messages, and she knew she needed to resolve her past to make a new future. Why ignore him any longer? She should just talk to him and put him in her rearview mirror.

But… it had only been two weeks since he'd dumped her. Only? It felt like a lifetime ago. She couldn't imagine being with Cody now after having known Smith.

Still, the realization that so little time had passed cautioned her to slow down with Smith. Just because she happened to find a decent man under all his bluster didn't mean hearts and flowers and forever would follow. That was nonsense.

So she kept her smile in place, asked the right questions at the right times, and enjoyed the rest of her day with Smith. Then she went home to fetch Tilly's dinner and fell asleep in her own bed by herself. Wondering when she'd stop feeling so alone and be content with her own company.

SMITH DIDN'T KNOW WHAT HAD GONE WRONG. HE COULDN'T pinpoint when Erin's attitude had changed, but he had a feeling he'd ruined things by getting all emotional in the coffee shop. She still laughed and smiled with him, but she seemed distanced.

Or he could be imagining it all, because what the hell did he know about women?

"Hey, dickhead, watch where you're going," a large man in fatigues and a short haircut yelled at Finley, who was trying to move a monster of a table by himself down a hallway. Finley ignored him and managed to find the elevator.

Friday's schedule needed everyone out in the trucks. Smith would love to know who'd made the assignments. Today he had a three bedroom move in an apartment that fortunately had an elevator. They'd parked the truck outside, with Stan, one of the ex-air farce guys, as he liked to call them, guarding the truck. The neighborhood fell on the dark side of shady, and the sheer number of questionable types in the building and the surrounding area reinforced the notion. He could see why the small family of five wanted to move.

Between Stan, Smith, and Finley, they had the house covered. Stan guarded the truck while Finley and Smith moved the family's belongings. Only Mr. Chen stayed behind, his wife and kids already at the new place in Tacoma.

"I've packed up the last of the kitchen items," the man told Smith, who nodded.

"Thanks. We'll have it moved out and all set to go in no time." Smith figured another two hours at this rate. They could move faster if they'd had one more body, but with everyone so spread out, they'd made do with what they had.

They needed Stan right where he was. A truck full of goodies had drawn too much interest, in Smith's opinion. He would have helped Finley move a few items, but he didn't trust the neighbors not to help themselves to Mr. Chen's boxes. And Mr. Chen would be little help. The guy seemed afraid of his own shadow.

The large man moving down the hallway lingered by Mr. Chen's open door. Smith stood just inside and stared at the guy. A few feet shorter but bulked up with more meat than muscle, this nosy neighbor would prove to be a problem. Smith could feel it.

He wanted to tear the guy a new one, especially when the fucker made eye contact and sneered. "You leaving anytime soon? Your guys are blocking the hallway and hogging the elevator, asshole."

Smith wore his work uniform. Not a good idea to go off on anyone without provocation. Not liking the guy's looks wouldn't cut it. He knew beating up dickheads went beyond the scope of his employment. But it would be so satisfying to break this guy in half. He'd been casing the apartment since they'd arrived that morning.

Smith decided to answer the man. He stepped forward, until they stood nose to nose. More like nose to forehead. "Yeah. I'll be leaving as soon as all of Mr. Chen's things are moved out. Not one single box had better go missing, or I'll have to stick around and look for it." He glared at the guy. "We're a full-service company, and we take our clients' security seriously."

The big dude snorted and scrubbed his military short hair. If this dick had served a day in any service, Smith would eat two helpings of Naomi's gross chocolate cake—which he prayed she didn't serve the following night.

Finley returned. "Excuse me, No-neck. We have shit to do."

Smith would have called him on it except Finley had been talking to the asshole blocking the door, not him for a change. Though slighter than Smith and a lot more glib, Finley had done his time in the Navy as a Master at Arms, what the Navy called their military police. The guy joked too much, had a stupid sense of humor, and liked to perform magic tricks that Smith would never in a million years admit stumped him. He didn't seem all that intimidating, but Smith had a feeling Finley could hold his own.

He wondered if he was about to watch shit go down. No-neck turned to Finley and glared. "You talking to me?"

Finley grinned. "Well, I'd call him No-neck" —he nodded at Smith— "but I have other names for him. Like Staff Sergeant Grumpy. Or Thanos. Or Satan, which seems to fit the more I come to know him."

Smith tried not to laugh. Showing amusement would only encourage the Navy idiot.

No-neck looked confused, and Finley slipped by him to grab a box.

Smith did his best to be professional. "Buddy, you're blocking the door. We need to get done so we can get out of everyone's way."

The guy took another step forward. "Tell you what. Me and my bros are gonna come in here and see what we need. We'll take a few boxes off your hands. Maybe a TV or stereo. Then you guys can have all the time you want." He whistled and two of his friends appeared from a door down the hall. Neither looked too intelligent.

From what Smith could tell, they didn't carry weapons. The shorter blond man looked more pudgy than muscular. His dark-haired friend had muscle but walked stiffly, as if injured or recovering from an injury. Both men looked up to no good, though, and they backed up their friend with mean smiles.

Smith grinned back. "Thanks so much for this," he said with all sincerity to No-neck. He turned and spoke to Finley behind him with a nervous looking Mr. Chen. "Finley, can you help Mr. Chen get the rest of the stuff staged in the hall and living room? I have something to take care of."

"Need help?"

"Nah. But lock up, would you?" He shoved No-neck back as he stepped forward into the hall. The door locked behind him. "Now, I'm warning you. I'm unarmed, just here to do a job for Mr. Chen." He cracked his knuckles and rotated his shoulders, feeing the adrenaline surge. It had been *so* long since he'd gotten to break something.

He laughed. "Okay, which fuckhead goes first? You gotta hit me though. Then I can claim self-defense when I end you."

The guys behind No-neck looked at each other then turned and walked away. Crap. "Hey, No-neck. Your pussy girlfriends left." That would set the guy off.

Smith wasn't wrong. The bulky man aimed for Smith's face, but Smith ducked back.

"The gut. Go for my stomach."

No-neck frowned but aimed at Smith's stomach. Smith tightened his core and stepped back to mitigate the blow. It packed little enough punch. But the impact made it okay to hit back.

A minute later, the idiot lay on the floor with a broken nose and clutching his dick. Smith hadn't broken a sweat. He waited, praying for someone with balls to join in. No one did.

The bully on the block lay in agony, his groupies apparently too scared to make a move with their illustrious leader on the floor. Smith leaned down to grab the collar of No-neck's sweatshirt and pulled the jerk down the hall.

"Which one is yours?"

"17," the guy wheezed, pulling at his sweatshirt to keep it from choking him.

Smith turned to see Finley once again carrying boxes toward the elevator, Mr. Chen grinning widely behind him.

Finley looked at him and shook his head. "Show off." The pair disappeared into the elevator.

Once in front of Unit 17, Smith banged on the door.

A sullen teenager answered it. "Yeah?"

The kid looked down the man on the ground and started laughing.

"He yours?" Smith asked.

"Unfortunately. DNA can be a bitch."

Smith smothered a laugh. "Well, keep him locked up before he hurts himself. He ran into a door by Mr. Chen's. It's pretty slippery down there."

The kid gave him a thumbs up before glaring down at his… father? Brother? Something. "Yo, Ma," he yelled over his shoulder, then shot a grin at Smith. "Petey tripped in the hallway and broke his nose." The kid left the door open but made no move to help Petey inside. "Thanks, dude."

Smith shrugged and left. A glance behind him showed Petey crawling into the apartment. Then the door slammed closed.

He passed another few doors until one opened, showing a little girl. She carried a stuffed dog and wore a tiara over rows of braids tied back with light blue fasteners. "Hello."

He stopped, a sucker for kids. "Hey. I like your dog."

"This is Pup-pup. Ruff, ruff." She made the dog pretend lick his leg.

He grinned.

Behind her, a frantic woman, probably her mother, rushed behind her and gave Smith a wary look.

Smith held up his hands. "Just passing by. I'm with Vets on the Go! moving Mr. Chen out today."

The lady paused, then looked out the door, up and down the hall. "Everything okay?"

"Yep. No problems."

She nodded, looked pensive, then asked in a hesitant voice, "Do you think you could do me a little favor? It wouldn't take but a few minutes of your time. I can pay you."

Not much, from the state of what he saw inside and the condition of the apartment complex. But she looked a little desperate, and the kid was adorable. "Let me finish with Mr. Chen. I'll be back."

She smiled. "Thank you."

After he finished helping Finley move the rest of Mr. Chen's items, Finley and Stan drove the truck to the new address. Smith would take his truck to the next move on the list to help out the Jackson brothers.

Mr. Chen was so grateful tears came to his eyes, which made Smith feel awkward.

"It's no trouble. Seriously."

But Mr. Chen refused to let him leave without giving him a few vouchers for his new restaurant in Tacoma. Something Smith didn't think he'd ever use, but he accepted the gift all the same to soothe the man's pride.

He knocked on the door of the stuffed dog handler and her mother. It opened quickly. Again, the lady looked up and down the hallway before encouraging him to enter.

The apartment looked clean and neat though rundown, the furniture beaten, the paint on the walls dingy. A little house had been fashioned from sheets and pillows over a table, a collection of stuffed animals and dolls surrounding her castle. The girl waved a magic wand made from a wooden spoon tied with sparkly ribbon and addressed her many toys as her "royal subjects."

He waved. She grinned and waved back, showing a missing front tooth.

The mother drew his attention toward the kitchen, where a medium-sized refrigerator stood near an empty space. The woman shrugged. "I paid good money for the delivery, and the guys just dropped it off and left since I refused to pay them an extra fifty!"

He frowned. "You should call the store and complain."

She rolled her eyes. "Honey, if I'd bought it from a store I would have. This came from Abe's downtown." At his blank look, she said, "Abe's has all sorts of stuff you might need at a discounted rate."

"Sure." Made sense. She hadn't said it was a pawn shop. And he didn't ask where she thought it might come from. "So, you need help moving it back and installing it?"

"I have twenty-five bucks I can give you."

Money that would be better spent on her kid and herself.

"Hold that thought." He had no problem muscling it into place or plugging it in. It fit without a problem. When done, he turned to her. "Look, while I'm here, you need anything else moved?"

The woman brightened. "Actually, I do."

He spent the next hour using her tools to fix her bed and her daughter's broke-ass dresser. He also moved the couch against the far wall, where the woman, Martha, had wanted it in the first place.

"You, Smith, are a lifesaver." Martha beamed. "I can't thank you enough. Will forty dollars cover it? I can do forty."

He straightened to find the little girl staring at him.

She frowned. "Are you my daddy?"

Martha clapped a hand over her face, her cheeks pink. "No, Sherri. That is not your daddy."

He grinned. "I'm not lucky enough to have a kid like you. You're too cute."

Sherri beamed and darted back to her castle.

Martha tried to hand him two worn twenties. He stepped back. "No can do. I have to do one good deed a day to keep myself from going to hell. Since I pounded some guy down the hall, I figure this makes up for it."

She grinned. "Actually, I'd say that makes two good deeds for the day."

"It felt good, I can tell you that." He walked toward the door. "Keep the cash. But if anyone asks, you have no idea who hit that dickhead in 17."

Martha nodded. "Not a clue." Then she shocked him by hugging him. "Thanks so much. You really helped us out."

He left, feeling not so down. Until Cash called, bitching him out for being late to pick him up at the warehouse. Apparently, Cash was waiting to ride with him to their next job. Which they'd be doing *together,* without the Jackson brothers, who had been tapped for a same day emergency move.

Smith hung up and banged his head on the wall. "This is so not my day."

CHAPTER NINE

Smith didn't say much to Cash as they worked, though he felt his brother's gaze on him throughout the move. The customers had thankfully opened the door and left, promising to return in several hours. Smith and Cash were to lock up after they finished.

To Smith's pleasant surprise, when Cash kept his mouth shut and did nothing but work, he wasn't so bad. Although it almost became a contest to see who could move more, faster.

They finished ahead of schedule, making the Friday an early one. As they moved the contents to a storage unit in West Seattle, Cash started talking.

So much for a quiet ride back.

"So. You're going to Reid's tomorrow night."

"Yep."

Smith fiddled with the radio and finally settled on a country station through all the static. The sky above looked like rain.

"I hate country music," Cash muttered.

Smith turned up the radio.

"Such a dick." Cash turned it off.

Smith sighed and looked out the window. Traffic backed up on 99, and he bit back a swear. *Shoot me now.* A glance at Cash showed the asshole grinning at him.

"Gee, this gives us more time to talk."

Smith swore aloud this time. "Shit. What do you want?"

"Well, just…" Cash swallowed and gave him a forced but pleasant smile. "How are you doing?"

"This is painful. I mean, it hurts all over."

Cash sighed. "I know. I promised Jordan I'd try to be nice. It's awful and makes me nauseous to be nice to you. I hate it."

"Great. Then shut your pie hole and put the music back on."

"Then again, knowing how much you hate talking to me makes it all worth it." Cash's green eyes glowed with mirth, his dark hair and muscular form so similar to Smith's that it felt odd to look at him.

"Tell me what I can do to shut you the hell up," Smith growled.

"Maybe you can explain why you're such a dick, for starters."

Smith smiled. "It's genetic."

"Oh, that's clever." Cash rolled his eyes.

"Look. We share the same mom and dad. Big deal. You already have a brother and a family. What the hell do you want with me? Because I really want to know."

"I don't know." Cash looked puzzled. "If you'd never come to Vets on the Go!, maybe I wouldn't have such a problem keeping to myself. I'd have read about you in Angela's journal, but you wouldn't be real to me. But you're here, and you hate us. And I get it, because I hate you too." That seemed to cheer him. "But then that makes it even more obvious how alike we are, and that's irritating."

"You got that right." Cash had a point. Smith sighed. "What do you want to know?"

"Well, we told you about Angela and dickhead Charles." The man's supposed father. "What was Meg like?"

Smith felt irritable, sad, and angry at mention of her name. "She was a bitch, okay? Can we drop it?"

Cash glanced at him, and Smith swore he'd belt the fucker if he saw one iota of pity. But Cash just nodded. "Charles, my dad, turned on me when I was just a kid. Went from father of the year to shithead of the year. He found out I wasn't his, and he never let me forget it. Mostly I heard how useless and lame I was. A few times he hit me. He treated Reid like gold, which made it all worse. Reid felt guilty for stuff that wasn't his fault."

Smith watched Cash's fingers whiten on the wheel. "What did Angela say about it?"

"Not a goddamn thing." Cash snorted. "She was so wrapped up in TV and books she never noticed us. I think that hurt more than the stuff the old man said."

They remained quiet as traffic broke up.

Smith kept his gaze on the cars outside and tried to separate emotion from fact. "Meg spent my childhood telling me how precious you fucks were, how her sister had the absolute best kids anyone could have, and wasn't it sad all she had was me. Uncle Allen would come over. We'd play a game together or mess around with toy cars. Then he'd go fuck Mommy Dearest for a few hours. He'd leave. And I'd be stuck with her ranting and raving about him until the next month when he rolled back into town."

"Hold on. You met him?" Cash sounded incredulous.

Smith turned to him. "So what? At the time I thought he was a friend of my mom's. The 'Uncle' was like an honorary title. Turns out she had a thing for him, but he only wanted Angela." Smith allowed himself a cruel smile. "Only thing I can thank him for. He made Meg's life a living hell. She wanted him. He loved Angela; but he couldn't have her, so he did the next best thing, using Meg as a stand-in. Best part was she knew it."

Cash stared at him for a moment before turning his attention back to the road. "Damn. That's harsh."

"Life is harsh."

"Can't argue that."

They continued the rest of the drive shooting the other side glances and pretending not to be interested. Arriving at the storage unit, they moved the clients' belongings in no time and returned to Vets on the Go! Cash parked the truck. Smith paused, and they sat in the dark, not speaking.

Then Cash asked, "Do you ever still see him?"

"Allen? Nope. I was a kid when he visited Meg. He'd come once a month for a while. Then he just stopped coming. She never heard from him again, and he never tried contacting me either. Hell, I don't know if he ever knew I was his kid. I only know who he is now because Meg felt it was her God-given duty to tell me the full truth of my hated existence the day I came home from the Corps. You know, in case I thought she and I would live as Mommy and Son happily ever after." He snorted, ignoring how much it still hurt to know the truth—that he'd never been wanted by either of his mothers.

He opened the door to leave.

"Hey," Cash said, stopping him.

"What?"

"Ah, have a good time at Reid's. Naomi can seem a little intimidating, but she's actually pretty nice."

"Yeah. Okay."

Now if he could just reassure himself that Erin would come with him, and that she still wanted anything to do with him…

SATURDAY AFTERNOON, ERIN SAT WITH TILLY IN TILLY'S apartment, making marionberry scones for Tilly's book club on Monday. Apparently, Rupert, Willie, and a few of Tilly's other friends gathered once a month to discuss erotic fiction.

Erin suppressed her desire to ask *so many* questions. Instead, she worked on the scones and watched Tilly polish off the casserole from last night's dinner.

"So, you're all fixed up now?" Tilly looked worried. "You sure the heat is working, right? Because that's all I need, for the furnace to be going out."

Erin reassured her. Again. "The heat is fine. Apparently, there was something stuck with the thermostat, but Smith fixed it. Oddly enough, the thermostat is also the problem with the oven. The oven still works. I just need to rely on a separate thermometer, so I don't burn what I'm baking."

"Bah. We'll get that fixed after the hot water heater issue and the electrical mess I'm now dealing with in 7B." Tilly groaned. "First 6B, then 7B. When it rains it pours. Everything has been working just fine for years. Then suddenly, it all goes to shit." She eyeballed Erin, her gaze narrowed with speculation. "Right when you arrived."

Erin laughed off Tilly's suspicions. "You can't blame me for things breaking down. Besides, you said you love the amazing meals you've been eating. That's got to be worth a few thermostats."

Tilly eyed the tray going in the oven. "Well, I suppose. Say, is that white glaze going over the scones when they're done? I like 'em on the sweet side."

"Yes, ma'am."

"And you're going to prep everything for Monday too, right? My coffee, the table settings, all the doodads and flowers and crap? Going to set it all up for me then skedaddle before our book club?"

"Yes, ma'am."

"House cleaned up a day early in time for the guests?"

Erin suppressed a sigh. They'd already been over all this. "Yes, ma'am."

"The good towel out for my powder room? The monogrammed one?"

"Yes, ma'am."

"You bumping uglies with Smith yet?

"Yes, ma'am—I mean, no!" They hadn't bumped much, though they had touched and kissed a good bit. But no way she could call anything on Smith ugly.

Tilly smirked. "It's only a matter of time, I suppose. I know how to read people. And you and that boy had *it* at dinner the other night. *It.*" She nodded. "Just like Rupert and Willie. I put those two together, you know."

"Good Lord."

"Yep. I'm magical when it comes to matchmaking. Inherited that talent from my me-maw."

And that was Erin's cue to change the subject. She'd learned early on that stories concerning Me-Maw had a bad habit of turning sexual or scatological, and one time a little of both. She cringed at the remembrance. "Smith and I are friends, Tilly. We're going out tonight to hang out with his brother and girlfriend."

"Oh-ho. Meeting the family, eh?"

"Kind of. But not like you're making it sound," Erin said. In this light, actually, Tilly looked a little bit like Grandma Freddy, and the sight made Erin smile.

"What's so funny?"

"You know, you kind of remind me of my grandma." Erin's pleasure felt bittersweet. "I still miss her."

"Ah. Passed away, did she?"

"Four years ago. She was so funny. She had all these rules about being a lady, teaching me life lessons to make some man a good wife." She snorted at that. "She was the only one in my family that would talk about the naughty side of life with me."

"You mean sex?"

"Yes, sex." Erin had no idea why she turned pink saying the word. "Grandma Freddy had some old-fashioned ideas about catering to a man, but she always told me the truth when I asked for it."

"Catering to a man? Well, I suppose that's not too bad. If the man caters to you too."

Erin sat and drank her tea, pouring another cup for Tilly. "Did your husband cater to you?" She'd seen a few framed photos of Tilly and a man, presumably her husband, around the house. But since Tilly had never before mentioned him, Erin hadn't brought up the subject.

"Hell, yes, he did." Tilly's fond smile took years off her face. "Hank and I met when we were in high school. Fell in love at first sight, that's what he told me. Took me a little longer to see what a gem he was. We were married for fifty-six years until he died. Five years ago next month marks his passing. And each year I celebrate his life by getting drunk and partying, the way he wanted it."

"You must have really loved each other." Erin envied her.

"Oh, we did. But he used to get on my last nerve, and he knew it. Said that made him special, because I only got that mad with him and the boy." Tilly sighed. "Hank Jr. I miss him more than I can say sometimes."

"Hank Jr?" Erin asked, seeing a softer side to the normally cussing, outlandish Tilly.

"I loved that boy to pieces. He was just like his daddy with an ornery spot of me in him." Tilly grinned. "Poor fool had a patriotic streak a mile wide too. We lost him in Vietnam."

"I'm so sorry."

"Me too." Tilly's eyes looked suspiciously shiny, but since she glared at Erin as if daring her to mention it, Erin focused on the glaze. Tilly harrumphed. "War is hell. It's a fact. But he went out the way he'd wanted, and his daddy and I were so proud of the man he'd been." Her voice turned thoughtful. "Probably why I took to Smith right away. He reminds me some of Hank Jr, but don't you dare tell him I said that. He hears I'm going soft, he'll try to weasel out of working for me."

Erin didn't see that happening, but who was she to say? "I won't say a word."

"Yep. That Smith Ramsey is one big pot of trouble. Sasses and swears like a Marine for sure. But he helps me when I need it. And sometimes even when I don't." She scowled. "He had the balls to tell me to watch myself on the stairs. Said I should be taking my old ass up and down in the service elevator. Can you believe that?"

"Somehow I can see him using those exact words."

Tilly's eyes crinkled with amusement. "He's a horse's patoot. Must be why I like him."

Erin could name a dozen reasons why *she* liked him. Her date Thursday had blindsided her, making her feel so much she wasn't yet ready to handle. She didn't want to talk out of turn, but she needed Tilly's opinion. "I learned a few things about him when we spent the day together downtown." She noted Tilly's attention and continued, "Smith had a pretty bad childhood. Lots of drama, and now he no longer talks to his mom. It's sad."

"Huh."

"But he found out he has family he never knew about, and he doesn't know how to deal with them. That's the family I'm meeting tonight. A brother he just learned he had. I want to help him, but I feel kind of out of place."

"Why?"

"Well, because…"

"You're his friend, aren't you? So, go with him and be his friend. Don't focus on being his mattress. He needs emotional support from you right now."

Erin nodded. "That's what I figured. Being there to help him." Then what Tilly said penetrated. "Wait. Did you say not to focus on being his mattress?"

"With a man that big, it would have to be king-sized. You're kind of tiny for the position, ain't ya?" Tilly hooted. "Sorry. Sometimes I can't help myself. I mean it though. Be his friend. We all need 'em." Tilly brightened. "And on that note, Rupert said he's going to give you a phone number so you can make your own kinda friend. I guess you made an impression on my nephew. And don't forget about the Hall-o-ween party on the 31st. We like to give out candy for the kids in the building, and the McCallisters like to hold open houses for people to mingle and get to know each other. It's nice. The McCallisters serve good booze."

"I'll keep that in mind." Nervous about just who Rupert might be trying to set her up with, she said, "Rupert doesn't owe me anything. I'm actually doing pretty well on friends now."

"Yeah? Who do you know?"

"You, Smith, and Reid—his brother."

"That's just sad."

Erin sighed. "I know. I'm trying. I haven't been in town all that long."

"Funny, feels like you've been here forever." Tilly grinned. "And not in a lingering-fish-smell-in-the-fridge kind of way either. The nice kind."

"Er, thanks." Erin finished the scones, listened to Tilly's gossip about Mallory and Jill Keen fighting over Jill's supposed affair, about Mark Johnson's apparent addiction to wine, because who the hell drank fifteen bottles a week, and Brad Battle's shoe size, because all the women Tilly talked to thought he just might be that impressive "where it really counted."

Finally, Tilly ran out of gossip, and Erin managed a word edgewise as she finished with the scones, now drizzled in white glaze. "If you're saying all this about my neighbors, what do you say to others about me?"

Tilly wiggled her brows. "I tell everyone you snagged the unattainable Smith Ramsey. Seriously, everyone wants to meet you at Hall-o-ween."

Good Lord. What would Smith think of that? "Tilly, stop gossiping."

"I swear I will…the day I'm dead and buried. Ha! Now go on and get ready for your hot and heavy date with my handyman. But you be nice, Erin Briggs. I need him happy and in one piece. Without him around, this place would go straight to hell."

Erin read the serious undertone of worry in Tilly's voice. "I have no plans to hurt your handyman. Let's just hope he doesn't break my heart. It's barely mended from Cody."

"Nah. That was just an infatuation with a little prick. And I mean that literally."

Erin ignored the sad truth of her statement.

"Smith's a man. He'll take care of your heart if you give it to him. But that's the kicker. You have to hand it over, honey. He might act like a brute, but he'd never take what wasn't willingly given."

Then Tilly physically pushed Erin out the door and slammed it behind her.

"Well, that was just rude." Erin went back to her apartment, showered, then spent half an hour trying to figure out what to wear, all the while thinking about what Tilly had said about Smith not taking what wasn't willingly given.

Erin knew that, believed it. And that fact made it that much more difficult to remain distant from a man who started to scare her. Badly. Smith was someone she could grow to love.

Already the lust she felt for him had transformed into a desire mixed with warmth and respect. As much as she didn't want another relationship like the one she'd had with Cody, she had some kind of "ship" with Smith, and they both knew it.

But how to handle him when he turned awkward or sweet and gentle? When he acted human?

"You are killing me, Smith Ramsey." If only he'd remain an arrogant blowhard. But even that aspect of the man hid something precious, a need for affection she was dying to give.

She kept holding clothing up to the bathroom mirror, stepping back to get the right angle to see herself, when someone pounded on her door. Crap. She tossed on her only robe—in baby blue cotton it reached her midthigh—over her bra and panties and looked through her peephole.

She opened it and dragged Smith inside. "You're early."

"You're late." He looked over her with an appreciative grin. "Not that I mind, but you might want to get dressed before we go over. Reid will like the outfit, but Naomi might get jealous."

"Just… Hold on." She hurried into the bathroom and grabbed the two outfits she'd narrowed her choice down to. "I'm going to wear jeans. But with this shirt or this one?" She held them both out for his inspection.

He looked baffled. "It's just a top. Who cares?" His look turned sly. "But I'll help you pick out a bra. Or, you know, you could go without."

"Choose." She shook the shirts at him.

He shrugged. "The sweatshirt."

She gasped. "It's not a sweatshirt. It's a pullover."

"Jesus. Fine. The Tee-shirt, then."

"It's a blouse," she corrected.

He groaned. "I'll be at my place, waiting. When you're dressed and ready to go, or naked is fine by me too, come on over. We'll go in my truck." He stalked to her, gave her a quick kiss on the lips, then left.

Breathless, she stared after her closing door. *"Be his friend,"* Tilly had said. But Smith didn't feel anything so casual as a friend. Yet if not that, then what was he?

After a few minutes, she chose the pullover and dressed for casual comfort. Minimal makeup, cute earrings, and a spritz of perfume she'd picked up for herself the other day—she'd tossed the perfumes Cody had once bought her.

She knocked on Smith's door. It opened right away, and she shoved the plate of lemon meltaways at him. "We're bringing this. Here."

He looked down at the plate, puzzled. "Reid said not to bring anything."

She snorted. "Please. I go to someone's house for dinner, I always bring something. It's only polite to bring a dish or wine." She frowned. "Darn it. I should have picked up a bottle."

He blinked at her, as if having discovered a new species, and grabbed his keys. After locking up, he drove them a short distance toward Naomi and Reid's house, also in Greenwood, but more toward Green Lake. After giving her a brief background about Reid—former Marine and genius behind a desk—and Naomi— PR guru and successful boss of her own company, he had thoroughly intimidated her. Though she tried not to show it.

"Don't worry about anything," he told her. "They say anything that pisses you off, we're outta there. And Naomi isn't a bad cook, so I hear. But she does have a thing about chocolate." He grimaced. "If you don't want to eat something, just pretend you like it, choke down a bite, then shove it around on your plate to look like you ate some."

His instructions amused her. At first. But she heard his buried nerves and felt his unease. This had to be so hard for him, learning how to deal with family he'd never known existed. And knowing him, as she did, she could see how his abrupt attitude might put others off.

She put a hand over his knee. He tensed all over. In a soft voice, she said, "It'll be fine. I have you with me, don't I? We'll be okay."

He sighed. "I sound stupid, don't I?"

"Not at all. Being social isn't easy for a lot of people. I don't mind it, but then, I never have to see these people again. You do."

He shot her an odd look, but they'd pulled to a stop in front of a cute Craftsman-style house Erin would have loved to call home. It had a small though well-tended front yard, a driveway and unattached one-car garage, and a dark plum color with white shutters and a wood porch bracketed by potted evergreens.

"Wow, this is so cute." She studied him, aware of his frown and stiffness.

"Well, we're here. Let's get this over with."

From the way he spoke, she expected Reid and an ogre of a girlfriend.

She encountered something very different.

Reid was just as handsome, polite, and charming as she remembered. Naomi Starr, his girlfriend...wow. A gorgeous, leggy redhead, she had bright blue eyes and a killer smile. Her house looked as if it had been designed by someone on a home and garden show, and the power couple looked too pretty for words.

Plus, Naomi was genuinely nice.

On behalf of cute, short people everywhere, Erin wanted to hate her on principle.

"Oh, you brought lemon bars. I love lemon," Naomi gushed. "You didn't have to do that." She shot Reid a side glare.

Reid held up his hands in surrender. "Don't blame me. I told them not to bring anything."

"See? Told you," Smith murmured to her.

Erin rolled her eyes. "It's a girl thing. Or maybe it's a Midwest thing. You always bring something for the dinner or the hosts. We should have brought wine."

"No, no." Naomi nodded for Erin to join her in the kitchen. "This is perfect. I have a sweet tooth."

Erin smiled. "Me too." She felt gauche next to Naomi's tailored gray slacks and peach tank. Erin Briggs—frump deluxe. Erin had dithered for an hour about what to wear. She'd bet Naomi had picked something at random from her closet and still looked like a million bucks. "So, Smith mentioned you do public relations work?"

Naomi nodded and returned to the salad she'd been tossing. "I run my own PR firm. That's how I met Reid. I stopped by to help his floundering business, and we connected."

"Hey. I heard that," Reid called.

Naomi grinned. "It was terrible. He, Cash, and Evan, their cousin, started Vets on the Go! to give veterans jobs. Something we all needed—local moves in the city done by reputable people. They were doing okay, barely, when Cash ended up saving a boy and his grandmother from a mugging. The news got wind of it, and Vets on the Go! got a huge rush of popularity they're still riding," she paused and, in a whisper, confided, "thanks to my team. The gang is great, but they needed help to capitalize on it."

"Nice." Impressive. Not only was Naomi beautiful, she was super smart and successful too. Great. Now Erin felt even more outclassed.

"So, what do you do?"

Fail at life. "Oh, um, I work from home, mostly. I edit for some agricultural magazines and do some cooking and cleaning on the side."

"Tell her about the cooking show thing," Smith barked from the other room.

"Quit listening in on my conversation," she yelled back. Then she blushed when she saw Naomi watching her with interest. "Sorry."

"No, no. I love it." She laughed. "I've been dying to meet the woman who can handle Smith. You seem to be doing a good job of it." She leaned closer and whispered, "Don't you find him a little intimidating? Smith is so big and, well, he's kind of snarly."

"Kind of?" Erin snorted. "He's a gruff giant who likes to loom over you. He's a loom-y kind of guy." She smiled. "But I like that about him. And I have to say, he makes me laugh."

Naomi blinked. "He does?"

"Yeah. Because any man who would call this a sweatshirt has to have a sense a humor." She plucked at her fashionable pullover.

Naomi shook her head. "That is too funny. You look great. Sweat-shirt? God, that's something Reid would say. Men can be so stupid."

The men in question popped their heads in the doorway. "I heard you call for stupid," Reid said with a smile. "So, I told Smith you needed him."

Erin shook her head. "Oh yeah. They're brothers."

CHAPTER TEN

*S*mith didn't know what he'd expected from a couple's dinner with Reid, but it wasn't…this.

"Okay, now I get to ask a question." Erin laughed at the goofy face Naomi made. "Answer this correctly and you might move ahead two spaces. Answer incorrectly and we can steal. Play or pass?"

The trivia game they were playing had turned out to be much more interesting than Smith might have expected. Especially since he knew a lot of the answers.

Naomi studied Smith and Erin, then glanced at Reid and nodded. "We'll play."

Reid grimaced. "But the category is animals."

"I like animals."

Reid laughed. "You like fake leopard print skirts and faux fur rugs."

"I have a cat." She glanced at the lazy feline licking itself while it watched them from its spot on a chair in the living room. "Rex counts."

"I don't think he's really a cat," Reid mused. "More like a demon in fur and whiskers." He turned to Smith and confided, "Sometimes he finds my toes under the bedspread in the morning. And he's got claws. It's like he takes great pleasure in scarring my feet."

They all looked at the cat who didn't miss a beat, now cleaning his paw.

Smith had thought about getting a pet. He'd tried as a kid, but Meg had claimed allergies. Allergic to love, more like. Now, living in a place that didn't allow pets and being so busy all the time, he didn't think having something small and furry, depending on him, would work for his lifestyle.

He glanced at Erin, saw her eyeballing the cat with caution, and thought she looked a little wary to be a cat lover. "A demon, huh?" she asked.

"Can we just answer the question?" Naomi said with a huff.

"Fine by me." Reid shrugged. "But don't blame me if Smith or Erin take us back to yellow."

"Oh, the loser color?" Erin asked with a wide smile. She winked at Smith.

He let the warmth flow through him and smiled back at her, happy and no longer hiding it. At first, he'd guarded every word and expression around Reid. But over the course of a pretty damn good steak dinner, some decent enough beer, and conversation, he'd eased, allowing himself to share in the fun, as well as bask in Erin's laughter.

He could tell she was enjoying herself. She'd held his hand under the table a few times, and it had been all he could do not to show off how much his girl liked him.

His girl.

He kept thinking about her in those terms, naturally pairing himself off since Reid had Naomi. Except Reid and Naomi planned on getting married. Smith just planned on getting Erin in bed. Or at least, that *had* been the plan. He wanted her, no question. But lately, just being around her eased him. Seeing her smile made everything around him feel right. And that emotional response unnerved him, because he hadn't felt that kind of need for a woman in a very long time. Sex he understood. Love and affection were foreign entities best experienced by normal people with normal families.

And normal had never been in his make-up.

Erin tapped him on the shoulder. "Pay attention."

"Hey, no cheating," Reid said.

"Telling Smith to wake up isn't cheating."

Reid scratched his head. "It has to be. He knows all the answers, or you do. This is not a fun game."

Naomi sighed and stroked his arm. "Hey, at least you're pretty. That's gotta be worth something, honey."

"Thanks." Then he blinked. "Wait a minute."

Smith saw Erin bite back a grin. He out and out laughed. "Yeah, at least he'll marry well."

"Shut up." Reid crossed his arms over his chest, scowling at everyone.

Erin shook her head. "I can't believe you're telling us not to cheat. We should be saying that to you guys. Who keeps looking at their phone for 'the time?' Please, Naomi. I can see Google open from here."

Naomi flushed.

Smith shrugged, biting back a grin. "Let her. We have a ten second time limit."

"Since when?" Naomi tried to pretend she hadn't been on her phone.

Even Reid groaned. "I thought you were good at this game. Naomi, they're crushing us. This is embarrassing." Then he gave Erin a wide, super insincere smile. "Or you could read between the lines and see that we wanted this evening for us all to get along, so we're letting you win."

"Um, yeah." Naomi's bright smile hurt to look at. "Way to spin it our way, Reid. I think good PR and marketing is wearing off on you."

Erin and Smith sneered at the same time. A united front in mockery. He was so proud.

Naomi groaned. "You two are unnatural. Your tiny brains are in sync or something."

"Tiny brain? I'm from Kansas, Naomi. We're all about big there."

"That's why she loves me," Smith teased, saw the startled expression come and go on Erin's face, and prayed he hadn't ruined things by trying to be funny. Then he realized he wouldn't mind if Erin loved him for his size, his brain, or just because.

Huh. What to make of that?

Erin cleared her throat. "Naomi, the question is, how many species of bear are there?"

Naomi and Reid conferred, and Naomi asked, "Like, American species?"

"The card says *global* in parentheses." Erin sounded apologetic, but the little faker liked winning as much as Smith did. He would never have figured her to be so cutthroat.

"I, er…" Naomi made a comical attempt to hide the fact she consulted google again.

Smith cleared his throat. "That's ten seconds. Your answer?"

"Twelve species."

Smith shook his head. "Nope. It's eight."

"Correct. Smith, not you, Naomi." Erin waved the card at her.

"You guys have to be cheating," Reid accused with a suspicious look at Smith. "Who the hell knows species of bears?"

"I'm a guy with hidden talents," Smith growled. "And I can name you each of them too." He ticked off his fingers. "The American Black Bear, the Asiatic Black Bear, the Brown Bear, the Giant Panda, Polar Bear, Sloth Bear, Spectacled Bear, and Sun Bear."

Reid gaped at him and stole the card from Erin's hand to verify his answers.

"Hey."

"Wow. The species aren't listed on here." Then Reid used his phone for the answers and asked Smith, "What? Is it national bear week or something?"

Naomi yanked another card out of the box. "Okay. What are a group of bats called?"

"I know this one," Erin said. "A colony."

"A group of bats *in flight*," Naomi corrected, looking smug. "You didn't let me finish."

"A cloud," Smith answered. "And before you ask, an aglet."

"Huh?" Reid frowned.

"The question on the back of the card is 'What's the plastic end of a shoelace called?' It's an aglet." Smith sighed. "It's so hard being a know-it-all."

"At least you don't have to worry about marrying well," Erin piped in with a grin. "Not with that big brain on top of your big body."

"In his big fat head," Reid muttered.

"Well, bigger is better." Smith gave him an evil smile. "But again, you'll marry well, so don't worry, bro." Smith grinned.

Reid blinked, then grinned back, his eyes warm. "Whatever. I still get dibs on Erin's lemon bars." He vaulted over the couch faster than Smith would have credited him.

Smith shook his head. "So weak. And they're lemon meltaways."

"You tell him, Smith." Erin nodded.

His heart felt too full, the unfamiliar sense of belonging and camaraderie foreign, and so missed. He'd experienced that kind of acceptance in the military for a time. But a need for change had clawed at him during his time in service, and Smith had made the decision to leave.

He missed that brotherhood the most. So odd to find it here, with Reid and his girlfriend. And with Erin, a woman he wanted like his next breath.

Erin stood with Naomi, oblivious to his self-discovery, and the two laughed as they walked to the dining table together, where Erin's lemon treats and a strawberry rhubarb pie sat waiting. Reid brought coffee and cups on a tray from the kitchen, his mouth full of lemony goodness.

He looked shamefaced at Naomi and said with his mouth full, "I'm sorry, honey. I had to. They're *so* good."

Erin blushed, looking pleased at the compliment.

"She's pretty awesome," Smith agreed, and dared to wrap his arm around Erin's shoulders. She looked up at him, her cheeks pink, and it was all he could do not to lean down and plant a soft kiss on her lips, his feelings overwhelming and confusing at the same time.

Instead, he squeezed her in a half hug then sat in front of the desserts.

"I didn't bake anything chocolate this time," Naomi said to him. "So you don't have to pretend to like it."

Caught, Smith looked up to see the kindness in her eyes. Something he wouldn't have credited the woman who regularly chewed out Reid and Cash on a weekly basis.

"Oh, ah, that's okay. The cake was good, I just—"

"He's allergic to chocolate," Erin flat out lied. "He hates to admit any weaknesses, but he gets hives if he eats it. He didn't want you to feel bad is all."

Smith just looked at her. What the hell was she talking about?

Reid slapped him on the shoulder. "Hey, no problem, bro. We all have our weaknesses."

Smith didn't know if he liked Reid calling him bro, but since he'd done the same earlier, he couldn't exactly complain. Reid seemed happy, and Smith, for once, didn't want to ruin his good mood.

"What's your weakness?" Smith asked, sincere.

Reid stared at him. "A need to make everything right for my family." His hand tightened on Smith's shoulder. "*All* my family, even my annoying little brother who never asks for help but should."

To say the dessert fell into an awkward silence wouldn't have done Reid's statement justice. Erin waited, watching the brothers weigh the other, the quiet a heavy oppression on an otherwise fabulous evening.

"Um, Erin, could you help me with the tea?" Naomi rose from the table.

"Gladly." Erin darted into the kitchen with her. Though the dining area could be seen easily from the kitchen, by backing toward the fridge, the ladies kept out of sight from the brotherly combatants measuring each other over the table.

"Wow. This is one of those times where you feel like you can actually cut the tension with a knife. And Reid was doing so well, too." Naomi sighed.

"Do they normally get along?" Erin had seen an easy sense of acceptance from both men tonight, and the dinner had been a lot of fun. Her misconceptions about Naomi sat like rocks in her belly. Naomi was as goofy, entertaining, and as sweet as she was beautiful and poised. Erin really liked her.

"Reid gets along with everyone," Naomi explained in a quiet voice. "But his mother did a number on all her sons. She ignored Reid and Cash and tossed Smith away. Now Smith is back and upset with the world, and if you ask me, he's envious of the way Reid and Cash grew up together. He had no one."

Erin nodded. "But I think he wants that." She hoped she wasn't being disloyal by speaking up. "He's kind of like me, alone and wondering why. Well, I know why I'm alone. I moved away from home and got dumped by my ex."

Naomi frowned. "That's terrible. Good riddance, Erin."

"I know." She truly believed that. Mostly. She still needed closure with Cody, but that could wait until she was ready. "I met Smith at a low point in my life. He didn't seem like he would be so nice, but he's been a sweetheart about all of it. Helpful and kind, and he's never taken advantage." *Even when I wanted him to.*

Naomi nodded. "He comes across as rough and a little angry, but there's more to him."

"Tonight means something. I can tell."

"Good. I want Reid happy. And he wants to make Smith happy, part of the family. But I keep telling him not to force things."

The men started talking in a tone Erin could hear, not about family or brothers, but about soccer, of all things. Erin didn't follow much of the conversation, but she and Naomi found it safe to return to the table.

After coffee, dessert, and feeling like a stuffed cow, Erin thanked her hosts, promised a rematch of trivia, and left with a silent Smith.

In the truck, she reached for his hand. "Are you okay?"

"Yeah." He gripped hers before letting go. "Thanks for coming tonight."

"Of course." Then she did what she'd been wanting to do all night. She leaned close to kiss him on the lips. A small, tender touch. But the familiar spark between them flamed bright all the same.

He kept sneaking glances at her on the drive home. The Smith she was used to would have made innuendos or teased her about getting sexy at some point. This quiet, introspective Smith did nothing but peek at her now and again. He parked and walked her to her door. There he paused, asked for her key, and when she gave it to him, opened her door.

He nudged her inside but remained in the doorframe, watching her. Waiting for her to invite him in, maybe? His gaze was tender when he said, "Thanks."

"Um, sure." She waited for the kiss that never came. "But you already thanked me."

"You deserved it. So, ah, can I see you tomorrow? Breakfast on me." He shoved his hands in his pockets. "If you're not busy, that is."

Kill me now. He was doing that uncertain, shy thing again. The sincere man breaking through all the antagonistic, arrogant barriers he normally flipped at the world. Killing her resistance smile by smile, Smith waited with patience.

"I'd like that," she said against her better judgement. So much for not getting involved with a man so soon after Cody. She was in so deep she could barely see past the need to make Smith happy.

His smile, when it came, made the butterflies in her belly flit all over the place. "Come on over when you get up."

"But what if you're asleep?"

"Knock and I'll wake up. I'd rather be with you than dreaming."

He left her staring after him, hopelessly ensnared and no longer unsure about it.

She knew what she had to do or go completely insane.

SMITH OPENED THE DOOR THE NEXT DAY AT SEVEN IN THE morning. He'd finally fallen asleep at two a.m. after a brutal time of trying to calm himself down. Just because Erin had agreed to breakfast with him didn't mean anything had changed. They were still dancing around each other, and he had no idea if she'd agree to sleep with him. But he found he didn't mind waiting, and that had never happened before.

He'd never had to chase after a woman. Typically, once he'd made his interest known, it didn't take all that long to get her in bed. Smith had looks and a decent body. He knew this. He also knew how to please a woman, and he'd never had a problem giving a woman an orgasm. Smith respected his bedpartners. He might not love them or want to be with them for more than one go in the sack, but he didn't lie to get them there. His lovers had known the score.

Did Erin? Because he sure as hell didn't know what he was doing with her. Frustrated with himself, Smith put on sweats and running shoes and went out for a four-mile run. He let the physical exertion work on his mental kinks, trying to iron out his thoughts and feelings while figuring out what it was about Erin that felt so different from all the others.

All the others? He snorted. Smith wasn't as big a player as he might like to think. Women gave him physical pleasure. But they wanted too much or not enough from him when it came to relationships.

Neither Meg nor Angela had wanted him. Rejected by two moms.

His first real girlfriend had wanted to play around, and he'd lost his heart at only fifteen. But hell, they'd been young, and he couldn't blame her for their breakup. Not that he would after seventeen long years.

In the time since, he'd dated only seriously once, fucked around, and generally had sexual fun with women while keeping his heart behind a Kevlar vest. His time and energy had gone to making a living working construction and odd jobs before joining the Marine Corps. The Marines had definitely helped mold the man he'd become. The odds were still out on whether that was a good or bad thing.

He stepped up his pace, dodging moms with strollers and a few couples jogging together. The crisp October morning promised more sun, and he ran hard to work off the pie and meltaways from the previous night.

He clenched his fists tighter, still able to feel Erin's hand holding his, to remember her mouth, her taste, her sweet scent as she'd kissed him in the truck.

Fuck, but he loved being around her. She made him feel as if all things could be possible. Happiness just within reach. So damn weird to feel that way for a woman.

The Corps had given him that for a while, a sense that he had a greater purpose to fulfill and was doing something good for once. He didn't get into trouble, was promoted early, and generally enjoyed being a Marine.

Yet something nagged at him the longer he'd been in, that sense he was missing something. Coming home obviously hadn't been the answer, because Meg cared even less about him now than she had when raising him. Her truths didn't crush him the way she'd probably thought they might. In a way, she'd started him on a new path, giving him brothers. At first to hate, and now to… what? He didn't hate them, no matter what he'd told Cash. That slippage last night, calling Reid "bro" had eased something between him and Reid. He felt it.

But it was Erin who preyed on his mind. Erin with whom he wanted to share his spare time.

He ran back home, winded, his muscles tired, his mind wired but also eased by his self-admissions.

He didn't mind having brothers, though he wouldn't call any of them close.

He liked his life right now, especially without Meg in it.

He especially liked Erin, as more than a friend. Hell, he was crushing on her big time.

And they planned on breakfast soon. Smith forced himself not to knock on her door, letting her come to him. Working out his upper body on his weight bench, he did several reps with the bar and hand weights, then finished his routine with sit-ups and pushups. He'd just taken off his shirt, sweating like a beast, when she knocked.

At least, he hoped it was Erin.

Unfortunately, he opened the door to Tilly.

She gaped at his bare chest.

He couldn't help himself. "Shouldn't you be in church, praying the sin away?"

"The devil's scared of me. He's smart." She poked him in the shoe with her cane. "A hell of a lot smarter than *some.*" She stared at his left pectoral and shoulder, where an Eagle, Globe and Anchor—the Marine Corps symbol—sat in a bed of snakes and smoke and the grim reaper decorated the outside of his upper arm. "I didn't know you had a tattoo."

He shrugged. "I don't know your shoe size. We're even."

Her lips thinned, but he could see her trying not to laugh.

He bit back a grin as well. Fucking with each other was their special way of communicating.

"So, what's the deal with the plumbers? They scheduled to come yet or what? You did call McSons, didn't you? If I'm going to pay through the nose for a plumber, I want to be entertained."

"Thought you said they were reasonable."

"Spending money on a water heater isn't reasonable. Spending money on fine beer and that *50 Shades of Grey* movie? Now that's reasonable."

He grimaced at her taste in films. "Whatever you say. McSons are coming next Tuesday to inspect the pipes in 6B as well as the hot water heater. I'll make sure you have appropriate leering time."

"Well, Pat used to clog her toilets on purpose to get them out there. At least my problem is legit."

Smith shook his head, his mind already on how to deal with the possibility Erin might not show. Breakfast was no big deal. And so what if he'd gone out and bought a ton of shit for them to eat? If she didn't swing by, he could eat it himself for days.

Tilly remained standing there, staring at him.

He wiped the sweat from his face with the back of his forearm. "What now?"

"You all alone in there?" She sounded disappointed.

"Nope. Got a date."

"Erin?" Tilly smirked, looking way too smug.

"Nah." He lowered his voice. "I met this one through work. Name's Naomi. Red hair, stacked. She's sweet." He winked at Tilly, who glared back at him. "What?"

Erin opened her door and closed it behind her. When she noticed Tilly talking to Smith, she paused. "Is this a bad time?"

"Apparently. He's got some woman in there," Tilly barked, turned, and muttered to herself as she made the long, slow journey back to her apartment at the end of the hall.

Erin looked upset and tried to hide it. But man, was she bad at masking her emotions. That she didn't like the thought of him with someone else gratified him. That she'd intended to join him for breakfast made him giddy with joy.

I am such a moron.

Smith nodded her closer. Erin, still frowning, took a few steps in his direction. He said in a low voice, "She was being nosy, so I lied. Get your ass in here." He tugged her off balance and into his apartment, then closed the door.

She stared, not at his gym equipment, that he needed to put away, but at his bare chest.

"Oh. Wow." She swallowed audibly. "You're all sweaty. And you have a tattoo."

Was it just him, or did her voice sound breathy? Aroused?

Or turned off. He realized he didn't smell so good.

"Damn. Sorry. I was going to go shower after working out when Tilly came by." Smith looked Erin over, taking in the loose navy pants and sweatshirt—pullover. She looked dressed for comfort, not seduction. Simultaneously disappointed he wouldn't be getting sex and thrilled she'd come by to be with him, he tried to shrug off any feelings of discomfort. She kept staring at his tattoo.

"That's so cool. Did it hurt?"

He wanted to invite her to trace it with her finger. Then her tongue. He coughed and prayed he could get to the shower before he showed her just how hungry he was. "Ah, I don't remember. Hey, make yourself at home. In fact, would you mind making us some coffee while I shower? Then you can sit back and relax. I'll make breakfast."

"You can cook?"

"Passably. But when it comes to breakfast, I'm a master." He turned away, glaring down at an erection he could no longer hide. "I won't be long. I swear."

He had himself in the bathroom and clean in minutes. Before he could turn the water temperature to cold, to relax his still aroused body, he heard the bathroom door open.

Then a knock. "Smith?"

He pulled the curtain back to peek around it and saw Erin standing there.

Naked.

He couldn't speak.

168

"You told me it was up to me."

"Up to you?" Had his voice ever sounded so deep? *Fuck me. She's naked.* And goddamn gorgeous. He couldn't look away.

"Yes." Erin walked forward, pulled back the curtain, and stepped into the shower with him. "I'm saying when. Right now."

CHAPTER ELEVEN

*S*ince Smith couldn't seem to form words, just staring at her and making her more than self-conscious, Erin brazened it out. She'd been going over this moment since last night, when she'd come to the realization that Smith meant more to her than just a friend.

Though Erin would have loved to be able to have a booty call and leave it at that, she didn't feel comfortable having sex with a stranger. She knew Smith, not as much as she wanted to, but enough to know he protected those he cared about, wasn't a user, and didn't like playing emotional games.

And wow, did he like her. She tried not to focus on that monster between his legs, but a woman would have to be unconscious not to notice his size and excitement. She'd already had two orgasms from the man but had yet to see him naked. She could honestly say she'd never seen a better-looking man in all her life.

It wasn't that he was handsome. He was, but she'd seen prettier and more refined men. It had to do with the way he'd been put together, all muscle and form, and the way he moved.

Well, maybe not right now, because he seemed frozen in the shower.

"Um, you're blocking all the hot water."

He continued to stare at her, looking her up and down, his gaze focusing on her breasts and below her belly, where she'd carefully groomed in preparation for today.

It had taken a lot of courage to make the first move. But he'd told her he'd wait for her, and good as his word, he continued to wait.

"So, um, are you interested? In me, I mean?" A stupid question, obviously, but the more he didn't talk, the more nervous she became. Was it possible she'd misread the whole situation?

Then Smith let loose a barrage of swear words, burning her ears. He moved to the side so she could get some hot water, then he backed her against the cold tile, his hands on her shoulders.

"You... I just..." He looked into her eyes once more, and his strong hands settled on her shoulders. "I could come just looking at you."

"Aw, you say the sweetest things." She grinned.

He groaned and closed his eyes. When he opened them, they looked so dark, the green blending with his pupils. "I didn't think we'd get to this today. Maybe not ever."

"Really?" She stroked his chest, watching the water trickle down over so much dense muscle. His abs clenched and his cock bobbed. Up close, it was even more impressive. Smith really wanted her. The realization warmed inside and out.

"I mean, I've been wanting you from the first. But..." He swallowed. "I thought maybe after our day at the market that I did something wrong."

"No. It was me, not you." She traced his ribs, enamored with how he reacted to her touch.

"It's all you." He lifted her hand from his ribs and kissed her palm. "I want to fuck you so bad right now. But I'll come in like two seconds."

She met his gaze, saw his need, and knew it matched her own. "Me too." She sighed. "I'm so ready for you. I don't think it would take much more than you coming inside me."

His eyes narrowed. "You okay with that? We haven't talked about it."

"It?"

He pushed some of her hair behind her ear. He didn't smile; he seemed too intense for that. But something in his expression softened. "Condoms. Sex. I'm clean, and it's been a while since I've been with anyone. What about you?"

She knew they should have talked about this before. "This is so embarrassing."

"Why?" He kissed her left cheek. Then her right. But when he planted a soft kiss on her mouth, she sagged, only his hands and the wall keeping her steady. "Sex is natural. I want you. Do you want me?"

"Way more than I should," she confessed.

A slow smile lit up his face. "No such thing." He drew a hand down her shoulder, over her breast and down her belly. Then he slid that hand between her legs, rubbing his fingers between her folds. "Oh, baby, you're wet. Tell me. You okay with no condom or should I get one?"

She groaned. "I'm protected from babies. I've been on birth

control for years." She felt her cheeks heat. "I haven't been with anyone for a while either. That's part of why I had issues with..." She didn't want to bring Cody up just now. "Why I had issues, and why I'm single." She'd never told Cody she was on the pill, liking that he wore condoms when they made love, as infrequent as it had been. And now she was doubly glad, wondering how long he'd been cheating on her with someone else.

She confessed, "It's been months since I was with anyone. He always wore a condom. And then, well, it wasn't that good." She stared into his eyes, needing him to know. "Not ever like it was with you. And technically we didn't even have sex."

"We really need to make that right." He leaned down to kiss her, and she moaned into his mouth.

He continued to slide his fingers through her sex, grazing her clit time and again. Making her insane. Pushing her past reason.

She yanked her mouth from him and reached for his cock. "Oh, God. In me. Right now."

"Not yet," he growled and pulled her hand away. "Keep your hands on my shoulders."

"You're too tall," she complained, waiting for him to kiss her again. What had she been doing keeping them from experiencing this for so long?

"Not now," he said as he moved to his knees. He drew her leg over his shoulder, spreading her wider.

"Smith, what are you—Smith!" she keened as he put his mouth over her. The added stimulation of his mouth and his clever fingers shot her into an intense orgasm.

He didn't wait for it to end. He hurried to his feet and pulled her into his arms in one move. She wrapped her legs around his waist as he positioned himself at her entrance and pushed.

The whole of him, right up into her.

The intrusion shot her into an even bigger climax, and she might have screamed. She didn't know. But she watched him in awe as she clenched him inside her, his shaft so big and thick, filling her right up.

He pounded into her with a ferocity that shattered as he thrust once more and stilled, coming so hard.

She kissed him again, thrilled when he kissed her back, his hunger unabated.

Smith pulled his mouth away and ground up into her, their connection complete. "Fuck me. Erin, oh, Erin, baby." He kissed her again and again, still moving in and out of her in slow jerks.

"Didn't you come?" she asked, feeling shy and silly for having to ask.

"Yeah. But I'm half-hard. And I want you again." He withdrew and gently eased her back to her feet. "Let's get clean first, okay?"

"Sure. That sounds great." *Whatever you want for more of what we just shared. My apartment. My life savings. My soul…*

But getting clean to Smith meant spending an inordinate amount of time soaping up her breasts, her ass, and between her legs. The man touched her everywhere. And in between he planted kisses along her wet skin.

"You're driving me insane," she accused.

"Good. Because I've been one massive hardon since I met you."

He turned her around to face the wall. "Now let me get your back."

He kissed his way down to her feet, the moved back up with soapy hands that had her shivering with need. And when he rubbed his erection against her back, she couldn't help pushing against him.

He sucked in a breath and dropped the soap. Then his hands came around to hold her breasts and he rocked against her, sliding that massive hardon over the small of her back. "What's your favorite position?" he murmured into her ear as he continued to push against her.

"I-I don't know."

"You like it from behind?" He nipped her earlobe, and she groaned his name. "It feels really deep that way. I could get so far into you."

"Then do it and quit teasing," she ordered, breathless and more than a little desperate.

He chuckled and pinched her nipples. "You like giving orders for someone so little."

"Too little?" she couldn't help asking.

"For everyone but me, yeah." He knew just how to touch her breasts, because she was on fire to have him and unable to stop from begging.

"Please. I need you."

"That's right. You need me." He sucked on her neck, and she cried out and grabbed one of his hand and thrust it between her legs. "Oh, right here? Is this where you need me?"

"You are so going to get payback for this."

He chuckled. "I can't wait."

Sᴍɪᴛʜ ᴍɪɢʜᴛ ʜᴀᴠᴇ ʙᴇᴇɴ ᴀ ʟɪᴛᴛʟᴇ ʙɪᴛ ʜᴀsᴛʏ ᴡɪᴛʜ ᴛʜᴀᴛ comment. Minutes later, as he stood in his bedroom, waiting for Erin to finish drying him off, he realized the woman had a sadistic streak. He'd dried her quickly, ready for them to fuck in bed already.

But she took her sweet-ass time. Could she not see his dick ready to explode? A slick shine of precum glazed his tip, and she kept rubbing the towel over his balls, the friction from the towel between his legs its own kind of torture.

She knelt before him, next to the bed on the floor. In one move he could have her bent over on the bed while he fucked her from behind. He'd been dreaming about doing that forever.

But now, with her on her knees between his legs, her mouth so very close…

"Eat me," he ordered, then groaned when she dropped the towel and licked him from the tip of his dick to his balls. "Fuck. Please. Put that mouth over me, Erin. Suck me dry. I can't…" His eyes rolled back in his head when she licked him again. He trembled and put a hand over her head. Not pushing her, just there to guide her should the vixen say yes.

She blinked up at him, sexy as hell yet still pure, something innocent radiating from her golden gaze. "What do I get if I do?" She smiled and turned him from a logical, thinking man into a chaotic beast.

"Whatever the fuck you want. I am so hard, right now. I want you. So much," he moaned.

"Whatever I want. I'll hold you to that."

"Anything. Everything. *Please.*"

Then she put her mouth over him, her ripe lips drawing him into the hot recess of her mouth. He didn't move, scared of freaking her out with his size or being too rough, too needy to be gentle.

But then he didn't need to. Erin put her hands on his ass and moved him, in and out, her mouth and tongue better than anything he'd ever known.

He watched her, unable to look away, and saw her close her eyes, moaning and she drew out his pleasure.

He didn't know what he said, only that he kept praying her name, his hips snapping in time with her grasping hands. "So good. *Yes, yes.*"

She licked under his cockhead, and he shuddered on the verge of coming. As much as he wanted to release, he couldn't without asking.

"I'm too close," he panted. "So ready to come."

She cupped his balls and twirled her tongue around him.

"Motherfucker." He swore and almost lost it. "Erin, if you don't pull back, you're going to swallow. A lot. I'm not kidding," he growled, giving her a chance to back away.

She only sucked harder, fondling his sac and stroking up between his legs, right along the crease toward his...

"Erin." He jetted into her mouth, lost to everything but her small hands and magically skilled tongue.

He couldn't stop, out of his mind with pleasure.

When she pulled away, she replaced her lips with her hand and milked him dry.

He felt lightheaded, completely done in by the smug woman on her knees.

"Anything I want, you said."

He nodded and fell back on the bed, working to catch his breath. When he could speak, he promised her, "Anything. I fucking swear."

She joined him on the bed, adorable, sexy, and wicked. "I'm going to save this 'anything' for later."

Smith could only nod, still trying to make his mind work. He felt her small hands stroking him, calming him down, and a surge of affection struck him mute. God, he'd never felt this good in his life. Nothing had ever come close to what he'd shared with Erin.

And then he felt horrible, because he'd just come and she hadn't.

"Damn it. I'm sorry."

Her hand stopped, so he nudged her to continue petting his tattoo.

"For what?"

"For not giving you an orgasm before I came."

She chuckled. "That's okay. I love knowing I made you lose your mind."

"Just my mind?" He grabbed her and pulled her over him, so that she straddled his waist. Another position he'd fantasized about. Unfortunately, he needed a break before he'd be ready to go again. That's if she hadn't broken him entirely. He had never, ever, come so hard.

Erin smirked. "You sure did seem pent up."

"Would this be the wrong time to tell you that you just had one of my special protein shakes?"

Her eyes grew wide. "That's a thing?"

"What?" He scowled when he realized what she meant. "Woman, I haven't had sex in months. And never like *that*." He flushed. "I was joking."

"Oh. Good." She planted her hands on his chest and leaned closer, and it was all he could do not to stare at her amazing breasts. They fit perfectly into his huge hands. "Because I'm not sure where we go from here, with us being more than friends, but I think it should just stay between us. No other women for you."

He remembered Brad Battle being super friendly. "And no guys for you."

"That's fine with me."

They nodded at each other. He let her look him over. She seemed fascinated with his body. And he could relate. Hers was so feminine, so soft yet resilient. And so fucking pretty.

"You have the prettiest nipples," he said as she stroked his. "I mean, I keep thinking I want to caress them, but I also want to suck them. Or fuck them." Her cheeks turned bright red.

He laughed.

"Oh, you." She tugged at his sparse chest hair, and he winced. "Thanks so much for my protein shake, but I think I need real food. And not one word about your sausage, either."

For some reason that struck him as hilarious, and he laughed so hard he knocked her off him.

She shifted to his side, still on her knees as she watched him and started laughing herself.

Once they'd sobered, he pulled her down for a kiss. "Sorry. I'll keep my sausage and my protein shakes to myself." He snickered. "Man, that was funny. Okay. I promised you breakfast. Let me dazzle you with more than my cock. How about some eggs and waffles?"

He loved how coarse words made her blush. And how mention of his cock had her looking there. He hoped she understood they had only just begun. Because he really hadn't gotten his fill of her yet.

A smaller, scared part that he refused to acknowledge muttered, *And you never will get your fill of her. Not now, not ever.*

ERIN LET SMITH PUT HER IN ONE OF HIS TEE-SHIRTS SINCE IT FELL to midthigh. For her sanity, he'd put on a pair of shorts, allowing her to ogle his amazing body while he cooked.

"It's the tat, right? It's like meth for chicks," he teased as he fixed them omelets.

Not used to having someone cook for her, she sat at the kitchen island and sipped her coffee. She'd made it darker than he normally drank it, and it amused her to think of drinking her coffee all manly-like while he doctored his with cream and sugar.

"Lightweight," she murmured as he drank from the USMC cup she'd poured for him.

"I heard that." He shot her an amused look over his shoulder.

This Smith had been buried under the arrogant Marine? Though the tougher version of Smith has always seemed sexy to her, this relaxed, handsome, *smiling* Smith kept digging at the walls around her heart. She knew she was making too much of their sex, but glory be in a basket, he'd played her body like a friggin' maestro. And he refused to let her get dressed.

She had a feeling he had more planned for them.

As if reading her mind, Smith winked. "Gotta make sure I keep you fed and energized. That was a pretty pitiful round one. We've got a bunch more to get through before I'm letting you out of here." His eyes narrowed. "I owe you some out of body experiences, I think."

"You up for it?" she taunted with a glance at his hips. With him facing the stove, she couldn't see the front of his shorts. But there was no way he could be raring to go again so soon. Could he? *Oh, please, be raring to go again.* Some insatiable sex goddess had taken root inside her.

He scowled. And that mean look did nothing but turn her on. "Oh, I'll be up for it, Cupcake. Just you wait."

"Cupcake? Is that the nickname you use when you can't remember their names?"

He laughed. "Trust me. There's no way I'll ever forget *your* name...Cupcake."

"Ass."

He chuckled. "Oh yeah. *Erin.* You made me crazy for you. But payback's a bitch."

"Named Smith." She snickered.

His eyes crinkled. "A bitch named Smith. Very funny." He

paused. "You're kind of obnoxious under that cute façade. It's like we're made for each other."

His happiness did something to her. It touched her deep inside, in the places she kept hidden, for fear of falling in love and losing herself. Even with Cody she'd kept part of herself separate. The physical distance between them had mirrored the emotional distance that had grown. His need to be the Person of Importance in their relationship obvious from the beginning.

But with Smith, Erin felt like they met on the same playing field. She liked him, he—amazingly—liked her. Not only had he driven her insane with lust, but she'd done the same to him. She'd never been so in charge before, and she'd *loved* it. Smith had begged her for mercy.

If she recalled correctly, he'd growled, "Eat me." That sounded dirty, and she shivered remembering every lick, suck, and swallow. Smith was a big man, and he only got bigger when aroused.

"I'd ask what you're thinking about," Smith said as he slid their omelets onto plates, then scooped hotcakes off the griddle to add to their calories. "But I feel like I already know." He set her plate next to his. "Now if you want to eat, pay the toll."

"Toll?"

He dragged her close for a kiss that had the room spinning. "Yeah. You kiss me, I feed you. Then after, when you deserve more of my amazing cock, I'll give it to you."

"Amazing, eh?" She would have sounded more disgruntled if she could catch her breath. "Well, it certainly does get big enough."

"It does more than that. It's magically delicious."

"I will never, ever, eat my cereal the same way again." She cringed.

He laughed and kissed her, and her desire spiked. But instead of finishing what he'd started, he placed her on the chair next to him and put a fork in her hand. "Eat up. You're going to need it."

"You're bossy." She dug into her food, famished. "And a good cook, surprise, surprise."

"Well, I don't mean to brag."

"Seriously?"

"But when it comes to eggs, I can do no wrong."

"Is that right?" Too hungry to give him more than that weak challenge, she gobbled her food. "This is really good."

He chuckled and started eating. "We'll have to have a contest. Best cook gets to be on top."

"That's a win-win."

"I know." He kept eating and casually said, "Watching your tits move up and down while you ride me, that's so hot. And I love looking at your face when you come. You get all soft and sexy. It makes me hard just thinking about it."

There had to be something wrong with the fact he'd gotten her hot and bothered over eggs. But he did put her hand over him, and to her delight, he'd gotten thick and long. She decided to play and slid her hand inside his shorts, stroking him while he ate.

He watched her, his appetite for the food on his plate diminishing. She, however, needed some energy. She had a feeling, by the size of his ever-growing "amazing cock," that his sooner than later was right around the corner.

. . .

An hour later, Smith had done what he'd promised.

"You…really are a…bitch," she said, panting, on her hands and knees while the man with an ungodly amount of stamina plowed her from behind. She'd already come hard from his talented tongue and fingers.

But he'd refused to give her the rest of him, intent on driving her out of her mind in lust. Just when she was ready to climax, Smith pulled back. He'd been toying with her forever, and even the feel of him pumping in and out from behind, so huge and thick, didn't give her the ease she needed.

"Fucking you is the highlight of my life," he said, slowing down.

She felt every inch of him slide inside her before those same inches pulled away. He withdrew until only the tip of him remained, then he started again.

"You're mean and so—" she paused as he shoved in one hard push and caught her breath on a spike of ecstasy "—big. Please, Smith."

"Say it, Cupcake. Tell me what I want to hear." He'd gotten off on the dirty talk. Lord knew Erin had turned ridiculously easy to please when he said those four-letter words or told her what he intended to do to her. Smith was good at it. Creative, descriptive, and inventive about sex.

Though she'd never been a fan of the C-word, when he talked about plowing her, she melted. Or as he liked to say, she creamed all over him.

"I want you to…" She lost her train of thought when he reached around and put his thumb against her clit, rubbing in circles, soft, then firm. With him still inside her as he touched her, he started the countdown to O-mageddon. Yet again.

He stopped, and she swore, which made him laugh. "You're so fuckin' hot when you're mad. Have I told you that?"

She looked over her shoulder at the man buried balls deep inside her. As much as she wanted to yell at him to stop toying with her, she couldn't help falling closer to loving him. She made a memory right then and there. His smile, his joy. And the sight of him connected to her in a way no one ever had been before.

"Smith, you're destroying my will to live."

He withdrew completely and flipped her over. "Can't have that." He leaned on his elbows above her, thankfully not crushing her. "This is going to sound a little weird, but I promise it's not."

She wrapped her arms around his neck and kissed him, on fire to feel him in her. "Mm-hmm."

"You're the perfect size for me," he said between kisses. "Small and posable." He paused, his smirk impossible to ignore. "You're like a sex doll. All tits and ass and fucking beautiful. Then you ruin it when you talk." His naughty grin dared her to get mean.

"Asshole."

"Yeah, that gets me going." He nudged her legs apart and settled between them. "I'm bigger and heavier. I can make you do whatever I want you to do."

"Damn it. You can't." She struggled to get free, not wanting to, but trying. Because she *loved* that he overpowered her. Perhaps telling him that after pancakes hadn't been her brightest move, because he used it against her, keeping her on a sexual edge of insanity by taking charge.

When her ex had taken charge, it had been to assuage his needs. She'd let him, though she could have escaped Cody's hold at any time. He wasn't that much stronger than her, nothing a well-placed kick wouldn't manage.

Smith took charge because *she* got off on it. She couldn't move him and craved his dominance.

"Oh, Cupcake. What will you do if I push inside you? You can't get free, can you?" he taunted and took her hand to his cock. He used her to guide him inside her, exactly where she wanted him. "Any excuse I have to get your hands on me, I'll take it." He stared into her eyes as he started fucking her.

It was raw and passionate. Nothing scripted about Smith taking her. Raunchy and dirty when he used the words he whispered into her ear. She couldn't get closer, and she needed to. She clawed at his back, dragged him close, and kissed him with all she had.

His thrust grew rougher, faster.

And each movement put his body over hers, touching her right where she needed it.

"Gonna come inside you. All inside your pretty pussy," he whispered and rotated his hips, hitting another spot deep inside her that shocked her into one mother of an orgasm.

She cried out and tightened her legs around his waist, arching against him.

When she could breathe again, she felt him thick inside her.

"You are seriously killing me."

He grinned, and a lock of hair fell over his eyes. His boyish smile didn't fit with the carnal desire between them, yet it did. And then he was drawing them both up, so that she sat over his cock. He kissed her and cupped her breasts, playing with her all over again.

"It's like you're a cat and I'm your ball of string," she whispered, his to command. And he knew it.

"Oh, no, Erin. You're the pussy, and I'm the dog with a big dick dying for a piece."

She stroked his hair and kissed him. "You want my pussy?"

He shuddered and moved her hips over him, touching her so deep inside. "Keep talking. You get me so hard when you talk like that."

"Like what?" she whispered and drew his ear to her lips, loving that she could make him shiver. A big tough guy like Smith, putty in her hands. "Don't you want to come inside me? Give me that thick cock and make me all wet inside?" She licked his ear.

He groaned and moved her faster, up and down over him. But that wasn't enough, apparently, so he laid her flat back on the bed and went to town. Touching every part of her, body, mind, and what really scared her—soul.

Erin whispered words of encouragement no lady would ever think about, let alone confess to. When Smith moaned her name and filled her up once more, she didn't think she'd ever had such a religious Sunday, in or out of church.

CHAPTER TWELVE

"Okay, what the hell?" Hector Jackson, one half of Smith's support on the Wade move, stared at him in consternation. "You've been smiling all damn day, and it's freaking me out."

His twin, Lafayette, nodded as he drew abreast of them in the client's basement, wrapping a cord around a floor lamp. "Seriously. I like a happy guy, but it just doesn't look natural on you, man."

The pair had been in the Navy, and for a couple of squids, they were okay. Built like bricks, the Jacksons could haul what he could. Both guys had smarts and sense, which did not always go hand in hand, and worked hard. Smith couldn't fault them for anything except their constant good cheer.

Because who the hell wanted to be happy all the time? "Blow me," he told them.

As one, they sighed.

"Ah, that's better," Lafayette said, his mirth clear to see. "Thought for a minute there you were someone else."

"Like who?" Hector asked with a smirk. "Cash, maybe? They do look alike."

"Fuck off." Smith glared at him. It was no secret he and Cash looked alike. But from what he gathered, none of the Griffiths—Cash, Reid, or Evan—had said a word about his connection to the guys. The fact that they acknowledged Smith as a brother was too new to understand.

"Yeah, they are *so* alike," Lafayette nodded. "Come on, Smith. Just 'fess up. You guys have to be related."

Hmm. Would the others want to keep the connection under wraps? They seemed to like bossing him around well enough. Despite the fact they employed him, Cash wanted him to visit again, and Reid had texted him a ton yesterday about how great the evening had gone. They seemed to want him around. Evan did, no question. But Evan was different, not a true blood relation at all, so the fact he didn't mind Smith's parentage had less effect.

Smith liked the guy anyway. Evan's girlfriend and aunt had been nothing but nice to him.

But Cash and Reid. Their existence put a different spin on things. His perfect cousins Meg used to go on and on about.

Though he'd been doing better about dealing with his repressed rage, sometimes it flared up out of nowhere. And even memories of Erin's amazing smile and kick-ass body couldn't suppress it.

"Yeah, we're related. What of it?" he snarled, his good mood dead and gone.

Hector and Lafayette shared a glance before Hector added in a soft tone, "No worries, Smith. We were just hassling you. It's nobody's business but yours."

And now Smith felt like a fucking idiot. They'd been razzing him the way he would have been razzing them—and had, he remembered—when they'd been all smiles and dopey in love. "I'm not dopey in love or anything," he muttered more to himself than to them.

Lafayette scratched his military short buzz cut. "Um, sure, man. So, is it okay if I'm dopey in love with my man? Simon is so amazing."

Hector rolled his eyes. "Please. No more Simon. He's giving me hives."

"He likes Lila."

Hector's new girlfriend, a hot piece of crazy. Smith had met her a few times. And yeah, she was beautiful. But she put him way too in mind of an Amazon. Not like Erin, who made him want to cuddle her and care for her. To keep her safe and...

"What?" he barked when the guys kept staring at him.

"Ah, nothing, chief. Just might want to be careful with that smile. Or someone might think you're more Hannibal Lector-happy than Mr. Rogers-happy." Hector made the sign of the cross and slowly backed away

"Smart ass." But the guy was funny all the same. "Sorry, okay? Cash and Reid get on my last nerve. And yeah, we're related. Not by choice." Which was kind of obvious, but whatever.

"So why are you smiling and happy today? Got plans to disembowel them later?" Lafayette asked. At Hector's puzzled look, he explained, "Been watching a *Saw* marathon on TV. Sorry."

"I don't know how good Simon is for you," Hector muttered. "*Saw*. Please."

"Oh, as if that's not better than the Housewives of Major City Can We Please Have Drama," Lafayette said. "And don't even pretend you don't watch that shit. I know you."

Hector looked shamefaced. "Keep it down, would you?"

"You guys are ridiculous." Smith shook his head, hiding his amusement. Hector's addiction to the same reality TV he teased Cash about was a well-known fact. "There's nothing good on cable"

"Well, that's true but—"

"Except for Marvel movies and comics. Not DC, because they suck. I'm talking Avengers, Dr. Strange, Spiderman…"

Hector gaped. "You— I can't believe it. You might be human after all."

"Hell no," Lafayette growled and planted his large hands on his hips. The guy looked like a shorter version of Michael Jai White, rocking those arms. "You did not just diss Superman."

"I sure the hell did. DC sucks ass."

They got into a loud argument about the different comic book publishers, arguing the merits of Dark Horse and Image—Wild C.A.T.S. anyone? —up against the megastars Marvel and DC. Then they segued into the strongest heroes and villains when Hector held up a hand and nodded over Smith's shoulder.

As one, they turned to see Mr. Wade, an older gentleman, standing with his grandson, who had to be the politest ten-year-old Smith had ever met.

Smith cleared his throat. "Sorry. We were on a short break and got a little carried away."

"I'll say." Mr. Wade left the bottom step into the basement and glared. "How can any of you possibly be a fan of the house that created Green Lantern?" he asked Lafayette. "Hal Jordan is a douche."

Coming from the mouth of a distinguished-looking older gentleman with a Porsche SUV in the driveway, *douche* made Smith's day. "Oh man, he so is. His big superpower is a magic ring that makes imaginary green things come to life. Lame." Smith sneered.

Wade's grandson, Billy, shook his head. In the tone of a college professor, he said, "Marvel isn't so great. What about Doctor Bong?"

"That's made up," Hector said.

Lafayette grinned. "But funny."

"Nah. He's real." Smith sighed. "I mean, he's a real Marvel super-hero. You got me there, kid."

The boy considered Smith with new appreciation. "You know who he is?"

"Doctor Bong doesn't really have powers. He's a genetic engi-neering genius who turned animals into humanoids. That's pretty lame in the grand scheme of things. Still, he's better than Asbestos Lady."

"That's true," Mr. Ward grinned.

"And Batman." Smith was on a roll. And there he lost Wade.

As Smith, Mr. Wade, and Billy argued obscure mutants and villains, Hector and Lafayette backed away.

"Who knew the big guy was a nerd?" Hector asked.

Smith smirked. "A super nerd."

Billy and Mr. Wade grinned, and Billy said, "I bet there's already a Marvel hero out there with that ability."

Smith looked at Billy and his grandfather, his good mood restored. "Mr. Wade, do I get a bonus if I noogie your grandson?"

Wade stared down at the boy. "For that slight on Doctor Bong, I think you have to."

THE REST OF THE DAY PASSED SWIFTLY. THE JACKSON BROTHERS made no more mention of Smith's new brothers, though they did tease him unmercifully about being a nerd. So Smith got them back by digging on them for pussying out on their significant others. Lafayette had a boyfriend, and for a time Smith had worried for the guy, about what Cash might do if he found out.

Turned out his brother was an equal opportunity asshole. Gay, straight, woman, man, white, black, and everything and everyone in between, Cash poked fun at everyone.

Smith couldn't care less about orientation. In the Corps he'd been good friends with a guy who'd had a crush on him. Smith had found it flattering, the idea of being wanted by anyone a compliment, though he and his friend had never mentioned it.

Was that why he liked Erin so much? Because she liked him back?

The idea bothered him while he drove home, tired after a full day.

So he wasn't in the best mood when he returned home and listened to his voicemail. He had five messages on his cell phone. And none of them had been from Erin.

The first two he deleted. Friggin' telemarketers. The next one was from Evan, bugging him about dinner at "their" aunt's again. Smith would call him back tomorrow. The last two froze him in his seat, and his mind blanked.

He replayed them, wondering if he'd been hearing things.

"Boy, you know it's me. Your mother. Not your real mother. Margaret. I need you to help me move. My back isn't so good anymore. And I can't exactly afford to hire an outfit to move me." She blathered on about how he owed her and his responsibilities as a good son, which shocked him.

The following message was worse. "I know you'll think about deleting this, pretending you didn't hear it. But guess what? I know something you'd die to know. I have a letter from *your father*. Yes, the man who fucked your mother and knocked her up. Allen Smith. He left a note for you six months ago. If you want to read what it says, you'll do what a good son should and help me out. I did my best to raise you, but you were such a selfish, egotistical…"

He tuned the rest out, replaying the part about his father.

Did he believe her? Could he afford not to? But did he want to learn anything about the fucker who'd cheated with Angela then disappeared? The same man who'd done nothing to help him and left him to Margaret Ramsey to raise?

Stirred up, he sat on his weight bench and curled twenty pounders for a while. The mindless reps helped him deal, so when he received a text inviting him to Erin's, he felt in a good frame of mind to visit.

He knocked on the door, and she let him in to a tiny apartment filled with the smell of something amazing.

He didn't know what to say. *Why did you ignore me all day? Am I being needy? Are you done with me now that we've had a marathon fuckfest? What should I do about the shitty woman who's now blackmailing me?* He settled on, "Hi."

Erin gave him a shy smile, and he hated that he wanted to forgive her anything if she'd still like him.

"Hi." She looked nervous, clutching her hands tightly in front of her. Then she groaned and darted into his arms for a kiss that shook him. "I wanted to do that all day. I also wanted to text you a bazillion times. But I thought that might be too clingy, so I didn't. But I missed you all day today. I'm sorry."

It took him a moment to understand her rush of words, and when he did, he felt ten times the man he'd been thinking he was. He put a finger under her chin and tilted her head up so he could see her eyes. "Is it bad that I missed you all day too?"

Her slow smile mesmerized him. "Good. I wouldn't want to think I'm forgettable."

"With those witchy eyes? No way. You scare me."

She frowned. "What's wrong with my eyes?"

He picked her up and settled her on the kitchen counter. "They're mesmerizing. I look into them, and I can't look away."

She locked her hands around his neck. "Oh. That's okay then." She drew him close for a kiss.

As usual, just her scent aroused him. The feathery touch of silk lips against his own made him hungry for more. But he caught her softening, a subtle care in the way she kissed him.

He drew back, studying her for some clue to the way she watched him. With caution and something more.

"I made you dinner if you want some."

He paused. "You did?"

"Yeah. How do hamburgers and fries sound? I made some for Tilly and had a hankering for some myself." She glanced down at his chin and said, "But I mean, don't feel like you have to stay or anything. I know you've got to be tired. It's late." It had passed seven. "And just because we slept together doesn't mean you owe me any—"

He hugged her, finding it easier to speak if she didn't look at him. "I wanted to call and text and tell you how I couldn't stop thinking about yesterday. Then I thought you'd think I only wanted sex, so I waited for you to text me. And I had to work with the Jackson brothers all day, and they're so fucking pleasant it's annoying. But then they said I was being too happy, and all because of you, I might add. The move wasn't so bad after all, but I got home to a bitch of a message from Meg." He sighed and drew in Erin's scent, needing the peace she brought. "I hate her, Erin." *She takes away all the good in my life and reminds me exactly how shitty I am.* "I was in such a good mood today. Then a call from her, and I'm right back into feeling like a loser."

She burrowed closer, and he never wanted to leave the warmth of her arms. How had he gone from being the protector to needing protection?

Erin drew him down for another kiss, and he took it. But it wasn't enough. He had to get closer, to show her what he felt, even if he didn't understand it yet.

Smith heard the hitch in her breath, felt the familiar tingle of lust and affection. Without asking, without questioning, he gave them both what they needed. He pulled back to scoot her jeans off, staring into her eyes the whole time.

She bit her lower lip but said nothing and helped him removed her panties as well. Then she unsnapped his jeans and reached inside for him.

Her touch rocked him back, and he came to that place where nothing mattered but Erin. No shitty mother, no miserable childhood, no remembrances of being discarded and unloved. He pushed down his clothes and let her draw him closer. Into her wet heat.

"Yes, more," she breathed and kissed him.

He kissed her back and pumped inside her, needing the respite of desire and care, if only temporarily, to heal that part of him that always bled when he thought of Margaret.

Reaching between them, he teased Erin, wanting her there with him when he came. Because it wouldn't take long. He fucked her with his mind and body, claiming her for himself, because she couldn't know how she affected him.

Two people in one place at one time, together, and she gave him everything, even if she didn't know it. Only after she'd cried out did he let himself pour into her, loving the mess he made, the claim that she belonged to him, in this moment.

Then he made the mistake of looking down at her and seeing in her eyes a possibility for a future he didn't deserve.

. . .

ERIN HADN'T INTENDED TO JUMP SMITH THE MOMENT HE GOT home. She'd missed him fiercely, so much so that Tilly had asked if she might be sick earlier. So, Erin had lied, claiming to be a little homesick.

She worried that she'd fallen too fast for Smith. Their amazing sex was one thing. Tender feelings for him because they'd made love was another.

After hearing about his day though, and how he'd thought about her but, like her, didn't want to seem too clingy, she wanted only to make him feel better.

God, how did he do this to her? Destroy her so that the sex evolved into affection, and one step closer to that dreaded L-O-V-E that had ended her life in Kansas?

"Damn, Erin. You feel so good." He moaned her name and pumped a few more times before withdrawing.

But of course he couldn't just wham-bam-I'm-out-of-here. He had to clean her then himself and tease them both about being quick on the draw while helping her prepare dinner.

He didn't make fun of her for having so little in her apartment. Nor did he try to take charge of the evening and be "the man," the way Cody used to. He asked her questions about her day and deflected more inquiries into his.

And he showed real interest in her editing job and her desire to restart her cooking channel.

"You need to film yourself making burgers. Holy shit, these are amazing."

Erin loved his compliments. Especially because they seemed so honest. The man was as likely to tell her she looked witchy as he was that she cooked amazing burgers.

"I'm washing dishes." He stood and collected their plates. Not that she'd ever argue over dishes—she loathed them—but that he offered without being asked meant a lot. Cody had taken for granted she'd assume the "woman's work." At first Erin hadn't minded. But her life soon revolved around Cody. His wants, his needs, his city far away from her.

She sighed.

"What's that about?"

She decided to be honest. "Cody." She thought he stiffened but couldn't be sure.

His voice remained even when he asked, "You miss him?"

"Like the plague," she said drily.

He snorted. "Same with me and Meg."

"I think it's different for you. You were just a child, and she treated you terribly. You never had any choice in being with her." She could see him listening, focused on her words. "I *chose* to be with Cody. Even knowing the way he was, kind of self-centered, but he was nice to me, I let myself fall for him." She sighed. "I'm the loser. You were just a poor little boy stuck with a monster."

He left the dishes to sit by her at her tiny table. Fortunately, the chair held under his weight. "Why do you think you went with Cody in the first place?"

She'd been thinking about that for a long time. "He was handsome and sweet. And smart. He works for an IT firm and travels a lot installing equipment. I've always been invisible. My parents' daughter. My older sister's helper. I'm there for everyone, but no one really sees me. You know?"

He nodded.

"I'm not complaining about it. It sounds like I am, but I'm not. I like being needed. And my first few boyfriends liked me for me, but I was younger. Those relationships didn't last. Then going to school took a lot of time, and I tried to do it on my own and be independent."

He reached for her hand over the table and stroked it with his fingers. "You're like me. We have to earn everything we get."

She agreed, wondering if that's why she felt so close to him, because they were alike that way. "Yes. I offered to help my sister when she was in chemo. I cooked meals, cleaned up, and helped with my niece and nephew. I loved it, and Tim, my brother-in-law, is a wonderful guy. They're a great family, and I loved feeling a part of that. Maybe…maybe I envied her. Wanting my own family. I don't know. I only know that when Tim brought Cody home one night for dinner, and Cody flirted and flattered me, I felt like I mattered, and not just because I was family.

"My parents love me. Joy loves me. They care, but it felt like they had to care because we're related. You know?" As soon as she said it, she realized her mistake. "I'm so sorry. But your mother should have cared."

"Which one?" He snorted, a hard gleam in his eyes.

"Both of them." She cupped his hand in hers, now stroking him. "You should have been surrounded by love. I bet you were an adorable baby."

"I'm sure I was." He smiled, but it looked strained. "But keep telling me about Cody. You wanted to matter to someone not family?"

She let him change the subject, not wanting him to dwell on bad memories. "Seeing it now, in hindsight, I feel stupid. I should have looked beyond what he gave me to what I really wanted. But he was handsome and treated me well. We went out on dates, and whenever he could he'd stop by Tim and Joy's, he always made me feel special. When I moved back to Colby, he'd come visit me there." She frowned. "Of course, I treated him like a king. I cooked, cleaned, did anything he needed. I pretty much catered to the man, because that's what the women in my family do. Except I didn't like doing it any more. Then he stopped coming around so much."

"Let me guess," Smith drawled. "It wasn't long before he gave you an ultimatum about moving to be with him, or you were through."

"Yes. And I'd repeatedly told him I loved Kansas. All my friends and family, well, except for Joy, are there."

"So, he never figured you'd move out here."

"That's the gist of it." She shook her head. "Our last conversation, when he told me I either moved, or we were done... He really made me think. What was I hanging on to? Love is worth moving mountains or moving cities. Suddenly, leaving for Seattle became an adventure, not something to be afraid of. So, I left Kansas for only the second time ever, and I moved here to be with him. And, well, you know how that turned out."

He was staring at her in a way that made her feel too open.

"Smith?"

"Do you think *I* ask you for too much?"

She didn't understand. "You barely ask me for anything."

"But you made me cookies. You just cooked me dinner, and we've had sex. Do you think I'm using you for, I don't know, food or something?"

She smiled, because he'd had to think about what he might be using her for. "No. First of all, I offered you cookies. I asked if you wanted dinner tonight. And the sex…" She colored. "I like being with you that way."

"I fucking love it," he said bluntly. "But it's only good if you're into it." He paused, and she sensed the vulnerability he masked with his gruff question, "Are you into it? For sure?"

She leaned closer to kiss him on the lips. "Do you really have to ask that after yesterday?"

A satisfied, very male smile appeared. "Yeah, that's true. You were all over me."

"Smith."

He chuckled, then his mirth fled. "I, ah, I need some advice, I think."

"Hey, you listened to me about Cody. I'm here for you."

"I know. And I have to tell you, that's new for me." He scowled. "You, Reid, Cash, Evan. Hell, the crew at work. I've been alone for a long time, and now people are all over the place. And they act like they want to help and be friendly. I don't mean you. You're real. I get that. But… Meg said she has a note from my birth father.

"I mentioned it before; my family is fucked up. My birth mom, Angela, had a family already. But she'd been fooling around with Allen. First, she had Cash. He's my full brother. She hid the part about him being Allen's, so Cash grew up thinking he had a different father. And that guy had no idea Cash wasn't his. Then she and that guy had Reid. He's a legit Griffith. But she kept having a thing with my old man, and she got pregnant with me."

Erin watched in rapt fascination. She nodded for him to continue. "I'm tracking."

"It's so convoluted. And just weird." He sighed. "Anyway, you know the rest. Angela hid her pregnancy, gave birth to me, and handed me off to her sister—Meg Ramsey. I don't think Meg ever loved me. But her husband had died, and she was lonely, I guess. Plus, it probably made her feel good to know she had her sister's son from the man she was in love with."

"Wait. You lost me."

"See, both sisters loved Allen—my birth father. But Allen only loved Angela. While I was a kid, Allen used to come visit me. Or Meg. I'm not sure which. He loved Angela, but he'd come over to fuck Margaret. He'd play with me some then take off. Once a month like clockwork, for years. Then he stopped coming. And it broke something inside her. She'd always been kind of cold, but after he stopped coming, Meg turned downright mean."

Erin could see him lost in bad memories, and she hated that he'd been subjected to such nastiness growing up. "I'm so sorry. So, you had no one at all to help you?"

He shrugged. "I had books and comics." He gave her a strained grin. "I had a pretty good imagination, and I used to dream about being a superhero. How my real parents would one day show up and take me to my home planet." He flushed. "Sounds stupid, right?"

"Not at all. It sounds like an amazing way to cope."

"I wasn't totally awful. I had friends, but not good friends. I was pretty much a loner in school. I got good grades, but I really shone on the sports field. Soccer, basketball, lacrosse. You name it, I played it. And I loved the intensity of competition. I've been trying my whole life to make Meg care, even a little bit. And since she was always telling me how much better my cousins were, I strove to beat them."

She shook her head. "But nothing you did could ever be as good as what they did, right?"

"Exactly. But one thing she'd said stuck with me. I ended up joining the Marine Corps because of Cash and Reid. At the time I didn't know anything about them. Just that my cousins were so much better than me. The Marines helped. I lived away from her, and I did well. Got promoted up the chain. Saw other countries, learned a lot. But it was never enough for me. When I left, I came home. Thinking maybe things would be different here."

"They weren't." She didn't have to guess.

"No. And she let it all out, how she wasn't my mother, about Allen, Cash and Reid, all of it. So, I joined Vets on the Go! to learn about them. And man, I hated those two perfect brothers, my birth mom's precious kids. She threw *me* away but she kept *them?*" The conversation had riled him up, but Erin couldn't blame him.

She caressed his cheek, and he froze. "I think I might hate Margaret Ramsey." *And I might be seriously falling for you.*

CHAPTER THIRTEEN

*S*mith stopped his rant, embarrassed he'd told her so much. Yet part of him felt so much freer getting it off his chest. Someone besides Smith knew the truth. Even better, she was on his side.

"You didn't have a choice," she'd said, and that resonated, easing a burden he hadn't been aware he'd carried for so long.

"I'm sorry. Is that wrong?" Erin asked, her hand still on his cheek as she leaned over the table. "Do you still love her?"

"Hell no." But he wanted…something…from the blasted woman. Not affection. He'd lost the need for her love long ago. But an acknowledgement of how she'd wronged him, that he craved. "I can't stand her. But she's holding a note from Allen—to me— over my head. I have to help her move. If I don't, she won't give me the note. I might help her move, and she might burn it to ash. With her, who knows?"

"That's so messed up." Erin's eyes blazed. "She's an awful person. To treat a child with such cruelty is just wrong. But then to not give you what's rightfully yours? He was your father, even if he never told you."

"To be honest, I'm not sure he ever knew." A sudden thought occurred.

"What's that look?"

"Come to my apartment with me?" He wanted her to see something. Because coward that he was, he didn't want to read Angela's journal alone.

"Sure." Erin grabbed her keys and locked up behind her.

Once inside his apartment, she settled on the couch while he grabbed the journal and returned to her. They sat side by side, and her presence gave him the strength to open the book.

"This belonged to Angela Griffith, my birth mother. Reid and Cash gave it to me to read, but I only managed a few pages before I had to close it."

"Oh, Smith. Is it too painful?" Erin put an arm around his waist.

His emotions surged, a powerful longing for Erin to never, ever leave. He cleared his throat to dispel the knot of feeling making it difficult to speak. "Um, no. It's just fucking bad. She writes all this shitty prose. Like, it's a very bad daytime soap, but with flowery language and euphemisms all over the place."

Erin tried to bite back a grin. "I can't believe it. You're a literary snob."

He flushed. "I am not. I read comics and fantasy for fun. I like books—*well-written* books."

She snickered.

He found himself smiling. "Oh, stop."

She laughed. "Smith Ramsey, the man who taught Tilly the word 'fuck-knuckle,' has definite ideas on well-written books."

"Shut up."

She finally quieted. "Okay, so you don't want to read her book, maybe because learning certain things, no matter how poorly written, might hurt."

She'd hit it in one.

He sighed. "Yes."

"Give it to me."

He handed it over. "This makes me a huge pussy for not having the stones to read the truth on my own, doesn't it?"

"Not at all." She pulled him close for a kiss that comforted. "Now I tell you what." Erin opened the journal, and his heart raced. "If you make me a nice cup of tea, I'll just sit here and read some of this. Will that work?"

"Um, sure. Yes. Great." He stood and stepped toward the kitchen then stopped. "What kind of tea?"

"Surprise me."

An hour later, Erin closed the book. She frowned, and her mouth remained a flat line. "Smith?"

He sat next to her on the chaise, sprawled out reading the next in a fantasy series he'd found at the library, one of his favorite places to go when he had any free time. He'd lost himself in the book, used to escaping the shittier things in life with make-believe.

Smith set his book aside. "What?"

"I think you should read this." She scooted next to him and pointed to a passage written in very neat cursive.

> *Charles has no idea, and it's best I keep it that way. If he knew Allen's name, who Allen really was, I fear he'd kill my love.*
>
> *But my baby boy, my little Riley. So special. I miss him every day, but at least he's in good hands with Meg. I miss my sister. I miss my son.*
>
> *And it happened. As I'd feared, I made a mistake. Charles heard Cash talking about what should have been our little secret, my private nickname for my boy. Charles came to me and demanded to know why I'd called him that. And it all came spilling out. How much I missed Allen. How Cash reminded me of his father.*
>
> *Charles hit me that day. Only once. A slap across my face.*
>
> *And then he cried. My big, strong husband cried like he'd only cried that one time before. And I knew then I should never think to leave him. Not when my love meant so much to him. I saw the depth of Charles's pain, and it moved me so.*
>
> *I swore I'd never see Allen again. And from that day forward, I meant it. Allen was heartbroken. But Charles. He glowed with joy, that I'd chosen him over my true love.*
>
> *I tried to hold onto that joy. But so lost without Allen, I turned inward. And found happiness in the words of others.*

Erin said quietly, "I wonder if that's why he stopped coming around, because Angela told him it was over. I've read through most of this and don't see anywhere that she told Allen about you. I have a feeling she kept you a secret."

"But he used to visit me all the time." Smith paused. Or had he?

Allen had come and played with him, yes, but the majority of the man's time had been spent with Margaret. Maybe he'd been kind to Margaret's "son" to keep her happy. "So, he might not have known about me." He for damn sure couldn't trust Meg's version of the past.

"I don't know. I've still got a few pages to read. But you're right. Most of this reads like a bad romance." She flushed. "I read, you know, and the stuff I like is so much better than this."

He nodded, distracted. Now more than ever he needed to read Allen's letter.

Erin turned back to the journal. Smith stopped her. "No. You've done enough. I should read this."

"It's bad. And there are more spots like this passage, earlier on, that are…" Her eyes welled. "I don't think Angela was all there, but her feelings were real. She loved her children, all of you." She sniffed. "But she didn't show it well at all. I feel so bad for your brothers. I know Meg abused you."

"She didn't—"

"She did." Erin frowned. "Verbal abuse is just as bad as physical abuse. There's no excuse for it."

Having her in his corner felt so fucking amazing. "Thanks."

She nodded. "And though Meg was awful, I don't think living in Angela and Charles' household would have been any better."

"Yeah, but I wouldn't have been all alone." And that, there, was the crux of it. Smith was so damn tired of being alone.

Erin didn't look at him as if he were pathetic for admitting that. Instead, she sighed. "Yeah. That has to be the worst. Being sad and afraid and having no one to turn to." She looked at him, straight in the eye. "I'm so proud of you, and it makes me feel a little bad about my own problems."

"What? Why?" He swung his feet over the chaise and sat up straight, watching her try to express herself. Her eyes started to grow shiny, and he didn't like it.

"You had no one to help you grow into the kind, loving man you are today."

His cheeks felt hot. "Nah. Don't make me—"

"You hush," she said and wiped her eyes. "When I was at the lowest point in my life, you were there. You helped me. You *held* me. And you never once took advantage or did anything but look out for me. No one showed you how to be a good man, Smith. You did that all on your own." She sniffed. "I have silly problems. A broken heart. Broken hearts heal. But what was done to you could have broken your forever." She leaned close and cupped his cheeks. "You're so much more than you see yourself. I see you." She put his hand over her heart. "See how it races? Because you're near. Because you're so amazing, and you can't see it."

His eyes burned. No one had ever said that kind of stuff to him before. Sure, he could bring a woman to orgasm. Yes, he had large muscles and a decent enough face. But Erin was really looking at him and seeing something that made her truly happy. Proud, she'd said.

He blinked to keep mortifying tears at bay.

"Can I ask a favor from you?" She wiped her eyes.

"Ask anything."

"Can I sleep over tonight?" Before he could deny her, knowing she had to be making the request of out pity, she added, "You said a lot about how you feel. And it made me realize something. We're only alone if we allow it."

He dropped his hand from her chest, not able to handle feeling her racing heart any more. Smith felt for this woman, something strange and beautiful and terrifying. And every time she said something meaningful and deep, she made it worse.

"I don't want to be alone tonight. I want to sleep next to you and know that you're there to keep me safe." She flushed. "That's not very independent minded, is it?"

"Stay." He cleared his throat, aware a gravel truck seemed to have parked there. "Just to sleep, I swear. I'd like that."

Her bright eyes crinkled, and her lips curled up in a smile. One that never failed to shock his pulse and warm him deep inside.

"I'd love to. And I'll read the rest of that tomorrow." She pointed to Angela's journal.

"No. That's for me to read. You helped me, so much. But it's time for me to stop avoiding the truth."

"Are you sure?" She looked up at him with concern.

So loving and tender, always trying to help someone else. Was it any wonder he'd fallen for her? "I'm sure." He led her into the bedroom. While they took turns getting ready for bed, he turned down the comforter.

He wore his underwear, and Erin wore one of his favorite shirts, dwarfed by the Avengers.

"You really do like comics, don't you?" she teased and plucked the thin cotton from her body.

It settled over her pert breasts again. Too emotionally and physically drained from the night's revelations, he patted the bed. She joined him, and when she turned on her side and snuggled closer, he breathed in her scent and kissed the top of her head, in love and uncertain about where to go from there.

"Good night, Erin."

She kissed his chest, above his heart, and he swore the shriveled organ cracked its outer shell and started beating just for her. "Good night...Riley."

He blinked more tears, not sure who he felt simultaneously sad and happy for. The man who had finally found a treasure to care for, or the boy who had missed so much in his life?

Erin snuggled deeper. "Nah. Good night, Smith. That's much better." He swore she murmured something that sounded like "sweetheart" before she drifted off.

He just held her and drifted into a contented sleep better than he'd had in years.

ERIN AWOKE THE NEXT MORNING, UNSURE ABOUT HER comfortable surroundings and glorious warmth, until she remembered last night. Poor Smith. God, the look on his face as they'd talked about his life. It made her want to cry all over again. Such an amazing man to come from such a start in life.

Was it any wonder she'd come to care for him on such a deep, lasting level? This was nothing like the "love" she'd felt for Cody, the crushes she'd had in the past, or even her first love in high school. Smith was a man with a man's needs, and for the first time that she could remember, she felt as if she could partner with him, so that they might help and love each other.

God, she'd admitted it. The L-word. Too soon, too soon. Yet she felt it all the same.

An arm tightened around her, bringing her closer to Smith, who spooned her from behind. She had to sneak away to use the facilities, but instead of staying awake—she blinked at the 5:00am on the alarm—she carefully crawled back into bed in the position she'd just left.

Smith murmured her name and tugged her closer. So strong, so big, he surrounded her with care and heat. Such wonderful heat.

Erin used two blankets over the air mattress in her apartment to combat the cold, and then threw more on top of her when she slept. But just one Smith and she felt toasty, comfy, and...aroused.

He pulled her into his body, his erection thick against her back. She wondered if it would be in bad form to explore him. Probably, though she doubted he'd mind.

The big sweetheart murmured her name and kissed her neck. "You awake?" he asked, his thick voice sexy as heck.

No, sexy as *hell*. Erin wiggled her ass against him. "I am if you are," she whispered.

He chuckled and jostled behind her, then raised her shirt up to expose her panties under the blanket. She felt his naked flesh against her back and froze, realizing he'd removed his underwear.

Morning sex. She shivered, remembering how it used to be, feeling a part of a couple, sharing intimacies with someone she... loved. Erin didn't want to think about her confusing emotions just now. She wanted Smith.

She pulled his hand between her legs. "Take them off me."

He did, then slid his fingers inside her, finding her slick and ready. "Oh, yeah. You're so hot." He pumped his fingers in and out of her, rubbing his erection against her back, then positioning himself between her legs, resting against her folds but not penetrating.

"In me," she breathed, wanting him to be a part of her, this wonderful man who had been through so much yet gave her so much joy.

"Yeah. In you," he agreed and angled himself inside her.

On her side, with Smith behind her, the penetration didn't get far enough. Then he shifted her leg over his, widening her, and pushed.

She gasped; he groaned. And his movements grew jerky while he rubbed her clit, the race to climax speeding. "Yes, oh, I'm coming." She keened and ground his hand against her, the aftershocks of passion making her tremble.

He gripped her hip and pulled her back, shoving so deep inside she felt him *move*. He shuddered, sawing in and out of her as he came, and she wanted it. Him. As close together as two people could be.

"Erin." Smith sighed and rested his forehead against her shoulder. "Fuck. You're amazing."

"An amazing fuck?" She heard herself say it and blushed.

"Hell, yeah." He chuckled but didn't withdraw. Instead, he stayed inside her, joined. "Man, I never want to move ever again."

"Don't."

"Trust me, if I could freeze like this, I would. But I'm getting soft, and you're about to get messy."

"Dang it."

He pulled out and she raced away to the bathroom. She'd finished cleaning up when he knocked. She was washing her hands when he moved to the toilet. "No."

He stopped moving.

"Don't even think about peeing in front of me," she warned. "We're close but not that close."

"Oh?" he sounded annoyed.

"Smith, we could be married fifty years with forty grandkids, and we still wouldn't be that close. The only person who pees in front of me is me."

He grinned. "Forty grandkids? So how many kids is that?"

"Oh." She left the room, feeling like an utter fool. Why the hell would she mention marriage or kids at all? She might be thinking about how much she liked and lusted and yes, loved the man. But she had so much baggage in her own life, and Smith clearly had a truckload in his. The poor guy constantly helped her out of messes, yet no one ever helped him, and look at how remarkable he'd turned out to be?

Erin paused in his bedroom. It had just turned six, and his alarm went off. She searched for his phone, found it, and hit a button to silence the racket.

"You want to shower here or at your place?" he asked, standing naked in the doorway.

She couldn't help staring at him. "You're not embarrassed about being nude at all are you?"

"Nope. And I pee in front of other people all the time."

"All the time, really?" She quirked a brow.

"In the men's bathroom, Cupcake. And when I was in the Corps, if we were out in the field or on patrol, we took care of business. No big deal."

She felt embarrassed but figured they might as well talk about it. "Okay, here's the deal. I like you. A lot. A lot-lot." The wide smile he wore looked good on him. "But I have my own quirks."

"Right. No peeing in front of you."

"Right. And that includes all things that involve the toilet."

"What about puking?" His eyes gleamed.

"Well, Mr. Pain-in-the-Butt, how about this? If it comes out of you below the waist, I don't want to see it. Same goes for me. I will *not* do my business in front of you."

"Okay."

"And no farting either." She wished she hadn't started all this. "It's gross. Guys think it's funny. I do not."

"Gotcha."

She had to give it to him. He was working hard to choke back laughter. "And another thing. I expect honesty between us. I liked sleeping with you. And I loved what we just did. Maybe we could keep doing this."

"This?"

"Us."

He watched her in silence, enough to make her uncomfortable.

"I'm sorry. Did I push for too much?" she asked.

"Just making sure you're saying that because you like me. Not because you pity me or anything," he muttered.

"You are as thick as a brick."

He glanced down at himself and shrugged. "I know. Thanks for noticing."

"No, you idiot. Not your penis. Your head."

"Huh?"

"I like you because you're sexy and sweet, but you can be kind of an asshole." Only Smith could make her cuss.

"Oh, you said a bad word."

"Shut up. I like being with you. You make me laugh. I feel good around you. And I know you'd never treat me the way Cody did."

He stepped toward her, stopping so close she had to look up to read his expression. "Never. I like you too." He sighed. "A lot. You're sexy and funny, and let's be honest, you make me hard. But you never leave me hungry." He grinned. "We should date. For real."

"For real?" She tensed. Had they been fake dating?

"You're my girl. Only mine," he warned.

She understood and relaxed, letting him take her in his arms. "So, you want to be my boyfriend."

"Yep."

"So, I'm your girlfriend."

"Uh-huh."

"But we don't live together, right?" she needed some clarification on that.

He opened his mouth and closed it, and she wondered what he'd intended to say before he'd changed his mind. "What do *you* think about the living arrangements?"

"I think it's too soon," she said, though she fantasized saying, *Yes, let's do it. I love you. Let's start making babies and live happily ever after.* To which Smith would run for the hills.

"Right."

They stared at each other.

Smith glanced at his alarm clock. "It's still early. Do you have time for another round?"

She smiled, feeling so in sync with this man. Erin whipped off her shirt. "Great minds think alike."

"Yes, Cupcake." His hands followed the trail his eyes had made. "They do."

CHAPTER FOURTEEN

*L*ater in the morning, Erin stood with Tilly in Brad Battle's unit, having accompanied the insistent older woman to avoid being nagged for another hour about the hot plumbers coming to fix her pipes.

Tilly laughed hard at her own jokes, but having been the recipient of Smith's ability with his larger-than-normal pipe, Erin laughed with her.

She'd been on cloud nine all morning. Erin had a boyfriend. Smith Ramsey was officially hers.

She hadn't yet told Tilly because she wanted to announce her new status the right way and prepare herself to answer a million prying questions.

For now, the sexy plumbers of McSons Plumbing occupied Tilly, so Erin kept her great news to herself.

She frowned. She had no one but Smith and Tilly to tell, anyway. And Reid and Naomi, she added, wondering how they might feel about her dating Reid's brother. Would Smith tell anyone? Did she care if he didn't? She didn't rightly know how to process her affection. She loved him. She knew it was crazy. And part of her didn't care.

But the other part did.

"Oh, they're almost here." Tilly sounded giddy as she stared at her phone and texted back.

A glance around the apartment showed a neat bachelor's pad. Brad had good taste. Nice, dark furniture against cream colored walls and upscaled appliances and countertops. He had a lot of photos of what looked like family, firefighters, and fellow Marines. Geez, there sure seemed to be a lot of them around here. She wondered if Smith had known Brad before, when he'd served in the Marine Corps, and figured to ask him later.

Some portraits of landscapes decorated the walls. Using Tilly's nosiness as an excuse, Erin had looked with her, seeing a neat space full of personal items that showed an organized mind. Brad had set up his second bedroom as an office, and he had a desk and computer and everything in its place.

This apartment must have cost more than hers, for sure. Maybe more than Smith's too, because it looked like Brad had two bedrooms, and the unit felt more upscale.

Tilly noticed her looking around. "Nice, eh? I updated most of the spaces on the B floor two years ago. I charge more for 'em, but the tenants are great and always pay on time. And speaking of which, rent is due on the first."

"I know. I can pay you."

"Six hundred, flat."

"What? That's—"

"The deal. Take it or leave it," Tilly growled.

"Tilly, that's less than what we agreed." Great. Now Erin felt as if she were taking advantage of an old lady.

"Look, your unit needs a lot of work. You cleaned it. You also cook for me and clean, though your dusting needs some work."

Erin rolled her eyes. She left the unit spotless, and Tilly knew it.

"And you don't mind helping with other stuff. You have my offer. Take it or leave it."

Erin didn't trust the militant look in Tilly's eyes, so she shrugged and gratefully took the gift for what it was. "Fine. But if you go broke because you're undercharging people, I expect to be the first one you kick out."

"The very first. My foot on your tiny ass as I shove you out the door."

"Thanks, so much."

Tilly snickered. Today she wore a pretty blue blouse and jeans over white orthopedic shoes.

"I thought Smith was supposed to be handling this," Erin said. She knew Brad had been notified, but Smith typically handled maintenance issues, even the ones subcontracted out.

"He was, but he's coming in half an hour when he can get away. He thought it would be sooner, but he said someone was out sick this morning and he had to fill in on a job farther away."

He hadn't told Erin any of that, but then, why would he? She was supposed to be working in her place. She had to be careful not to fall behind. She had two new articles to edit, one on almonds and another on fire prevention. And she was way past due to film something new for her cooking channel.

Two men appeared in the open doorway to the apartment. Both extremely handsome, wearing jeans and white McSons Plumbing shirts, they came with a toolkit, friendly smiles, and a lot of muscle. Erin now understood why Tilly had been so keen on having these particular plumbers solve her problems.

"Hi. Mrs. Cartwright?"

Tilly moved faster than Erin had ever seen her, flying toward the plumbers and barely using her cane. "I'm Tilly Cartwright.

"I'm Brody Singer." The sandy-haired man with the killer grin notched a thumb at his companion. "This is Flynn McCauley, my talented employee."

The dark-haired man glared at him. "He means partner." Then he turned on the charm and had Tilly laughing and flirting in seconds.

"I'm so glad you're here," Tilly cooed.

Erin just stared at her landlady, in awe of Flynn's power.

"And you are?" Brody asked, friendly but not too friendly. She noted he and Flynn wore wedding rings, and she appreciated him being more professional with her. The guys couldn't have been too much older than Erin. She imagined they did *a lot* of business through referrals, no doubt from the single lonely-hearts of Seattle.

"I'm Erin." She shook their hands. "I'm with Tilly. She's the boss. I'm just here to do what she says."

The guys grinned. "Sounds good. Now Tilly," Flynn said. "The guy who called said something about the shower not heating up?"

"Yes. Follow me." Flynn followed her while Brody remained behind.

He asked her, "I don't suppose you know where the hot water heater is in the building."

"Sorry, no."

Brody shrugged. "No problem. Tilly mentioned Smith Ramsey, our point of contact, should be arriving soon."

She nodded. "Smith does all the handyman work around the place." She started to say more when she saw a cat sitting on the kitchen counter. "Um…"

Brody followed her gaze. "Hey, kitty."

It allowed itself to be held and petted while Flynn and Tilly spoke in the bathroom. Tilly kept laughing at whatever Flynn said.

"Erin." Brody motioned her over.

She joined him near the cat and petted it until it drew back a paw. Man, she did not seem to have luck with felines. "What?"

"Please tell me she didn't flush anything down a toilet."

Erin blinked. "Huh?"

Brody sighed and in a lower voice explained, "One of our clients, the one who referred us to Tilly, has a habit of flushing stuff down her toilet for us to come fish out. I'm not lying when I say we've been to her house half a dozen times. The woman is in her eighties. And no, she doesn't have grandkids or anyone who lives with her. I think she has a crush on Flynn."

Erin bit her lip, amused by his telling. "I'm sorry, yet amused."

Brody grinned, his light brown eyes glinting with humor. "So am I."

"Emerald Estates really does have a plumbing problem. Tilly—"

"What the hell is this?" Smith barked from the doorway. He glared at Erin, standing close to Brody.

She smiled. "Ah, my boyfriend." It felt good to say. "Smith, come meet Brody, one half of McSons Plumbing."

Brody looked relieved. "Oh man. Glad to meet you. Erin was just telling me Tilly really has a problem."

Smith looked puzzled. "That's why we called you."

Erin chuckled and whispered, "But Tilly's friend who recommended these guys has a crush on Flynn. She keeps flushing stuff down the toilet so he'll come fish it out."

Brody smirked. "She's eighty years young, and Flynn's on her must-do list."

Smith quirked a grin. "Ah. Got it."

Erin liked that he smiled so much more now. He looked so handsome when he let himself enjoy life. Then again, he turned her on when he sneered.

Brody held out his hand, and after introductions were made, Erin excused herself to go back to her apartment to work. But not before giving Smith a big kiss.

They forgot everything before Brody cleared his throat, then they sprung apart.

"Ah, you know, your blossoming romance makes everything brighter. But Smith, do you think you could show me the hot water heater?"

Erin laughed and left, just as Smith called Brody a wiseass.

SMITH HADN'T LIKED ERIN STANDING TOO CLOSE TO TILLY'S plumbers. Because yeah, he could see why the old woman had wanted them to "service her unit" as she'd said, laughing, over and over again. The guys looked to be around his age, give or take a few years. Brody was smart, had a sense of humor, and knew his stuff.

Smith's first reaction to seeing the guy standing near Erin had been rage. Jealousy. An ugly realization that she'd been flirting and not meaning any of that close crap about them being a couple.

The pain had been vicious. For all of a few seconds. Then he'd come back to earth and realized they were doing nothing but talking. He'd heard Erin call him her boyfriend for the very first time.

I have got to get a grip.

Brody followed him outside after setting down the cat... "Is that yours?" he asked the guy.

Brody shook his head. "Found him in the kitchen."

"That's gonna cause a problem." Tilly was firm about no pets.

Then again, she might not notice because she'd been back in the bathroom with Flynn for a while. "Should we rescue your partner?"

Brody sighed. "My brother. And he's got a lot to learn. I'm teaching him the ropes, but he's not as quick at catching on as I'd hoped." He grinned. "Make sure you tell him I said that if he asks."

"Ah, sure."

"I'm totally kidding. Guy is super smart. But he's annoying."

"I get that." Cash had been over him like a rash all morning, asking questions about the dinner with Reid and Naomi, about Erin, and about what Smith might be *feeling*. It had been pure hell.

"So, the water heater…"

Half an hour later, Flynn still hadn't joined them, but Smith had learned it was only a matter of time before the water heater crapped out.

Brody shook his head. "This thing has gone beyond its prime, if you ask me. It's a good piece of gear, but one of these days it's going to break, and then you'll be out of luck and taking cold showers." Brody wrote down a few names. "Check on these. I recommend the top two as your best bang for your buck. But it's your call."

"Tilly's call," he said as he read the brand names. "And you guys will install it? How much?"

Brody rattled off some figures. "Let us know what you want to do. Once you know what you want, we'll order it for you and schedule to install it. Won't take long to come in. Should be anywhere from 2-4 hours to install, but we'll allot extra time in case something goes wrong. We'll remove the old heater, which means disconnecting the power and water supply, then remove the tank. We put in the new heater, a tank if she's not going tankless, then we have to fit the thing. Then reconnect it. It's not a huge project unless we find issues when we remove your tank."

"Okay. I'll let Tilly know."

"Depending on her homeowner's insurance, she might be covered for some of it."

They walked back to Brad's apartment and found it locked.

Brody frowned. "Did he leave without me?"

Freakin' Tilly. "Come on." Smith led them to Tilly's apartment and banged on the door.

"Hold your horses," he heard her yell.

"You think she has my brother tied to a chair? Forcing him to do unnatural things?" Brody whispered.

"With Tilly? Probably." He smirked at the wary look on the guy's face.

Tilly finally answered the door, a flush on her cheeks, wearing a huge grin. They found Flynn at her kitchen table munching on some of Erin's cookies.

"Dude," Flynn said to Brody. "You have got to try these. They're insane."

Brody took one and agreed.

Tilly beamed, glanced at Smith, and said nothing.

Smith knew it would come out eventually, so he said, "My girl-friend made them." He refused to look at Tilly's smug expression, though he unfortunately heard her loud, "I knew it!"

"You should marry her," Flynn said as he inhaled another one. "Okay, Tilly. I really do have to go." He stood and patted his flat stomach. Tilly, the lecher, watched his movements like a hawk.

"You fixed Brad's shower problem. Have a few more."

"I'll grab them," Brody said with a wide grin.

Tilly gave him a flirty smile, and Smith wanted to gouge his own eyes out.

"I gave Smith the details, Tilly," Brody said with a napkin full of apricot rugelach. "You decide what you want installed and when and call us." He glanced at Flynn and said with a sly smile, "And thank Pat for recommending us. She's a sweetheart, isn't she, Flynn?"

Flynn gave Brody the same look that Smith had used earlier on Cash. Maybe it was a brother thing.

"Oh, yes. Please thank her." Flynn turned to Smith. "Call if you have any questions." Then he shook Tilly's hand, his smile sincere. "It was a pleasure meeting you, Tilly. Thanks so much for the cookies." Flynn slapped Brody on the back, hard enough to make him stumble. Then he grabbed his toolbox and yanked his brother with him out the door, closing it behind them.

Tilly stared after them with a sigh. "My word. What a day." She turned back to Smith and smirked. "Now spill it, boy. What's going on with you and that girl? She's been dreamy-eyed all damn morning."

"Tilly."

"Don't Tilly, me, ass-munch. Talk."

"Well, when you put it like that, how can I refuse?"

ERIN HAD DELVED INTO HER MAGAZINE EDITS. NOT ONLY DID SHE work on articles concerning harvesting nuts like walnuts and pistachios, she'd just received two early December articles. One on pruning and the other on winter sanitation in the orchards for navel orange worm. She wanted to thank whoever knocked on her door to give her a break.

"Coming." She looked through the peephole to see Smith waiting impatiently.

She opened up, and he tugged her close for a kiss.

He let her go, and she sighed. "Well, hel-lo to you too." Talk about a steamy greeting.

"Sorry about before. I didn't mean to be so late."

"You okay?"

He followed her inside. "Yeah. Cash got chatty on the job. About drove me nuts."

She grimaced. "Please. Don't say that word."

"Cash?"

"Nuts." At his frown, she explained about her articles.

"Ah." He glanced at her open laptop. "Nice work, Ms. Editor. But I prefer the YouTube channel." He shrugged. "I looked you up. You're supposed to be filming new stuff this week."

She waved at her kitchen. "Where would you suggest I do that?"

He snuck a hand in his pocket and produced a key. "Well, I had a thought about that."

She stared at that key. It seemed to glow in his hand. She swallowed. "Is that yours?"

"Yeah. I had another made. Don't tell Tilly." He chuckled. "Look, you need a kitchen. I'm addicted to your cooking. How about a deal?"

"A deal?" He hadn't asked her to move in. She told herself to be glad, because she wasn't ready for that kind of commitment yet. Bad enough she thought she might love him. She needed to be smart about the falling for him part.

"You're looking at me weird," he said cautiously.

"Sorry. I've got nuts on the brain."

"Long as they're mine, I'm okay with that." He winked.

She blushed and tried to cover it with a frown, which made him laugh. "The deal?" she reminded him.

"Right. You need a kitchen. I like your cooking way better than mine. How about you use my kitchen whenever you want to do your food thing? I know it's not super fancy but—"

"It's just fine. I can work with that kitchen island." Excited at the prospect, she wanted to jump on his offer. "Are you sure this is okay?"

"Cupcake, I'm more thrilled with the idea than you are."

"I don't know about that."

"I do. What's the next thing on your list to make?"

She frowned. "I don't know. Some kind of dessert. You keep calling me Cupcake, and now I have a hankering to make cupcakes."

"Awesome." He grinned, a lot freer with his smiles than when she'd first met him. "I'll provide the raw ingredients for dinner, you cook it up, serve whatever you make on you show for dessert, and we're good. Yes?"

"Oh. So like I do with Tilly." She nodded. "That's fair." She went to take the key, and he closed his fist around it.

"You have to make enough for two to eat though. We'll be eating together. You and me. Is that okay? It's kind of a package deal."

He wanted them to eat together. "Only if I can pay for half the meals. It's only fair since I'll be eating it too."

"Nope. My house, my rules. You want to pay for something? Consider whatever you cook on the show your fee."

"Well, I guess." She studied him. "This isn't you feeling sorry for me or thinking I'm poor is it? I can afford my own food."

"It's actually me being cheap, because I'll be getting amazing meals at a quarter of the price. But it's no pressure if you say no. I'm not trying to strongarm you into being with me or anything."

Great. She'd tried to do the right thing by not taking over his house, and thus his life. But he seemed hurt by her hesitance. "Fine. I'm happy to cook at your place. But you have to promise that any time you don't want me to come over, you'll tell me. I don't want to be so intrusive you get sick of me." The idea that Smith wouldn't want her anymore caused a minor sense of déjà vu—watching Cody walk away.

Smith nodded and held out a hand. She took it, and the key, then gasped when he pulled her in for a kiss that turned her into a needy mess. He let her go, and she sagged against the nearby wall.

"Something else I have to tell you." Smith looked bothered, and not because of the kiss.

"What's wrong?"

"Well, you and I said we should be honest with each other. I'm not real good at the dating stuff. At least, I wasn't back when I dated."

"Which was how long ago?"

"A few years."

She didn't believe that for a second. "A few years?"

"Having sex isn't dating. I told you that before." He gave her a small grin. "Anyway, I wanted you to know that I didn't like those plumbers hanging so close to you. I felt...jealous." He blew out a breath. "I also felt like a horse's ass for being possessive. But before I could wrap my head around it, you called me your boyfriend."

"That was okay, wasn't it?"

"It was more than okay. I felt like a moron for being so happy." He sighed. "I've been a moron for the better part of my day."

She laughed and moved in for a hug. Wrapping her arms around his waist, she put her head against his chest and closed her eyes. "I like you being a moron."

"Thanks." His voice rumbled against her ear, deep and calming. "I'm sure I'll continued to be an idiot and make you deliriously happy soon enough."

"Smith, I don't want you to feel jealous, but I'd be lying if I wasn't glad you don't like me with other people. I feel the same way about you."

He glanced down at her as she looked up. "You do?" The hope on his face tugged at her to promise more. But she couldn't. Not yet. Not until she dealt with her past and figured out why she'd made such a mistake with the wrong guy—who hadn't seemed wrong at the time.

"I do." Crap. With the phrase *I do*, her thoughts immediately flashed to an aisle, a white dress, and a sexy, scowly groom. She hurried to wipe that from her mind and added, "We should always be honest with each other." She paused, wanting to get it out in the open. "At some point I'll have to talk to Cody to get some closure."

His face closed. "Why? Because you still want him around?"

"No. But I'm entitled to some answers. And he wants to talk to me. He's been leaving me messages."

He considered her for a moment. "Makes sense. He should apologize. I can come with you. You know. For moral support."

"No." He didn't seem to like that. "I have to do this on my own. But I'm so glad you offered."

He didn't seem mollified. "Just... there's no rush to see him is there? Take your time and settle in here more. Make your videos. Get your life back on track." His ghost of a grin started that fluttery L-word buzzing inside her. "You know, be with your amazing boyfriend and feed him all that good stuff from your soon-to-be famous show."

"I can do that." She tilted her face up and accepted his kiss, wishing he would stick around to finish what he started. But Smith had to get back to work.

And Erin had to make a phone call.

It was time to stop dithering and make some decisions.

She clutched his key in her hand.

CHAPTER FIFTEEN

"*A*nd that, friends, is how you make Carrot Cake Perfection cupcakes." Erin smiled and signed off her cooking channel, the video one she prerecorded so she could edit before posting.

Three days had gone by since Smith had given her his key. Three days since she'd been catching up on filming. She'd made unicorn whips, a mean chocolate mousse-inspired delight that Tilly had gobbled up in seconds, and today's carrot cake cupcake with out-of-this-world frosting.

Smith and Tilly didn't have a problem with her concoctions. Tilly gobbled up anything she made. Smith complimented her so much during meals she worried she'd start believing her own "godly abilities with a spatula." And of course, she capped off dinners by spending the nights at his place, either at his request or her own.

His complaint that he couldn't sleep in her tiny bed made sense. And she rationalized that she saved time and energy by staying over. Heck, they conserved water by showering together. She found it all too easy to make excuses not to leave. After they made love, they cuddled. She'd never met a man more insistent on physical affection that had nothing to do with sex and everything to do with caring.

They talked too, about everything and anything. Smith really did know his comics. She'd learned more about the Punisher and John Constantine than she'd cared to and realized that her boyfriend was really a big comic nerd. The contrast of tough guy to geek made her love him even more. Especially because she understood why his fictional heroes continued to be so important to him.

Like her, Smith didn't have many friends. Yet the more he talked about how annoying Cash was or how autocratic Reid could be, the more she heard that longing to accept the idea of family in his life.

Thoughts of family made her homesick. She missed her parents, her friends. Erin knew she needed to go out and meet people, but she had no idea where to start. Naomi, maybe? But Erin only knew Naomi through Smith. Would that be presumptuous to call Naomi out of the blue and ask her to grab a coffee some time?

Her phone pinged, and she looked at the message, expecting Smith telling her when he'd be home.

But it was Cody, again wanting to talk. Though Smith had told her to take her time, Erin didn't like putting off the inevitable. She wanted to move forward with Smith, despite her fears she'd moved too fast and was on the road to another heartache. Maybe if she knew what it was about her that Cody hadn't been able to accept, she could fix it so Smith never had that issue with her.

No matter how much Smith insisted Cody had been wrong—and she knew cheating hadn't been her fault—something had pushed the man to another woman. That had hurt. If Smith found someone better, she didn't know what she'd do. Cody hadn't mattered the way Smith did, and she needed to be sure she wouldn't be the cause of him leaving.

She texted Cody back. *"I'm ready to hear you out."*

"Finally." He texted her the name of a coffee shop in Queen Anne, one Rupert had showed her over a week ago. *"Can you meet me there in an hour?"*

"Yes."

Nervous and a little freaked out that she'd finally get to confront Cody for being such a jerk, she left Smith a note and locked up, then went home to pick the right outfit for the occasion, the one that said *screw you, you could have had all this, but you blew it.*

Erin settled on jeans and a form-fitting amber sweater that brought out the golden glints in her eyes. She brushed her hair until it shone and wore her favorite gold hoops—a gift from her sister, not the earrings Cody had once given her. Though they were pretty, she'd exchanged everything he'd once given her to a nice consignment shop in Greenwood not far away for credit. Cody had to be good for something, after all.

A short drive in the late afternoon had her arriving in time to find a parking spot. A miracle. She left her vehicle, praying it lasted another 179000 miles before she had to budget for a new car, and walked the short distance to the coffee house.

She found Cody sitting inside, looking dapper as usual. To her bemusement, she settled down at the familiarity, no longer so anxious.

He smiled and stood when she approached. Always the gentleman. Until he wasn't. "Hope you don't mind. I ordered you a cappuccino and a French macaron."

Her favorites. "Thank you." She sat, draping her jacket over the back of the seat, her purse by her side. She clasped her hands together on the table and waited.

And so it began. Polite chitchat. Manners and ladylike behavior. Wait on Cody to say what he wanted, when he wanted. Ugh. Erin was so done being what others expected her to be. With Smith she just acted the way she wanted.

She took a sip of coffee to fortify herself. "Explain." Ha! She hadn't said please.

Cody studied her. "You look as beautiful as always."

She had to fight the urge to thank him for the compliment. "Cody, I came because I want to put you and our relationship behind me." He looked startled at her blunt speak. She took heart from that and continued, her pulse racing as she threw her all into the confrontation. "Tell me why you couldn't have mentioned a girl-friend before. Why you didn't just break it off with me when I was in Colby. That's all I want to know."

He sighed. "I'm so sorry for how it went down, Erin."

But not sorry he'd cheated? "Went down? It's not a crime drama. You dumped me after I'd spent a fortune to move myself out here. Why?"

He cringed. "Not one of my finer moments. Look, you're so sweet and nice all the time. You took care of me, made me laugh, made me happy. But I never felt good enough for you. It was hard trying to measure up."

She blinked. "Wait. So, it's *my* fault you cheated on me and lied?" Her voice rose. People glanced at them, but she didn't care. "That is the saddest excuse I've ever heard."

A redhead with two toddlers glared at Cody. "You tell him, honey." She walked out, muttering under her breath.

Cody flushed, hating to be the center of attention. Normally Erin would be right there with him. But she'd been hurt and betrayed by someone she'd once loved. She hadn't seen his flaws back then. Would she be able to see Smith's now?

"Erin, please, keep your voice down." He looked around nervously.

"Why? Afraid your girlfriend might walk in and wonder why you're with me? Or is she in the back waiting to take you to another work meeting before dinner?" Okay, that was plain bitchy, and she knew it. But somewhere Erin had started to let herself go with the conversation. She bit into the macaron. Raspberry flavored. Yum.

"Fine, I had that coming." He guzzled his coffee. "I didn't want to hurt you by breaking it off. I thought if I made up some outlandish dictate you'd walk away. I honestly had no idea you'd come out here." He looked puzzled. "I mean, who does that?" His look turned to one of fascination. Not a good sign.

"Uh-huh." Had he really not known she'd come out here for him? "And the girlfriend? When did that start?"

He glanced at his coffee, toying with his cuffs. A nervous tell she used to find endearing. "Diane and I started dating a few months ago. And don't be mad. You and I were on the outs, and you know it."

"How can you say that?" His clear dismissal of what they'd had shouldn't have hurt her any more. Yet it did.

He met her gaze. "Please. We hadn't been together in months. And when we were, you always wanted to talk or go out." He lowered his voice. "We rarely had sex. When we did, you made me wear a condom."

"So, you had needs, is that it?"

"Damn it. Yes. And even when we were together, it always felt as if I wanted it more than you did."

She lowered her voice to match his. "Maybe I'd have wanted it more if I'd gotten some pleasure out of it instead of waiting for you to finish." *Oh my gosh, I said it!* She couldn't believe she'd told him the truth about their sex life *in public.* Her mother would be mortified, and Grandma Freddy would be turning over in her grave. A lady did not talk about sex in public. Ever.

He gaped. "What?"

On a roll, Erin added, "Cody, you had this weird idea that we could only have sex with you on top. You lasted maybe five minutes." She sipped her coffee, wondering if he'd spiked it. That or she was riding high on sugar and caffeine. Where had this sassy woman come from? "And foreplay is not a four-letter word."

He continued to stare at her in astonishment.

"You know what I've learned about myself, Cody?"

"What?"

"That I'm tired of always doing for others. I'm living in Seattle now. I have a job I like, friends"—okay, a little white lie, but she was working on that— "and a new boyfriend. He's amazing and treats me like I matter. And he's not afraid to tell me the truth." *I hope.* "All you had to do was tell me you didn't want to see me anymore. It would have hurt, yes, but I'd have gotten over you.

Unfortunately, our breakup cost me a lot of money and time it shouldn't have."

He had the grace to look shamefaced. "I'm so sorry about that. Sincerely." He tried to reach for her hand, but she tugged hers out of reach. "I'll reimburse you for the move. You can go back home if you want."

"I don't think so."

He shook his head. "Are you seriously telling me you want to stay out here? We constantly argued about you ever leaving Colby. Don't you remember?"

"Yes, I do. I also remember telling you I'd think about it, because our relationship meant more to me than where I lived. I just needed time."

"Erin, we were together for more than a year. You had time."

"And so did you. Enough to be honest with me instead of cheating and lying. Everyone told me you were no good for me. But I believed in you." The way she believed in Smith. "I loved you. Or at least I tried to."

He scoffed, but underneath his disbelief she swore she saw hurt. "You're telling me you didn't love me? Erin, you practically smothered me with it. Cooking my food. Doing my laundry. Anything I wanted, you'd give it to me."

"And that was a problem?"

"Hell, yes. There was no challenge, no thrill. You were about as close to being a human doormat as a woman could get," he snapped.

She didn't want to let him get to her, but dang it, that had been mean. "You really aren't nice at all, are you?" Smith might be an ass sometimes, but he'd never been cruel to her.

"Oh Erin. I didn't mean that." He ran his hands through his hair. "Please, hear me out. That's all I'm asking."

She should leave and never see him again, but she heard a ring of truth in his apology. "You have five minutes."

"We were good in the beginning. And that's the God's honest truth. You're beautiful, inside and out. And so sweet. I fell head over heels for you."

This was worse than him acting like a jackass, because that warm look in his eyes, the smile on his face, and the many compliments reminded her of the good times they'd had, the laughter and fun they'd shared.

"The distance hurt us, to be honest. I missed you so much in the beginning. But I got used to not being there, and then I felt empty without you. I'm not excusing what I did," he said before she could argue with him. "I'm explaining it. Erin, sometimes you had expectations I didn't feel able to fill. You always acted like a lady. Everything at your house was neat and perfect. It was like stepping into a Martha Stewart set, with everything just so." He sighed. "And as you can see, I'm a lot less than perfect."

She frowned. "You're saying I expected too much?"

"Yes. No. Look, I just found it hard to live up to what I thought you needed." He flushed. "If I wasn't as creative in bed, it's because I didn't know what you'd be okay with."

"And you couldn't have asked me?"

"Seriously? Anytime I mentioned sex, you turned scarlet. And when I asked what you wanted, you'd tell me what I wanted was good enough. Erin, you never complained. How was I to know I wasn't what you needed?" His expression soured. "Jesus. Now I'm a bad lover too?"

"But…" Erin thought about it and realized he had a point. "Okay, so maybe I was more closed off then. But can you tell me you tried all that hard to make me 'happy'?"

"You can't even say it, can you?" He shook his head.

With Smith she'd been bold and aggressive. "Fine. You didn't give me orgasms. How's that for bold for you?"

"Wow. That's quite a leap for you, isn't it? You're still blushing, but you said *orgasm* and didn't explode into a ball of holy fire." He chuckled.

"Shut up." She laughed with him, remembering their many discussions about sin and how hypocritical people could be.

He sighed. "I have missed this with you. Laughing, talking. I really am sorry I was so terrible about our breakup. It wasn't good of me at all, and I've been feeling guilty ever since. I was telling you the truth about giving you the money to get home. I owe you that."

"I don't get it. This is the Cody I dated. Where were you three weeks ago?"

"You caught me off guard on a really bad day. I was running late for a meeting about a possible promotion I've been working toward for months, and I've been having problems with Diane. She and I… She's nice, but she always came up short compared to you." Cody shot her a disarming smile. "I'm not saying that to win you back or anything, just telling the truth."

Okay, that feels good to know.

"We're working things out. But it's slow going." He frowned. "I'm sorry she hurt you like that. I think you and I would have broken up eventually. But never like that. Seeing her be so awful to you, especially after I did the same, it was eye-opening." He looked sad. "For both of us. I had no idea I could be such a dick. Or that Diane could be so nasty. Hell, maybe we do deserve each other."

They sat in silence, absorbing what he'd said. "So, um, did you get the promotion?" she asked.

He laughed, but he didn't sound happy. "Yeah. Can you believe that?"

"You were always good at your job."

"Just not so great at being a good person, I guess." He frowned and stood. "I think I should go. I know it's a lot to ask, but I'd like to remain friends. Think about it. I know we're over, but I... I miss you." He left before she could respond.

Huh. That hadn't gone at all the way she'd expected. Cody was supposed to flaunt his new girlfriend, tell Erin how naïve and silly she'd been to think she could have a worldly man like him, then let her down gently and treat her as if she hadn't a brain in her head.

Instead, Cody had apologized. He'd taken a little bit to get there, yes, but his words had been genuine. He didn't try to win her back, but they'd shared a little bit of the connection they used to share. He missed her.

Yet he'd also told her some things she'd needed to hear. Apparently, being kind could be a bad thing. Smith didn't seem to mind her, but what if by being together all the time, he saw the side of her that had scared Cody away? Smith wasn't the type to cheat, but she hadn't thought Cody was either.

Nervous, she ordered another macaron and thought over all her times with Smith, trying to dissect her new, wondrous relationship before it turned sour, the way hers and Cody's had.

WHEN ERIN ARRIVED HOME, SHE REALIZED SHE NEEDED TO TAKE Tilly's supper to her. She grabbed the casserole she'd prepared earlier and headed to Tilly's. She knocked and tried to open the door but found it locked. Puzzled, she set the casserole dish on the floor and fiddled with her phone, texting Tilly to find out what the woman wanted her to do. Tilly had talked about getting a key for Erin, but she hadn't had time to get one made. She'd been planning to put it on Smith's to do list.

Erin had to smile at that. Tilly and Smith had an odd relationship. One that didn't look like it would work but did. Tilly nagged and harangued Smith. He barked back at her and acted tough. But he constantly helped the woman, even when she hadn't asked. He took her dirty clothes bag down to the laundry room for her twice a week. He picked up her groceries when she needed odds and ends between her delivery service, and he constantly fiddled around in her apartment to fix things she hadn't mentioned needing fixing.

Tilly had told her all of that, because Smith didn't talk much about himself unless prodded, and even then, he had a habit of turning the conversation to Erin and what she thought or did.

She waited for Tilly to respond, and when she didn't, Erin figured the older woman must have gone out. Heck, Tilly had more of a social life than Erin did.

Erin grumbled under her breath and returned the casserole to her refrigerator. Thinking about Tilly and laundry made her realize she had a load to do, so she grabbed her basket and walked down to the laundry room in the basement. Unlike the creepy basements in horror movies, where the dim lighting and close confines contributed to the heroine getting mauled by a monster or serial killer, the laundry room in Emerald Estates had high basement windows, bright white walls, and plenty of overhead lighting. It wasn't cramped, and the six washers and six dryers had worked the entire time Erin had been in residence.

She'd put her wash in and used up the last of her quarters when she noticed Tilly's cane against the far corner, near the bathroom. Odd. "Tilly?" she called, not expecting an answer.

The thump from behind the bathroom door alarmed her. "Tilly?" she called again and put her ear to the door.

"In here. I hurt my hip."

"Oh no." Ein tried the door. "It's locked. Can you unlock it?"

"If I could unlock it, don't you think I would have?" Tilly snapped, which made Erin feel a little better. If Tilly could gripe, she couldn't be too hurt, could she? "Smith has a set of keys. Can you get them and help me out?"

"Yes. Wait right there."

"Do you really think I'm going anywhere anytime fast? Hell and damn, girl. I've been stuck in here for an hour." Then she grumbled, "Doesn't anyone do laundry anymore?"

Erin texted Smith, *Emergency. Tilly fell. Where are the apartment keys?*

Fortunately, he texted right back. *In top drawer to left of kitchen sink. Be home in half an hour. Soon as I can.*

"I'll be right back, Tilly," Erin called and ran upstairs. She found the ring of keys and raced back to Tilly. After going through a few, she found a key that fit the bathroom door. She entered to find Tilly in a state. The poor woman sat on the lid of the toilet, her weight shifted to one side, her expression one of pain. When she saw Erin, her expression lightened despite the tears in her eyes.

"Hell of a thing, getting old," Tilly said, reaching for Erin.

Erin hurried to help her to her feet, conscious that Tilly favored her right side. They walked slowly, grabbed Tilly's cane to use as extra support, and continued up to the first floor, Erin apologizing all the way. Tilly weighed less than Erin did, so assisting her wasn't difficult. But not creating more injury meant they had to walk so carefully.

"I'm sorry. I know this hurts. I'm so sorry. You're going great. Let's keep going."

"Just take me to my apartment. I'll be fine."

"I'm taking you to the hospital."

Tilly flushed. "Hell, no. That's a bother."

"You have insurance, don't you?"

"Yes, but—"

"No buts. Tilly, you could be bleeding internally. You could have broken something. You need a hospital."

"Fuck me sideways. Fine. But no ambulance."

"Right. Just…wait right here." Erin propped her against the

hallway wall and rushed to grab her purse and car keys. Then she returned, only to be ordered to grab Tilly's purse as well. Tilly held out a shaky hand with her keys.

Erin blinked back useless tears and rushed to get Tilly's things. Along with her purse, she grabbed Tilly's favorite shawl and a coat and then drove her to the hospital, all the while worrying about Tilly's pallor and her hip.

After checking Tilly in, Erin realized she hadn't texted Smith. She let him know where to meet her and waited. Then she wondered if she should text Rupert, the only known member of Tilly's family. Erin decided it couldn't hurt, so she let him know what had happened to Tilly but didn't hear back right away.

Tilly hadn't looked so good by the time they'd wheeled her into emergency care. After filling out a ton of forms and being directed to two different stations, Erin had nothing to do but wait and worry.

Tilly had become a surrogate grandparent in a lot of ways. She gave Erin advice Erin hadn't asked for, as well as a sense of support and kindness she needed. When Erin had had no place to live, Tilly had offered her a more than fair deal, from which Erin continued to reap the benefits. And one of them was having Tilly as a friend.

The thought of possibly losing her hit hard, and Erin had to wipe away tears, worried by all that could go wrong. Tilly was seventy-nine years old with a history of osteoporosis. She'd already had one hip replaced. Fortunately, not the one she'd hurt. Seeing her in pain had been awful, and knowing Tilly had suffered for a while, and might have continued to suffer had Erin not found her, rang warning bells.

Tilly might need around the clock care after this. Could she afford it? If not, who could help her? Erin wanted to offer, but did she need to be qualified to administer medication? Would Tilly even want her around all the time? And besides, Erin also needed to work. She had more editing awaiting her at her apartment.

Worn out from the shock of Tilly's fall and her meeting with Cody, she grabbed a magazine and settled in for some mindless reading about celebrities and their scandals and every day activities.

Two hours had passed. No word from the doctor yet, and Smith was stuck in traffic.

Gosh, she needed him by her side. With Smith around, she felt safe and cared for. Almost...loved.

SMITH COULDN'T BELIEVE HE'D BEEN SIDESWIPED BY SOME DRUNK asshole after being stuck in traffic forever. Wasting time while some young cop struggled to understand the concept of emergencies and needing somewhere else to be, it was all Smith could do not to clock the bastard who stood on the cop's other side, bitching about being late to a meeting.

"Look, officer," Smith growled. "*I'm* the guy who got hit on the way to the hospital, where my grandmother is in emergency care. I wasn't drinking or speeding," he directed to the rich asshole.

"Please. I'm totally sober." The guy's phone rang, and he stepped aside to answer it.

Smith had totally been speeding before he'd stopped at the stoplight. And by calling Tilly his grandmother, he hoped for a little more sympathy and urgency in dealing with the accident. "I was turning right on green when this guy plowed into me, running a red light. I can fucking smell him from here."

The cop sighed. "Yeah, so can I. I'm sorry. We're nearly done. There's one more thing I need to do, then you can be on your way."

"In that?" Smith growled, pointing to the tail end of his truck, which had been too badly damaged to drive. He studied the crumpled back fender and axel and swore, glowering once more at the driver swearing on the phone. The older man in a decked-out Land Rover wore a suit and tie and talked on the phone as if he owned all of Seattle.

The cop turned to deal with the rich dick, and Smith fumed. He'd already been running behind to get to Tilly because of their job across the city. Traffic was always bad, but today it had been off-the-charts insane, and then he'd been hit.

"What the fuck happened here?"

Smith groaned. Not the voice he needed or expected to be hearing. He turned to see Cash walking toward him wearing a huge frown. "Shouldn't you be at the job site?" He noticed Cash's SUV parked behind the cop car.

"If you'd listened to anything I said, you'd have heard me tell you to wait while I finished talking to Hector. I was going to drive you."

"Great. Then you would have been tail-ended by assface over there."

Rich guy heard him and scowled. "I want to make a complaint." He took a step towards Smith, who clenched his fists and grinned through his teeth.

The cop frowned. "Sir, I'm going to have to ask you to step over there. And Mr. Ramsey, please, don't engage."

"He won't." Cash waved at the cop. "I'm his brother. I'll keep the hot head over here."

"Thanks."

Smith wanted to hit someone. He looked at Cash.

"Don't even think about it," Cash warned. "If you'd have waited, I would have been driving, and we could have avoided all this."

"Huh? I didn't do this! Fuckhead over there did!"

"Yeah, but we would have left a few minutes later, so his drunk ass would have hit someone else."

The drunk ass in question said, loudly enough to be heard, "I am not drunk. And I want that man arrested for assault."

"Sir, he hasn't assaulted anyone." The cop sighed.

"Not yet," Smith muttered. "Yo, officer. Are we done here?"

"You can go. Contact your insurance company and let them know there's a police report." The cop turned back to the dickhead. "Mr. Murphy, can you please tell me the last time you had alcohol?"

"I haven't been drinking."

"What the fuck ever, pal," Cash snarled. "You smell like a brewery." He yanked Smith toward his SUV. "Come on. Your friend is waiting."

Smith tugged his arm back but didn't argue. Tilly and Erin needed him. He'd deal with Cash's attitude later.

CHAPTER SIXTEEN

*A*t the hospital, Smith found Erin slumped in a seat. He ignored Cash and rushed over to her. "Hey, you okay?"

She saw him, and her eyes filled. She reached for him, and he stood with her in his arms, just holding each other.

"I'm so glad you're here." She wiped her eyes. "Sorry for crying. Tilly's going to be fine. It's just been a heck of a day."

Smith blew out a worried breath. "Thank God she's okay. What the hell happened?"

Behind him, Cash cleared his throat.

Smith glared at him over his shoulder, but Cash raised a brow, looking from Erin to Smith. "Fuck. Fine. Erin, this is Cash. Cash, Erin. He's Reid's brother."

"Oh, hi. Nice to meet you." Erin sniffed and wiped her eyes. "Smith, put me down." He did, and she held out a hand to Cash.

Cash shook it and smiled, the soft expression odd on his normally frowning face. "Hi. It's nice to meet you too. I heard about you from Reid, but my *other brother* here hasn't said much." Cash smirked. "Tough to deny how much you look like me, little man."

"Oh, I'll give you a little man," Smith growled and took a step in his direction.

Erin stopped him by putting a hand to his chest. She stared between them. "Wow. You guys really do look alike. I'm so glad you came," she said to Cash. "Tilly means a lot to me and Smith."

"We were on the job when he got the call. But the asshole left too quick for me to catch up. We both got stuck in traffic, but I picked him up from the accident and—"

"Accident?" Erin turned and looked Smith over, running her hands over him. "Are you okay? What happened?"

He felt both embarrassed and thrilled that she fussed. "I'm fine." He ignored Cash's amusement. "Some drunk hit my car, or I'd have been here sooner. Sorry for that."

"I'm just glad you're okay." She drew him down for a kiss he was happy to give her. "Let's go get something to eat, and I'll tell you what happened."

In the cafeteria, the three of them sat and ate a late lunch.

"I was bringing Tilly her supper for later, but she wasn't home. And I remembered I had laundry to do. But after I threw my load in, I saw her cane by the bathroom door. She'd fallen and hurt herself in the bathroom but couldn't move on her own to get help. That's when I texted you for the keys."

"Damn. Good thing you were there," Cash said.

"Yes." She shivered, and Smith put his arm around her, not liking how sad and tired she looked.

"So, what's Tilly's deal?" Smith asked.

"The doctor took her for X-Rays, but I haven't heard back if her hip's broken or just bruised. Her pain isn't so bad, according to Tilly. Then again, she didn't want to be here, so she could be covering up how much it hurts. The good news is she seems in good health except for the hip."

"I want to talk to her."

"You should. She'll listen to you." Erin gripped his hand on the table.

He finished off his burger but refused to let her go. And he knew Cash saw it, though the guy made no mention of it.

They made small talk about work when Erin asked them about it. And they even got her to laugh a little. When she excused herself to use the restroom, Smith waited for the comments.

Cash just looked at him.

"What?"

Cash shrugged. "Erin seems nice."

"She is."

"And this Tilly. She's your landlady, but you seem to be friends with her too."

"So what?" Smith felt as if Cash were trying to corner him into admitting something.

"So, when you got that call, your face turned white, and you ran like a motherfucker for your truck. I knew something bad had happened. I didn't know what."

"Your point?"

Cash gave an awkward shrug. "I don't know. I'm just curious about the old lady, I guess. How long have you known her?"

It felt weird to talk about Tilly with Cash, though Smith didn't know why. "Look, she gives me a heck of a deal on my rent, and I do repairs around the building. It's no big deal."

"She means something to you."

"So?"

"Nothing. I just… that's cool. I'm sorry she got hurt is all."

"Okay." They watched each other warily.

"Ah, if something happens to you, do you have, like, an emergency contact person?" Cash asked. "You had to have filled that out on your application form."

"I don't remember." No. He had no one.

"Well, I mean, something like this happens to you, you might need to put someone down."

"I should add Erin's name then, I guess." Would she mind? Would that be presumptuous on his part?

"Sure, sure." Cash tapped is fingers on the table, jumpy.

Smith frowned. "You okay? You seem kind of wired."

Cash scowled. "I'm fine. I was just going to say you could put my number or Reid's down, you know, in case you needed to let someone know you needed help."

Smith froze. "Why?"

"Why else, asswipe? For an emergency contact. You know, you're dying or some shit, and you need to let someone know." Cash's eyes glittered. "It's not a big deal. Something happens, you need someone to water your plants or pick up your car or mail or some crap like that, you have someone to help."

"You have Reid."

Cash nodded. "And Jordan. Evan and Aunt Jane too." His eyes narrowed. "Did you call her back yet? Aunt Jane thinks you don't like her."

"What?" Smith blinked. "That's not true."

"So, go have breakfast with her. Don't be a douche. She's old and has feelings."

"I'm old and have feelings," Smith muttered. "Why can't I just keep to myself?"

Cash sighed. Loudly. "Look, dickbag, you have family now. You need to learn you have emergency contacts, people to hang out with, dinners to go to. You know, responsibilities."

Smith cracked a smile. "Seriously? You're giving me a speech about being responsible and family oriented? Okay, Dad. What's next on our afterschool special?"

"You are such a fuckhead." Cash called on his patience—Smith could see him trying to be nice and had to laugh at the guy's effort. "I can't help that you grew up without anyone. I had Reid; he had me. And though we never really thought about it, we could have had Evan and Aunt Jane too. Sucks that you had nobody, that Meg fucked you over. But man, now you have people. Looks like Tilly's special, and for damn sure you have Erin. Dude, she was clinging to you like a burr."

"So what? I like her."

"Exactly. And she likes you. You want to be pathetic and all needy with her? Or do you want to show her you have friends and can be social? Because most chicks seem to like social guys."

"Must be hell for you, eh?"

Cash groaned. "You have no idea. Reid and Evan are great with people. I think people suck."

"They do."

"Yeah. But the Vets on the Go! gang are okay. I mean, I love Jordan, and Naomi's cool. She liked Erin a lot."

"That's a no-brainer. Erin's easy to like."

"I can see that."

Smith frowned. "You look pretty damn smug about something. What?"

Cash watched him for a moment, then said, "I wasn't kidding about Aunt Jane. She's really nice, and for some reason she likes you a lot. It could just as easily have been her in here, breaking a hip. Life is short, bro. Don't waste the time you have." Cash stood and stretched. "I have to get back. I'm thinking you can get a ride home with Erin."

"Yeah."

"Okay then." Cash took a step and stopped. "In case it's not obvious to you yet, brainless, ask Erin to go with you to Aunt Jane's. Take your girl to your aunt's house and make everyone happy. Aunt Jane gets to see you, Erin feels special since you invited her to meet family, and I don't get nagged anymore to talk to you about how much you're hurting one of the kindest, gentlest women on the planet." He glared.

Smith rolled his eyes. "You are so dramatic. Fine. I'll call her and set something up. Okay?"

Cash's dark expression vanished. "Great. Thanks." He left without another word.

Smith stared after him, confused.

Erin rejoined him. "Everything good?"

He patted the seat next to him. "It is now. What the hell? I thought you'd fallen in."

She blushed and scowled. "First of all, you do not ask a lady what she was doing in the bathroom."

"But you're no lady," he teased.

She grinned. "No, I'm not, am I?"

"You look pretty happy about that. What am I missing?"

She ignored the question. "Secondly, I saw you two sitting together and figured you needed time to talk. So, I got a coffee." She held up a cup he hadn't noticed. "Everything okay? Cash seemed nice."

"He's an asshole," he said bluntly. "But he was okay. Was giving me a ration of crap about listing him or Reid as my emergency contact people."

Her eyes widened. "You know, that's a great idea. And me. Put my number down." She paused. "Would it be okay if I listed you in my phone as an emergency contact?" She flushed. "I have my mom and dad down, but they're kind of far."

"Stupid question. Of course." He took her phone from her and plugged in the info. Then he did the same to his phone with her number. When finished, he saw her watching him. "You okay?"

"Today, all I could think was that you'd come and make everything better." She didn't seem pleased about that. Instead she seemed…worried. "Is that a lot to live up to?"

"I don't understand."

"Is that an unrealistic expectation? I mean, I don't want you to have to make my world right. It's just, you're always so strong and capable. Do you feel like I'm pushing you to be something you're not?"

"Where the hell is this coming from?"

Erin looked sad and worried, and that fear triggered his own. Did he do something wrong? Had he failed her in some way?

Afraid of Tilly being hurt, he'd had a mini panic attack on his drive over, freaked the fuck out that she might die and leave him alone. Smith didn't know how he'd handle Tilly not being there. For all that he'd only come to know her the past eight months, Tilly felt like family. He liked her, damn it. And he wanted her to be around. She gave as good as she got, and she never minded if he was crabby or late or just quiet.

And now he had Erin, a woman who made his heart sing. He liked being with her more than anything. He didn't feel the need to imagine himself as better than he was, because around Erin he felt as big and strong as his heroes. She made him feel that away.

When she'd mentioned getting closure with Cody, fear had nearly stolen his ability to speak. He didn't want her getting back together with the loser. Knowing she had history with the guy she'd once *loved*, he didn't want her seeing him or talking to him. Not until Smith could convince her that she would never find anyone better than Smith Ramsey at her side.

He needed time to woo her, to get her to want to accept his key as more than a means to use his kitchen, but as a step to moving in together. To being a permanent couple.

He'd thought about it a lot. He'd never had a woman matter so much to him. In just a few short weeks, she'd come to mean so much.

He forced himself to sound calm. "Erin, I don't understand."

NEITHER DID SHE. ERIN KNEW SHE SHOULDN'T HAVE MENTIONED anything, not now, with Tilly in the hospital and them both on edge. But fear for Tilly, needing Smith so badly, and her talk with Cody had scrambled her thought processes. And now she felt like an idiot.

"I'm sorry. I don't mean anything by it. I just don't want to be a burden. And today, I kind of felt like I need you a lot more than you need me."

"That's bullshit," he said, his voice so low she had to lean closer to hear him. "You're fucking awesome. I love being with you, and I'd be with you more if you didn't freak out so much at us being together."

"What? That's not true."

"You looked like a startled deer when I handed you my key. I knew if I moved the wrong way, you'd take off on me." He sighed. "I'm happy when you're with me. I'm glad you found Tilly when you did. She was in shock. She could have died, you know." He glanced away, cleared his throat, and continued. "I don't know how it happened, but I care for the old bat. Don't tell her I said that."

She felt so much for him right now, seeing him vulnerable. "I won't."

"I want to see her as soon as we can. You know, to let her know not to worry about anything."

She loved him so much right now. "Because you'll take care of the place."

"Yeah. She just needs to work on getting better."

"Speaking of work, are you in trouble for leaving early?"

"Nah. And I have off tomorrow, so I can stick around and do whatever she needs. Or you need. I know you were working today. I hope this didn't put you behind."

Cody hadn't appreciated her job, since she didn't go to an office to work and didn't make much money. The job fulfilled her financial needs and satisfied her independence. Smith talked about her editing and cooking as if they really mattered. They did, but that he recognized it showed her he knew how hard she worked.

"Thanks, I'm good." She kissed him, a soft gesture of thanks. Of love. "I'll be glad you'll be home though. I miss you when you're gone."

"Me too." He smiled, his expression lighter than it had been. "I'd like you to be with me tonight and tomorrow. When you're not working, I mean. You always rush away to work in your apartment. I don't mind if you do your edits at my place."

She searched his gaze. "Are you sure?"

He sighed. "You always do this. Yes, I'm sure. If I didn't want you over, I'd tell you. I don't hold much back, you know."

She grinned, relieved. "That's true." Cody might have been too worried about hurting her feelings to tell her the truth. But Smith didn't seem to have the same hang-ups. "But if you ever—"

"Yeah, yeah. If I ever feel like you're over too much, I'll kick your ass out. I got it."

"Good."

He leaned closer and confided, "Here's what I want to happen. I go in and see Tilly, make sure she's okay and find out what she needs me to handle. Then you and I grab something to eat on the way home, so you don't have to fix dinner. I love your food, but I figure it's been a long day, and you're probably tired."

"Good idea." Though she loved to cook, sometimes Erin needed a break.

"Then we get naked, get clean—because I've been moving shit all damn day—and fuck. I want you under me tonight. I *need* you, Erin."

She heard something in his voice, saw it in his eyes, and prayed she hadn't imagined the care there. She nodded, mute, and let him take her hand.

Back in the waiting room, she saw Rupert, Willie, and two other people she didn't recognize. One of them, a pretty blond woman, stood with Rupert. The other, a tall, menacing looking man covered in tattoos, stood behind her. Smith had already left Erin to talk to someone at the main desk.

Rupert frowned, his eyes worried. "Aunt Tilly isn't doing so well, huh?"

"She'll be okay." Erin patted him on the shoulder, then explained to him and the others what had happened.

Willie grunted. "Good thing you were there. She coulda died."

"Willie," the intimidating man said. "Jesus, go easy."

The blond with him shook her head. "She didn't die, and she'll be just fine, Rupert."

"Right. Right." He clasped Willie's hand in his. "Besides, no way my Aunt Tilly dies in some bathroom in the basement. She'll either be robbing a bank or shacked up with some man forty years her junior. She's got style."

Willie laughed. "Sounds about right."

The woman and man exchanged an amused glance.

Rupert seemed to realize he hadn't made introductions. "Sorry. Erin, this is the gal I wanted you to meet. Ivy, this is Tilly's friend, Erin. And that lug behind Ivy is Sam, her boyfriend."

Sam nodded but remained quiet. Ivy greeted Erin as if they were old friends. She had kind eyes and a firm handshake.

"Oh, sorry." She lightened her grip. "I'm a massage therapist. Sometimes I forget I'm not at work."

"That sounds interesting." Erin smiled. "I edit for agriculture magazines, and I have an independent cooking show I'm trying to get off the ground."

"Oh, food. We should talk recipes." Ivy lead her away from Rupert, Willie, and Sam, who started talking about dogs to rescue. "Sorry. When they get started on dog and cat talk, I sometimes need a break. But I wasn't kidding about recipes. Sam eats a lot, and I'm always looking for new things to make him."

She glanced over at her man and smiled, and Erin saw the love pass between them. "Oh, I want that. That look where you just smile and know you have each other."

Ivy glance over at Smith, who had kept his eye on Erin. "I don't know. Seems like you have your own giant watching over you." Smith gave Sam an unfriendly glare, but Sam didn't see it, focused on an argument with Willie.

"Ignore his death glares," Erin apologized for him. "It's been a rough day. And when he thought something had happened to Tilly, Smith kind of freaked."

"Smith? That's his first or last name?"

"First." Erin grinned. "Everything about him is a little bit different. I like it. I like him."

"I'd say he likes you too." Ivy chuckled. "He must be the boyfriend Rupert thought you made up."

"He said that?"

"Yeah. But I wouldn't blame you. I met Rupert and Willie through Sam. They're all an acquired taste," she said with humor and affection. "Rupert mentioned you're new to town and trying to meet new friends."

Erin flushed. "Why do I feel like a kid whose mom tries to set her up on a playdate?"

Ivy laughed. "That's about right. But don't worry. I get it. It can't be easy to come to the city all alone."

"Yeah. I'm over the ex-boyfriend. Rupert no doubt told you about that?"

"He did. I can have Sam go beat him up if you want."

Erin was pretty sure Ivy was kidding. "That's okay. It's all I can do to keep my guy from rearraigning his face."

"Yeah. He seems like the type." Ivy leaned closer. "What is up with the giant men around here? Am I right?"

"Yes." Erin nodded. "Smith is only slightly taller than his brothers. And they were all Marines."

"Huh. Mine and his friends are all mechanics and felons." She winked. "Kidding about the felons thing. They just look the part."

Erin gave Sam a wary glance. "I'll say. How did you start dating?"

"Cookie brought us together." Ivy explained how a lost dog had thrown Sam into her life. They chatted about good places to eat and made a coffee date for the following week.

"Oh, wait. I saw your massage place on Queen Anne Avenue," Erin realized. "Bodyworks?"

"That's me," Ivy said with pride. "You know, business is all about word of mouth. You need a massage, I'm your gal. You need a mechanic, Webster's Garage won't steer you wrong. Want a pet? I can hook you up there too."

"Need to move? Use Vets on the Go!" Erin stuck a thumb in Smith's direction.

Ivy's eyes widened. "No kidding? He's with Vets on the Go!? I saw that piece in the news about them. Didn't one of the guys save some kid and his grandma from robbers?"

"I think so. That happened before I moved here."

"Good to know. And what about you?" Ivy asked. "What are you selling? You said you have a cooking channel? What's the website?"

Erin rattled off the URL, pleased and a little nervous to be treating her cooking gig as a real business. She'd always considered it her side project, hoping to grow it bigger. But the more she talked about it, and Smith talked about it, the more she realized how much she wanted to focus her efforts on that. The editing paid the bills, but her heart remained in her online kitchen.

Smith joined her side once more. After introducing him to everyone, they went back to visit Tilly.

She sat propped up in her bed dressed in a pale blue hospital gown. "Go ahead. Look your fill at the old lady who fell in a damn bathroom and had to be rescued off the toilet."

Smith grinned. "Sounds pretty damn funny when you tell it like that."

"Oh, shut up."

Erin heard more than saw the humor and let herself relax.

"Erin, when I get out of here, I'm going to stay with Rupert for a little while. He's got a one-story house with a caretaker who helps him. I'm going to borrow her for a few weeks until the limp is gone."

"A few weeks?" Erin wondered about the timeline.

"My hip's bruised, not broken."

"Good," Smith said, looking relieved.

"I can help you," Erin offered, not liking the fact that Tilly felt she had to leave her own home to be cared for.

"And you will. I hadn't gotten to that yet."

"Huh?"

Tilly sighed. "It's a lot to ask, but I'm going to lean on you some.

And to make it fair, I'm not charging you any rent until I'm back home."

"No."

Smith and Tilly stared at her.

"No, you will not give me a rent-free apartment. You're my friend, Tilly. I'll do whatever you need for free. You don't charge friends for help."

Tilly flushed and fiddled with her blanket. "Well, hell. Don't get your panties in a twist over it. Fine. But you'll use my kitchen and supplies for all that cooking stuff. I mean it. I want you to keep cooking meals for me and for the neighbor, the nurse's aide. Rupert already arranged for Fiona to help me instead of him. I told him not to, but he says he only lets her do his PT work because she's cute." Tilly harrumphed.

Erin bit back a grin but noted Smith didn't hide his.

"So, while I'm recuperating at Rupert's, I want you two to hold down the fort. Smith, you keep fixing shit that breaks. Erin, you water my plants and keep my place dust-free. And you keep cook-ing, but this time I need you to deliver the meals. It's a ways away in Queen Anne. Not far really, but you figure in the traffic and it's a bitch."

"It's not a problem."

"Well, it might be since this knucklehead has no wheels." She shook her head at him. "I told you that driving like a maniac would be your undoing."

"Please. I was hit by a drunk loser."

"So you say." Tilly's eyes sparkled as she argued with Smith, and

Erin could see a similar pleasure in her boyfriend as he crabbed with the old woman.

"Now Erin, I got to say a few things to the boy. Would you mind waiting outside? It won't be but a minute or two. Nothing but handyman stuff that'd bore you. And don't be fretting about me leaving my apartment. It'll be more like a vacation. Rupert has a hot tub in his backyard."

Erin didn't mind giving them space. "No problem." She leaned over to kiss Smith, knowing how much Tilly would love seeing her supposed matchmaking at work. Then she shocked Tilly by kissing *her* on the cheek. "Get better soon, and make sure you text me if you want me to make you something specific. Otherwise I'm planning the menus."

CHAPTER SEVENTEEN

"Okay, you old woman. What did you need to say to me that you couldn't say in front of Erin?" Smith had been so worried for Tilly until he'd talked to her. No matter what the nurse had told him of Tilly's condition, he'd needed to see her for himself.

"You have such a smart mouth for such a stupid man," she muttered, sounding as cranky as she normally did. "Look, asswipe, I'm getting tired. So, I'll keep this short. Do the Hall-o-ween thing. Make sure you introduce Erin to everybody at the McCallisters' party. The girl needs more friends than an old biddy like me and a sex-starved fiend like you."

"Really?" Was that how she saw him? Then again, she wasn't totally wrong. He was sexually starved for Erin at all times. He grinned.

"Such a horndog," she muttered, "When you get a chance, I need you to grab a bag and pack a few things for me. Try not to get too excited touching my undies."

He rolled his eyes.

"But make sure to pack the clothes I like. You know the ones I wear all the time."

He did. "You sure you don't want Rupert or Erin or somebody to pack for you?"

"Nope. You. Erin's gonna be busy cooking for me and Fiona." She paused. "Rupert said Fiona's young and a real looker. You interested?"

He snorted. "I have Erin. What do you think?"

She rubbed her hands together with glee. "I freakin' *knew* she'd be perfect for you. Knew it the first time I saw you two together."

He groaned, secretly pleased she had enough energy to gloat. "Yeah, yeah. What else?"

"I want you to pack my copy of *The Catcher in the Rye.* It's in my nightstand. It was Hank's favorite, and I like to read a page every night before bed. And bring me my picture frame too."

"Which one?" She had a bunch of pictures of her husband in the living room. He'd never been in her bedroom, though, so he wanted to make sure he got it right.

She studied him with an expression he couldn't read. "It's the one with me and Hank. And Hank Jr."

Shocked, because he hadn't realized she'd had a kid—she'd never mentioned it—he nodded.

"Never told you about him, did I?"

"No."

Her voice softened, and she said, "Hank Jr. was my heart, you know. I lost a part of that when he died after Vietnam." She watched Smith with a steady gaze. "He was a Marine too. Proud as a peacock because of it." Her eyes watered. "Now don't you think I'm getting soft. But if something happens to me, I want you to have his purple heart. Hank, my husband, he'd want that too. You understand sacrifice, and not too many people do nowadays."

Smith nodded, too taken aback to do otherwise.

"It was pure dumb luck I slipped and hurt my hip. I know that. But a body's got to be prepared. I have a will all made out so my family will get what little I have left to give."

He forced himself to remain lighthearted, while inside he rejected any notion of Tilly leaving him. "Yeah, whatever, Midas."

She grinned and wiped an eye. "But you need to know if something happens to me, you always have a home."

He frowned. "I know that. I can always find another place to live, Tilly. I'm not broke or anything, even though you seem to think I am."

"I mean a home at Emerald Estates, jackass. It wouldn't be the same without you there taking care of everybody."

He huffed. "I just do what you pay me to."

"Really?" She arched a brow. "Because I saw you tying Regina's shoes in the hall so she could keep up with her big brother. I know you out and out threatened Janet's ex with violence if he lays a hand on her. And that you keep an eye on the building. Haven't had a problem with burglars or druggies since you came on board."

DELIVERED WITH A KISS

He didn't like her looking at him like he was a nice guy. "I don't know what you're talking about."

"You're all about family, no matter how much you try to act like you don't give a shit." She smiled, and that sweet expression on her face freaked him out.

"You're not dying or anything are you?"

She laughed so hard she choked.

He handed her a glass of water, and she swallowed it down before sighing. "Ah, that's better. I needed that laugh. No, I'm not dying right this minute. Unless I have an aneurism because you made me laugh so hard. What I'm trying to tell you is that I love you, dumbass. And I want you to know you're like a son to me. And I don't say that lightly…and I won't say it again."

He looked away until he could look back at her with dry eyes.

She reached for him, her skin papery-thin, her grip weak, but she held on when he took her small hand in his. "You're a good boy, Smith Ramsey. Margaret Ramsey was one crappy piece of work. I told her that then, and I'd tell her that now if she had the balls to show her face. You remember that."

Her words meant everything. He couldn't speak, so he nodded to show he'd heard.

She tugged her hand back, and he let her go. "That girl out there thinks the world of you, so you do her right. And for fuck's sake, get her out of that crappy efficiency and moved in with you. Mrs. Fine's place needs a complete rehaul."

He grinned with relief, glad to be done with all the emotional drama. "Yeah. I know. But I'm trying to be stealthy about it. I gave her my key, and she almost fainted. So, I'm wooing her."

"Woo faster," Tilly snapped. "Now get out so I can get some sleep."

He was at the door when he had to turn around. He saw her lying in that bed, looking frail and old and ornery, as usual. He couldn't not say it. "I love you too."

He turned and left before she made a big deal of it and hurried to find Erin so he could get away from all the uncomfortable emotions sweltering inside.

"You okay?" she asked and reached for him.

He took her hand, thinking maybe not all feelings needed to be avoided. "I am now. Let's go home."

THEY'D HAD PLANS TO GET FOOD ON THE WAY BACK, SHOWER, then have hot sex. Unfortunately, they hadn't planned on running out of energy.

Erin had helped Smith pack up Tilly's clothes while he grabbed the other items on her never-ending list. He grumbled while he packed, but she noticed he took extreme care to put everything in Tilly's suitcase, and he'd chosen her outfits himself.

Erin didn't know what exactly had been said between the two, but it must have been emotional. Smith had been quiet for most of the drive home, and he'd made a few comments to convince her Tilly would be just fine—even though she'd expressed no doubt to the contrary.

The poor guy. She would have gone with him to deliver Tilly's things to Rupert, but he'd told her he'd be quick and for her to set out their dinner.

She'd done little more than put their takeout on plates then fell asleep while waiting for him to return.

Now she blinked at the clock in his bedroom, sensing she'd slept through Friday night into Saturday. She didn't remember coming to bed, so he must have carried her in. It still made her shiver, to know Smith could haul her around so easily. She'd had other boyfriends brag about loving her tiny size, but no one had made her feel weightless.

Erin turned on her side to study him, thinking that even in sleep, Smith looked hard, unforgiving. She stroked his face, loving his square jaw, the stubble on his cheeks and chin. He had looks, power, and stamina.

And a heart in need of mending.

Tilly's near miss had made her realize how much she missed her family, so while waiting for Smith to arrive yesterday, she'd called her parents and her sister. She missed them, but not as much as she'd missed Smith.

It was as if she wasn't complete without him. She smiled, knowing he'd roll his eyes if she said something so corny.

Meeting with Cody—had it been just yesterday?—had woken her to the reality she hadn't been blameless in their breakup. Yes, the sex had been underwhelming. But she should have said something. And while she found nothing wrong with catering to a man if *she* wanted to, part of her had resented doing everything for him since he had seemed to expect it. And that was on her.

Cody should have been honest with her, and she should have told him the truth of her feelings. She never should have moved out here to satisfy *his* needs and *his* demands. That she had still shamed her. But she'd learned.

At twenty-five years of age, she'd finally grown independent enough to move away from home, supporting herself on her own working two jobs, and she'd found a man she might love, not because she needed him, but because she wanted him.

And she wanted him right now.

He must have cleaned up before coming to bed because he wore nothing but the skin God gave him, and he smelled of the soap he had in his shower.

She leaned forward to kiss him, pleased when he kissed her back.

Normally she'd worry about morning breath or her hair sticking up, but she wanted nothing more than to make them both happy. She crawled on top of him, loving the feel of his large, callused hands on her hips. But she wanted them in other places, so she put his hands over her breasts and reveled in his low groan.

She deepened the kiss, felt him arch up against her, his erection digging into her thigh. She moved so that she slid over him, her wet response impossible to ignore.

He kissed her harder, trying to angle so that he could penetrate, but she stopped him by pinching his nipples and nibbling to his ear to whisper, "This is my fun. I'm in charge. You just lay there and enjoy."

She pulled back to see him staring up at her with dark eyes, the green not visible in the dim light streaming through his blinds. He lay in shadow, dark and big and sexy. And all hers.

Erin shimmied down his body, trailing kisses from his face down his neck, awash in emotion. He murmured her name as she kissed him, and he stroked her as if she were precious to him.

Smith didn't rush, he savored. And he was especially good at taking his time with Erin. So, she wanted to do the same with him.

She tried to show him what he meant to her with in each slow, deliberate kiss. By feathering her hands down his broad, muscular chest to the tight core of his abdomen and lower, past the dark hair surrounding that thick, jutting cock.

"Please," he rasped and arched up, moaning when she took him in her mouth and cupped his balls.

Erin rubbed him gently, then with firmer pressure while she nibbled her way up and down his cock, sucking and taking him deep, to the back of her throat.

She rubbed the insides of his thighs and toyed with his navel while pumping him with deep draws of her mouth.

When he'd get too close, she'd back off, trail caresses down his legs to his ankles, then start back up again. She explored his torso, fascinated with his nipples, so dark and hard, his chest so different from hers, that tattoo mesmerizing. He liked when she sucked him, so she teased him the way he had her. And it drove him wild.

He flipped her to her back and mounted her, lost in lust, but she stopped him. "Uh-uh. I'm in charge, remember?"

Panting and swearing, he rolled them both over, so that she straddled him once more. "Erin, baby, please. I'm so hard it hurts."

She felt no pity, wanting him to be on edge, needing her the way she needed him. "I love sucking you," she whispered against his lips as she went in for another kiss. She found her sweet spot, riding her clit over his hard shaft, loving how wet he made her, how her touch stimulated him.

"*Fuck*. Cupcake, I'm gonna come, and I want to come inside you," he groaned.

She continued to move, so slowly, over him. "You're so big. You fill me up so good," she said and licked his ear.

He shot up so hard he nearly unseated her.

She chuckled.

"Did I say you were nice? You're evil, making me want you so much." He tilted his head so she could suck his neck. "So fuckin' hot. I need you, Erin. Need to be in you."

She figured he'd had enough, and so had she. Time for the first of many orgasms.

Erin rose on her knees and reached for him. He palmed her breasts, his gaze on her hand around his slick cock.

"You're so wet," he moaned as she lowered herself. "Come on. All of me. Take me," he growled.

She kept sliding down, watching his beautiful face as he cried out, the sexual agony impossible to resist. She sat fully on him and leaned back, the position making him feel that much bigger.

"Yes, you feel amazing inside me."

"Move, Erin. Up and down, baby. Come around me."

She watched him watch her while she did all the work, lifting up and falling back down, her body so tight around him. They matched, a perfect fit, was all she could think as she took him.

"Come," he said again. "Touch yourself while you fuck me. I want that pussy so tight when I fill it up."

Oh, the dirty talk, it kept getting better. Hotter. He continued, whispering filthy things as she moved faster, unable to help herself as she rubbed the sensitive flesh between her legs, the combination of her hand and his cock an impossible temptation.

"I'm coming," she shouted as she let go, her orgasm stealing her breath.

"Yes," he hissed and shoved up so hard into her she shattered all over again. He gripped her hips and continued to thrust, his climax so strong the bed shook.

When she could see straight again, she slumped over him and felt him stroke her back.

The sex had been powerful and erotic. But this, the after, she loved this so much. Smith cared in every touch and taste, and he showed it in so many ways.

"Erin, I want to ask you something. You can say no."

She tried to push herself up to see his face, but he kept his hand on her back, and she didn't have the energy to struggle. "What's that? Mmm. I love the way you touch me."

He chuckled, and the rumble in his chest vibrated. "You're like a kitten purring on top of me. With the hottest little pussy."

She felt herself blush. "You had to say the p-word."

"Pussy? Better than the C word right?"

"Cock?"

"Cunt," he said and slid his hands down to pull her tighter against him. He'd started to soften inside her, but she could still feel him there. "As in, I want to fill up Erin's hot, wet cunt. Then lick her until she screams and do it all over again."

"*Smith.*"

He laughed and groaned. "Damn. I'm falling out. Let's hit the shower."

She let him carry her into the tub, which was way too small for them both to sit in, though she'd have killed to take a bath with him. Tub sex was next on her list.

They stood in the hot spray of water and just held each other.

"I am going to have to call McSons to fix the hot water situation."

"What situation?" she asked on a yawn, feeling very much like the contented kitten he'd described.

"The one we're going to have. It's only a matter of time before the hot water starts going out."

"Ah, work stuff."

"Yeah." He pulled back and grabbed his shampoo. Then he handed it to her. He loved when she massaged his head, and the sensual expression he made when she did it made it one of her favorite things to do.

"So, what did you want to ask me?" She lathered him up.

He sighed. "I love you."

She froze. "What?"

"I said I love this."

She forced a laugh, her heart racing, when she wanted to cry. She had no idea how much she wanted to hear him say it first. Then she could say it and not feel as if she'd scared him into saying it back. Or worse, confessed feelings that he didn't return.

She finished shampooing him then handed him her bottle. He

smiled down at her, kissed her, then shampooed her. "You should be a massage therapist," she told him. "You have great hands."

"I know."

"Braggart."

He chuckled.

"I met a massage therapist. Rupert's friend, the pretty blond and her lethal looking boyfriend, Sam. Remember them from the hospital?"

"I didn't like the way the guy looked at you."

She smiled. "That's sweet, but I think he was just making sure I didn't make any sudden moves to endanger his girlfriend. They're so in love. You can tell."

"Yeah? How can you tell?" He drew her into the hot water to rinse her off.

She blinked her eyes open when he'd finished and saw him studying her. "What?"

"I asked, how can you tell he loves her?" He held a bar of soap and proceeded to run it all over her body.

She'd been relaxed only moments before, and somehow, he had her sexed up and raring to go again. "I-it's the way he looks at her."

"Like how?" he asked and turned her to face the wall while he scrubbed her back, her butt, her legs.

"Like nothing matters but her." *The way I look at you.*

"That dreamy, dippy, stupid look?"

Well, that brought her back down to earth. She glared at him over her shoulder. "No. It's totally emotional and sweet."

He didn't look sweet at all to her. "Spread your legs for me, Cupcake."

She growled, wishing he hadn't ruined the moment, but spread her feet wider when his soapy hands trailed over her legs. Up and down, he touched her, and she wondered at his game.

When she turned her head to ask him, she was caught in his kiss, and it turned ravenous in a heartbeat.

Then he swore and lifted her, her front still pressed against the wall. "What are you—"

He slapped her ass, and she gasped when he ordered her to be quiet unless begging him to finish. Then he was there, pushing into her sex from behind, holding her in place and moving her where he wanted her without effort.

The helplessness of her position made everything better, and when she came screaming his name, he shoved home one final time and joined her.

The water started to turn cold. "Smith…"

"Damn." He withdrew and left her aching for him to return. She liked feeling him inside her. Besides being incredibly sexy, the physical closeness felt more like an emotional connection, at least to her.

"So, what I wanted to ask you…" He did a quick cleanup on them both, then toweled her off before seeing to himself.

And she loved him for that too. All the little things he did added to up to one amazing, giving man.

"Just say it already." She smacked him on the ass, and his startled look made her laugh and smack him again.

"Okay for that, you have to say yes."

"Yes." She smiled.

"Good. It's settled. We'll grab the ferry tomorrow at ten. And it's casual dress."

"Wait, what?"

He smiled back at her. "I agreed to go to my aunt's for brunch. She's been asking me to come over forever." His smiled faded. "I could really use you there with me." A pause. "This new family stuff isn't easy for me."

"Whatever you need." She tugged him close for a kiss, ignoring her sudden unease at the thought of meeting his aunt.

"You, I just need you."

She sighed, so in love.

"And a blowjob. That would be nice too."

She chased him down and forced him to make her breakfast for being such a smartass.

Because Smith had a terrible weakness she planned to put to good use.

THE NEXT DAY ON THE FERRY, HE WOULDN'T STOP COMPLAINING.

"Oh, stop being such a baby."

"I hate getting tickled." He glared at her, but he couldn't hide his smile. "Okay, fine. Since we both know I can outwrestle you, I guess the tickle thing evens the playing field. But I have to tell you, it's not sexy. Not at all."

"What, tickling doesn't put you in the mood?" she asked as they stood outside on the upper deck of the ferry boat.

"No, that smugness. It's really off-putting."

She gave him more smug, and he grimaced and tried to block out her face with a huge hand.

She laughed, having so much fun with him and totally repressing her nerves about meeting more of his family. She loved that he wanted her to meet his aunt, but if the woman didn't like her, Erin would feel awful.

"Hey, the world revolves around me," Smith announced. "Not anything else."

"You wish."

"I know." He looked so smarmy, and then he laughed.

It still amazed her Smith could be so normal and down to earth looking the way he did. So large, he commanded attention because of his size. But that intensity he wore like a second skin, that's what warned people to be on their guard.

I have my own personal bad boy. For real.

"Uh oh."

"What?" she asked.

"That smile of yours. It's evil. What do you have planned I don't know about?"

"Well, you said something earlier about a blowjob..."

His eyes grew comically wide. "Here?"

A few couples were on deck, though most passengers remained indoors, out of the wind.

"No, you dope."

His eyes narrowed.

She had to laugh. "I was just thinking that I'm dating a bad boy."

His boyish grin took her aback. "Yeah? Well I'm dating the good girl, so I guess we're even." He whispered into her ear, "And she's *so* good. She swallows."

Erin smacked him on the arm, and they walked back to her Jeep in the bay downstairs, laughing.

She'd asked Smith to drive, because she had no idea where they were headed. And she'd never driven onto a ferry before. But now that she'd seen it done, she wanted to drive them back.

"You know," she said as they entered the vehicle. "I'm learning a lot with you."

"Yeah? Me too."

"Like what?" she asked, unsure what the world-wise Marine could have possibly picked up from her.

"Well, I've learned that smaller is sometimes better." His eyes heated. "You fit me perfectly. I've never had better sex in my life."

"You think about sex a lot, it seems."

"Please. I'm a guy. I think about sex all the time; I can't help it. Especially if you're around."

"Ah, okay." She tried not to feel flattered about that.

"I also learned that carrots are amazing in baked goods. I have never had carrot cake before you."

"No way." She gaped.

He flushed. "Nope. Hey, I thought it was a fake way to get a kid to eat veggies. How was I to know it's real cake?"

She laughed so hard she cried.

The ferry docked, and people started their cars.

"And I learned something else."

"What? That zucchini is good in bread?"

He opened and closed his mouth, then gave her a sheepish grin. "Well, that too." As more of her laughter subsided, he said, "I learned that I don't want to live without you anymore. I want you to move in with me."

Cars started leaving.

She didn't know what to say or think and feared blurting "I love you too" might not be what he meant. She cooked, they had sex, they liked to talk and hug. But she hadn't known him all that long. Heck, they hadn't even had a real fight, just a few verbal skirmishes over dinner or what to watch on TV.

He winked at her. "Don't answer me right away. Think about it. And I'll go over a pros and cons list with you later tonight. I drafted it a while ago. I just wanted to give you some time to mull over the idea."

He patted her on the knee.

Just think about it? As if she'd think about anything else for the near or far future.

They arrived at his aunt's house, and he walked her to the door, her thoughts still frazzled.

"You're welcome."

"For what?" she asked.

He gave a smile filled with a healthy dose of male superiority. "For giving you something better to worry about than impressing my so-called aunt."

CHAPTER EIGHTEEN

*E*rin wanted to punch Smith in the head, but he seemed too pleased with himself. He could tease her all he liked about being nervous, but she saw the anxiety he tried to suppress with humor.

"Quit with the 'so-called.' She wants to think of you as her nephew. It's sweet. You be nice."

He raised a brow. "Yes, ma'am."

She huffed and crossed her arms over her chest.

He put an arm around her shoulders and waited.

The house looked massive on the outside, and situated on the water, not far from the ferry, it had to be worth a pretty penny. She'd learned from Smith that Jane Griffith, Evan's mom, was related by marriage, so she didn't actually have a blood tie to Reid or Cash. Her husband had been brothers with Reid's father. Despite learning Cash's father was not her husband's brother, Jane insisted nothing had changed. She loved her nephews and considered Smith family.

Erin liked her for that already.

The house though, that she'd have to take in bit by bit. Erin felt overwhelmed, the homeowner obviously one of wealth and means. Apparently, Jerome, the owner, was a retired geologist who'd made his money in oil before retiring to teach. Now fully retired, he planned to marry Jane, who'd been widowed many years before.

"Jerome is cool," Smith told he again. "A damn nice guy. And Jane—"

"Aunt Jane," she reminded him.

He sighed. "Aunt Jane is nice. Remember, she's older than Evan, around Tilly's age, I think."

"I know. Stop fretting."

"I'm not fretting," he muttered. "How long does it take to answer the damn doorbell? Are they five thousand miles away in the wine cellar or what?"

"Maybe the butler is otherwise occupied," she teased.

"Or he killed them all with the candlestick in the ballroom."

After a pause, she shook her head. "That was just bad."

He sighed. "I know."

The door finally opened, and a man who resembled Reid opened the door. Handsome, with a bright, charming smile and pale gray eyes, he looked well at home in khaki's, a white collared shirt, and loafers.

"What the hell are you doing here?" Smith asked.

She pinched him.

"Ow." He frowned down at her.

"Hi. I'm Erin. And you must be…Evan?"

"Good guess." The stranger shook her hand and drew her inside, ignoring Smith, who swore after him. "Jerome, my mom's sugar daddy—"

"Evan!" his mother yelled.

"I mean, her fiancé, is back in the city helping a friend." Evan chuckled. "He's actually a terrific guy. He wanted to be here but couldn't, so Mom asked me to help."

"We didn't want to be any trouble," Erin said, feeling like an unwelcome guest.

"Oh, you're not. He is." Evan nodded to Smith, who stormed in like a heard of elephants on over the hardwood floor. Evan chuckled at the look Smith shot him. "I'm kidding. I'd planned to do brunch with Mom since I don't see her as much with her living out here now. When she told me you guys were coming, I was even more excited to come."

"I'll bet." Smith showed a lot of teeth, but Evan just grinned.

He had a charming way about him, and before Erin knew it, she'd told him all about Tilly and her mishap the day before.

"That's terrible." Evan frowned. "Is she okay? Smith, if you need time off to help her, you know you only have to ask."

"I only get so many sick days," he said, sounding gruff.

Erin could feel a sticky sense of tension. "Evan, where's your mom?"

"Here!" Aunt Jane called from the kitchen.

They walked through a grand, open living area, past a study, and continued to the kitchen and the back living area. *Geesh, I could fit my entire apartment in here three times at least...on this level.* Then she saw the hallway leading to an area farther back and amended her estimate to five times.

Jane Griffith stood behind the sink, her cheeks flushed, her white hair pulled back in a clip. She looked like a wealthy older socialite in a gray sweater, pearls, and jeans. "Sorry, the maid's day off."

Erin smiled.

Evan chuckled. "She's kidding. There's no maid, just a hell of a lot of house."

"Well, Jerome does have a cleaning lady who comes twice a month."

"Damn, Aunt Jane. You're moving up in the world." Smith sounded different. More deferential, softer, somehow.

Erin met Evan's gaze and saw him nod. When Smith went to offer Jane a hug, Evan whispered, "He's mean on the outside, a softie on the inside. And he likes my mom."

"Quit flirting with my girlfriend," Smith ordered. "And speaking of which, where's Kenzie and Daniel?"

Evan smiled. "My fiancé and her brother are busy. Kenzie's doing some girl's weekend with Lila and Rachel—"

"Evil incarnate," Smith interrupted, which had Jane laughing.

"And Daniel's on a sleepover at his buddy Rafe's. Interesting fact: Rafe is Jordan's younger brother. It's like six degrees of separation in Seattle with Vets on the Go!"

"What?" Erin missed the joke.

Smith stepped away from Jane to rejoined Erin. "Evan means everyone knows everyone. Jordan is Cash's girlfriend. And her younger brother happens to be good friends with Evan's younger brother by marriage. Or soon to be marriage, if he doesn't screw it up first."

Jane nodded. "Exactly what I keep telling him—not to screw it up." She walked up to Erin and gave her a big hug. For being in her early seventies, the woman had a fierce grip. She looked lovely, happiness agreeing with her. "Erin, I'm so pleased to meet you. I've been bugging Smith to come by before now, but for some reason I seem to scare him."

They both looked over at Smith, to see him flushing. "I am not scared of you, Aunt Jane."

"Ha. Liar." Evan laughed at him, then struggled when Smith gave him a noogie.

"Not so sophisticated now, eh, *Cousin* Evan?"

"Ass."

"Evan, language."

"Sorry, Mom." When Jane turned away, Evan got free and put a finger across his throat and pointed at Smith, who gave a silent laugh.

Jane snickered. "Boys. So, Erin, tell me about yourself."

Jane ferreted all of Erin's history in between pastries from Sofa's —only the best bakery in all of Seattle, according to Jane— brioche French toast, and spinach and mushroom omelets. The conversation stalled when Jane left to get coffee and asked Smith, not Evan, to help her.

As soon as the pair left, Evan nodded for Erin to follow him out onto the back veranda overlooking Puget Sound. The sun glittered off the deep blue waves, ripples of wind pushing the dark caps and light-colored sail boats in the distance.

"Oh my gosh. This is beautiful!"

"I know." Evan sighed. "I'm so happy Mom is marrying a guy who can take care of her. We're not big money people. I mean, I'm a CPA, and I've worked with big money. Mom was in middle management in business. She had some money when Dad left, but not like this."

Erin hugged herself against the cold and blinked in surprise when Evan wrapped a blanket around her. "Thanks."

Then he took one from the outdoor closet for himself and smiled. "No problem."

"Does this ever make you nervous?"

"Why should it? It's just money."

"Maybe to you. It's overwhelming, I have to say."

Evan studied her.

"What?"

"I heard nice things about you from Reid, Cash, and Naomi." He nodded. "I'm glad Smith has found someone special. He's so much more than what people see."

"I know." She looked inside through the glass doors to see him drying dishes with Jane and laughing at something she said.

"He smiles now. Laughs too. He was so angry when I first met him."

"He's still angry," she said. "But I think he sees that he can be happy if he lets himself."

Evan nodded. "I do our accounting at Vets on the Go! But when Cash broke his arm, I filled in for him. They paired me with Smith a lot."

"I'm sorry."

He laughed. "Yeah, at first, so was I. But as I got to know him, to see beneath all the digs at Reid and Cash, the obnoxious comments to anyone who tried to, God forbid, be nice to him, I saw a pretty decent guy."

"He's a sweetie, but he'd rather die than admit it."

"Yep." They watched his mother snap her towel at Smith, who dodged and grinned. He saw Evan watching, and frowned. "The best Smith story, that just shows you who he really is, is the tea party story."

"I have to hear this."

Evan smiled, and she had to admit he had the looks and charisma that all the Griffiths seemed to possess. "We were moving this rich family, and they had a ton of stuff. So, I'm working, and I happen to go by the little girl's bedroom. And there, at the tiniest table known to man, sits Smith drinking pretend tea with the girl and her stuffed gorilla. It was so surreal."

She could easily see that scene happening.

"Then I overhear the sweetest conversation. She's sad because her parents are getting a divorce, and he's telling her it's never a kid's fault, that sometimes grownups have problems. I can't remember exactly what he said, but it really touched me. He was swinging her around and making her laugh when he saw me watching and turned beet-red. That's when I knew Smith was quality people."

She sighed, watching him through the glass, his image in no way distorted by anything she'd seen or heard. "Yeah, he's the best."

"He's also a major pain and refuses to see that he's worth more than he thinks he is. Keep that in mind when he pushes you away. Because if he hasn't yet, he will." Evan paused. "He never stopped watching you today. Even when he was talking to me and my mom, he had you in his sights. He's into you, Erin. I don't know how much, but take care with him. He's a lot more fragile than his big mouth would have you believe.

She had to laugh at that. They turned and watched a few boats in the water before Smith came to save his girlfriend from his lazy-ass cousin.

Evan tossed him his blanket before joining his mom for after-brunch coffee.

"We'll be right in," Smith called. "Okay, what did lover boy have to say about me? Did he warn you off?" His teasing couldn't cover his unease.

To cover how much she felt for Smith, Erin socked him in the arm.

"Ow. You may be tiny, but you're fierce."

"Hush, you. That's for teasing me about moving in with you."

He rubbed his arm and drew her inside with him, but along the way he whispered, "Who said I was teasing?"

THE RIDE HOME PASSED IN SILENCE, BUT NOT BECAUSE SMITH HAD

fallen asleep. Far from it. After telling Erin he'd been serious about her moving in, he waited for them to discuss it. Only she hadn't, and he didn't know what to think.

Brunch had been magical. Aunt Jane was all the moms and aunts and grandmas he'd always dreamed of having wrapped up in a caring woman who genuinely wanted him to visit whenever he could. Like, she *meant* that shit. Evan had been his typical self: charming, funny, and damned nice.

Smith had to admit he liked the guy, and he'd promised to bring Erin to meet Kenzie and Daniel at some future date, though he hadn't committed to anything specific. Not unless Erin confirmed it.

She'd been a little too quiet since being outside with Evan, and it freaked him out. Was it all too much? Had Evan dissed him without him knowing it? Did she see how much he didn't fit in with the Griffiths and now pitied him with no way out?

By the time they parked, he felt ready to come out of his skin.

They went upstairs to his apartment, and at least she seemed okay with that, because she followed him inside.

"Okay," he burst out, "What the hell?"

She frowned. "What?"

"Why are you mad at me?"

She gaped. "I'm not mad."

He started pacing, his nerves shot to hell. Today had been about sharing something good with her, but he felt as if he'd done something wrong. "Then why have you been giving me the silent treatment the whole way home?"

"Me? I thought that was all you."

"Huh?"

She poked him in the chest, and for some reason that turned him way on. "I have been wanting to talk to you all day about this living together thing, but you say nothing. Are you serious about me—I mean, serious about me moving in—or not?"

Smith had been through enough. He couldn't take their distance any longer. He knew one thing he was damn good at. One thing he couldn't screw up. So he kissed her, and he showed her exactly how much he wanted her. He stripped her naked in moments, his mouth and hands never stopping. He had her against the back of the couch and knelt between her legs, his mouth over her before she could do more than cry out his name.

He ate her up, licking and sucking her into a wild orgasm that tore his name from her lips.

Then he turned her around, a fantasy come to life, and unzipped his jeans. "Bend forward," he ordered and didn't recognize the grit in his voice. He took himself out, so sensitive, so hard, and spread her legs wider as she bent over the back of the couch, almost off her tiptoes due to the height.

He took himself in hand and angled at her entrance, so hot and slick. He shoved home, over and over, thrusting in tune to her cries for more. He couldn't stop, so fucking in love with the woman that where he ended and she began blurred.

His orgasm took him by complete surprise, the rush of ecstasy both numbing and exhausting and over too fast.

He stood behind her, shivering as he released, small shocks of bliss still pumping through his blood.

"Cupcake, you good?" he asked, feeling as if he'd run a marathon.

She held a thumbs up then flopped back over the cushions.

He stayed there a moment, feeling better than he'd ever thought possible. He'd been a part of something today, of a family, and he'd been treated just like everyone else.

With Erin by his side.

She made it seem right. Normal. As if he'd always belonged.

She *had* to move in with him.

He withdrew and carried her in his arms to the bedroom where he gently cleaned her up, more than satisfied to have left part of him inside her. Thoughts of a baby jolted him into a new reality, the idea he could have a wife and family, someone he loved and who loved him, possible.

Then he told himself not to get too excited because the blasted woman still hadn't committed to moving in with him.

After he'd cleaned up and stripped naked, he joined her on the bed. "Well?"

"Definitely a 10," she mumbled. "Man, that was wild. You wore me out, Mr. Mad. Are you still mad? I hope not. Because if that's how you make love when you're angry, I'm always gonna wanna fight." She sounded sleepy and satisfied.

He grinned and pulled her hair from her face so he could see her. "That wasn't making love, Erin. That was some hard fucking. Making love involves a lot more kissing and touching."

She hissed a breath when he took her nipple in his mouth and did just that.

"*Oh.*" She clutched his head to her chest. "Did you mean it about moving in with you?"

He pulled back to stare down at her, totally in love with Erin Briggs and her bright eyes and wide smile.

"I totally meant it."

"Can I tell you yes tomorrow, so my answer isn't clouded by great sex?"

His heart thundered, his feelings so fucking joyful he could barely contain himself. But he tried to act casual about it. "Oh, uh, sure." Smith cleared his throat. "So, do you want me to go down on you again? Or you want some straight up missionary?"

Her eyes widened. "Again? Right now?"

"When I get my second wind."

"Oh good. I need a tiny break." She laid the back of her forearm over her eyes. "But I won't stop you from nibbling on the rest of me to wake me up. Then we should do sixty-nine, because I haven't tried that yet."

Now he was the one looking stunned. "You can't be serious."

"Hey. We aren't all as experienced as Big Dick Ramsey."

He laughed so hard he cried. "Can I use that name with the guys? I love it."

"Shut up."

"Sixty-nine is a sacred number." He grinned. "Oh, Cupcake. You have so much to learn…"

Erin wondered if she'd made a mistake. If her nights continued like the past one, she might just turn bowlegged. In the morning, she gave Smith her tentative yes, and he swung her around until she grew dizzy.

But at least she knew he did in fact want her to stay.

The next few days passed in a blur. She would drop Smith at work in the morning, then cook for Tilly and Tilly's helper, after which she'd take the food to Rupert's. She edited her agricultural magazine articles during the day and filmed her cooking show at night at Tilly's, threatening Smith on pain of death to keep away.

But after editing her video, she'd decided to try another angle and asked him to film her making an assortment of Halloween treats she intended to share at the next night's Hall-o-ween.

He kept making her laugh until she smeared her mouth with chocolate and kissed him.

The only time she'd ever seen him cringe when kissing her.

After the segment, he congratulated her. "Wow. That was totally cool. It felt like I was on the set of a real televised cooking show." He nodded to the tripod she normally used when filming with her phone. Then he shot her a sly look. "Ever filmed yourself having sex?"

"No. Just no." She grabbed her phone and hugged it to her chest. "With my luck, I'd accidentally share it on YouTube, or worse, my parents would see it." She cringed.

"Okay, but you don't know what you're missing."

She paused. "You have?"

"In my wilder, younger days." He laughed.

He seemed like a different man since she'd moved in, though the actual moving in hadn't exactly happened yet. She spent her days and nights at his place while keeping all her things in the efficiency. He hadn't pressed her about it, and she hadn't mentioned it, but she liked having a cushion with her name on the lease. The fear that what had happened with Cody could happen with Smith refused to leave her mind. Not that Smith might cheat on her, but that something might happen between them making it impossible to live with him.

Unfortunately, talking to Smith about her fears caused him to clam up and grow defensive. She understood his lack of communication skills, but it didn't make it easy to talk to him about their future. And then she worried she'd once again jumped too fast too far for a man. But then he'd look at her like he loved her, and she'd forget about her worries and do her best to stay in the now, enjoying him.

Halloween came and went, and with it an amazing time at the McCallisters'. Smith kept his arm around her in a not so subtle attempt to let Brad and a few other singles know she was taken. But it didn't bother her either, because she didn't like the way some of the women looked at him, as if he were still available.

They laughed about it after, but she saw worry in his eyes. No matter how much she tried to convince him they were fine, he seemed on edge. And she still hadn't given up her key to next door.

TWO DAYS AFTER HALLOWEEN, ERIN RECEIVED AN INVITATION TO cocktails with Naomi, Jordan, Kenzie, and Aunt Jane. A little uneasy about being one of the Griffith girls, though technically Smith wasn't a Griffith, she nevertheless went out for drinks.

And accidentally got hammered. Much of the night remained a mystery, though she did recall a male review club and a bunch of ones Jordan had forced on her disappearing down a man's G-string.

"Hey there, big tipper." Smith's loud voice cut through her Sunday morning regret.

"Oh, my head."

"I hear you slipped on a few buttery nipples. That right?"

"Ugh. I had four drinks. Four."

"At the first club," he muttered, sounding amused.

She blinked open one eye and saw him looming over her, as he normally did.

"Whoa. You're a little scary hungover." He pulled her into a sitting position and sat watching her.

"I'm not a doll, you know."

He sighed. "Yeah, we haven't gotten to the doll fantasy yet, where you let me position you and you don't move."

"Don't move?"

"Like a doll. Then I have my wicked way with you."

She glared at him, or tried to glare past the tiny hammers intent on killing all her brain cells. "Stop looking so cute and hopeful." She rolled out of his bed and would have stumbled to the door if he hadn't picked her up and carried her to the bathroom. "Thanks," she muttered and slammed the door on him.

She took her time in the shower, letting plentiful hot water—

thanks to McSons Plumbing who'd installed an energy efficient new water heater just yesterday—sluice away her pain.

Afterward, she had a case of dry mouth, no appetite, and bad cramps. She'd been expecting her period, so she had supplies. But she didn't feel comfortable talking about it to Smith, and she knew it would come up in conversation. Feeling crabby and miserable, she wanted to go next door and hide for a week.

He saw her, his smile faded. "What's wrong?"

"I don't feel good."

"Aw, honey, you'll feel better soon. Just drink a lot of water."

"You don't know everything. Water won't help." Actually, it would. But so would a Midol.

"O-kay." Smith paused by the stove. "Want me to make you something to eat?"

"Noooo." She felt nauseous at the thought. She was never, ever, going to try to outdrink Aunt Jane again.

"You mind if I make something?"

"Go head," she mumbled into her arms and dozed off.

She woke to him placing her on the couch with a blanket over her. And it made her think of home, her mother, and her beloved Grandma Freddy.

Cramps twisted her insides. Her mother would have found her a hot water bottle and placed it on her stomach while rubbing her head.

She sniffed, suddenly so very homesick. She really needed for Smith to not see her like this. She hated being weepy, and he'd already seen her lose it when Cody had dumped her. Erin needed to get back to her apartment, but she didn't want to leave him. God, she hated feeling so emotional!

"Erin?" Smith stroked her hair.

She turned into his hands and cried. "I need to go home." *Back to my apartment,* she meant. But saying "home" confused her, because she'd started to think of belonging with Smith. He was home, safety, love. Yet it hadn't been that long ago that Kansas and the apartment next door had been home. Was she moving too fast? Making a mistake? Then why did she imagine Smith and feel so in love?

What a confusing mess. She cried some more, thought she heard the door close, but her head hurt too much to care. She'd nap away her headache and deal with life—and Smith—much later.

CHAPTER NINETEEN

*S*mith couldn't bring himself to talk to her. Two days after her pathetic crying jag, he felt like shit. He barked at the team, moved like an automaton, and dithered over whether to let her come to him or to demand they talk this out.

He hated talking. Talking lead to misunderstandings and bad news and dismay. But having her spend her time at her place or at Tilly's *hurt.*

He sat on his lunch break, rubbing his heart, his appetite gone. The temperature had chilled, freezing rains sweeping through, so instead of eating outside, he, Heidi, Cash, and Hector had driven to a nearby strip mall to grab some chow.

Inside the fast food place, he stared at the wrapped sub with no desire to eat. But to get everyone off his back, he pretended.

The great pretender, Smith Ramsey.

He didn't understand what was wrong with him. Smith was no pussy. He could take a breakup and move on with his life. But the idea Erin was done with him didn't register in his brain. Being without her, for even a few days, didn't work.

He didn't like her distance, and he liked even less that she didn't want to talk to him.

I want to go home, she'd said. What? Home like Kansas or home like next door? So far it had been next door. His knee bobbed, his frustration and anxiety building.

What the hell had those women said to get her so riled up? One night out with the girls, what should have been a fun excursion where she finally made new friends, had turned into a nightmare for him.

He'd tried asking Jordan what the fuck had happened, but she seemed as much in the dark as he was. He would have asked Reid and Evan to ask their ladies, but he didn't like everyone knowing his business. Or that he'd fucked up and had no idea how to right it.

The simple answer would be to ask Erin what was wrong. Except her possible answer, ending their relationship, terrified him.

He grabbed his sandwich when he saw Heidi outside, waving at him to come back. His phone rang, and he answered automatically, in case it might be Erin.

"You'd better be coming to help me," Margaret Ramsey insisted, every inch the ice queen. "Because you can bet your ass I'll burn this letter and any shot you ever have to get to know your father if you don't. I have to b e out of here by next week, and I'm done waiting on you. Be here Saturday, one o'clock. Or don't bother coming." She texted him the address.

"Fuck." He swore some more, ignoring the glares from several mothers with smaller children and stormed from the store, now feeling like a cretin for burning tiny ears.

"Yo, let's go," Cash nodded to his SUV. He'd been giving Smith a ride the past few days. Thankfully, Cash hadn't asked any questions about Erin or why Smith might be needing help to get to work.

Smith entered the vehicle and slammed the door behind him, then put his head back and tried to tune out everything. Inside he was dying, and he was so stupid for thinking he might have a future with a woman who meant everything to him.

"So, you and Erin," Cash said slowly. "Not working out?"

"Fuck off." He seethed.

"What happened?"

"Who the hell knows?"

They drove for a while, until Smith realized it wasn't back to the job. "Where are we going?"

Cash didn't answer, and Smith didn't feel like playing twenty questions, so he remained silent. They arrived at a large warehouse. A huge guy with a flat top stood at the back door in jeans and an olive drab sweatshirt. He didn't look military or on the up and up despite the military haircut.

Cash left his vehicle, and Smith joined him because he had nothing better to do.

He watched Cash and the big dude bro-hug. Money exchanged hands. "Thanks, Ritter. I owe you."

"Nah. This'll do. And I was never here, right?"

Cash nodded. He looked at Smith, locked the SUV with his

remote, and scowled. "Come on, fuckhead." He entered the warehouse without looking back.

Smith had had enough. "Who are you calling a fuckhead, asshole?" He followed Cash inside and stopped. The place looked deserted but for the small boxing ring off to the side, highlighted by long florescent lights overhead. Around the place, small cocktail tables gave the place a club feel, and a lot of paper stubs littered the ground.

"Let's go. You and me." Cash was putting on headgear and taping his hands. Then he took out a small plastic mouthguard from a sealed baggie by the equipment rack before fitting his hands into boxing gloves.

"Seriously? I'll hurt you. Then Jordan will be mad at me." And Reid and Evan and Aunt Jane... Or had the sweet older woman been faking the whole time at her house? Had she been the one to warn Erin off?

"Let's go," Cash said, muffled through the mouthguard. "Your piss-poor attitude is on my last nerve."

"Yeah? So's your sense of superiority," Smith sneered. "You no-neck motherfucker."

"Oh, words hurt. Boo hoo." Cash smirked at him.

Smith put the headgear on but didn't bother with tape. He put to use the mouthguard and gloves though.

Then he stepped into the ring and let loose his fury.

He wasn't too proud to say he'd beaten the shit out of Cash. But then, Cash hadn't hit him back much. He'd been blocking a lot, but the guy could have pounded Smith and hadn't.

Sometime later, Smith and Cash lay on their backs on the mat, panting as they tried to catch their breath.

Cash spit the mouthguard out into his glove. "You done yet?"

Smith did the same. "Maybe." To his surprise, he felt somewhat better. The rage had passed. Now he just felt grief. He took off the headgear and gloves and closed his eyes.

So, he wasn't prepared when Cash slugged him in the stomach. As he rolled to his side and wheezed, he heard Cash sigh. "Yeah, cheap shot. Whatever. I let you pound on me for fifteen minutes. You have some anger issue, bro."

"Fuck...off," Smith said in between painful breaths. *Shit, that hurt.*

"So, Erin dumped you. Life goes on. Man up. Just tell her you're sorry."

He leaned up on an arm and glowered. "Sorry for what?" he rasped. "I have no idea what I did. She just won't talk to me, says she wants to go home." His eyes watered, and he blamed the punch. At least she had a home to go back to. Without her, he had nothing.

"That's it?" Cash scratched his head. "Huh. Jordan told me you were being all pissy and bugging her about Erin."

"Bugging her?" Smith snorted. "I asked her one goddamn question about what happened Saturday night."

"And she had no clue. She told me Erin was happy and in love with you. Etcetera, etcetera."

"Yeah, sure." He wished. "And it's not just her." He hadn't meant to talk about it, but keeping everything to himself no longer helped. Instead he felt burdened, needing to share with his brothers. And that just sucked, because who knew how long they'd want him around.

"What else is there?"

"Never mind."

"No, tell me. You don't think I'll care? Is that it? Well, idiot, I care, okay? You're like a less mature, rougher sketch of me. And I feel sorry for you."

"Fuck. Off." Smith had no trouble saying that.

"What I mean is, when I lose it, Reid helps me. And man, I used to lose it all the time. How do you think I knew about this place? Ritter once took me here where I fought for fun. And, well, for money. But don't tell Reid. They closed the place down over a year ago… Anyway, that's not important. What's the deal? I got nothing but time, hero, so talk."

Smith rolled to sit up and rubbed his tender stomach. "You really want to know?"

"I just said so, didn't I?" Cash barked.

And Smith saw himself in a few years, older, more sarcastic, and hopefully less angry. "Margaret Ramsey is blackmailing me."

Cash's eyes widened. "Okay, *that* I hadn't expected."

"She has a letter Allen Smith left for me. Yeah, our dad."

"No shit. Wait. What's with the blackmail?"

"She wants me to do something for her, or she won't give me the letter. For all I know, it doesn't exist."

"But you have to find out."

"Do I?" Smith felt so tired. "Who gives a fuck? Angela didn't want me. Meg didn't either. And I never once heard from Allen. So who cares?"

"But you'll always want to know."

"Yes, no. I don't care about much of anything right now." *God, I won't cry. Not in front of him.*

"Oh, enough of *this.*" Cash stood over him, his hands on his hips. "What exactly did Erin say that put you in this funk? Did she or didn't she break up with you?"

"I don't know."

Cash stared at him, his mouth open. "How can you not know? Are you telling me she's pissed off, you have no idea why, and that's why you've been moping around like you just found out Old Yeller dies in the end?"

"Thanks, Spoiler Alert. I'm guessing that's the only book you ever finished so you just had to share."

Cash gave him the finger. "You are so very, very sad. Pathetic. Talk to Erin and find out what's wrong. You can't fix it if you don't know where to start."

"I know that," Smith snapped. "I asked her to move in with me. And she said yes. But she won't move all her stuff in, and I know it's only a matter of time before she leaves." God, he didn't want to think it, but he knew it was coming. Had known all along. "Why would she stay? None of them stay." *I'm such a loser.*

He heard his mother—Meg—telling him the same thing in so many ways over the years. The kids who didn't come to his party and never invited him to theirs. The girls who never called him back. Who used him until he'd learned they only took and took and never gave. His mothers, who had thrown him away.

Yet he still hadn't learned, thinking that giving Meg money and coming back to see her once he got of the service would make a difference. "I'm so stupid." A big ball of self-hate stuck in his throat, and he choked on it.

"You are a moron. I don't know if I'd say stupid…"

Smith rose and charged, knocking Cash to the ground. He started whaling on the guy, out of control and uncaring of anything but getting back the blessed numbness of his life. He felt himself get hit multiple times, but the pain didn't matter. And then he felt Cash's arm around his neck.

"Jesus, pass out, asshole. Before you kill me," Cash croaked.

And he knew nothing more.

When Smith woke up, he was lying in a bed in a strange room, his arms and legs tied to the frame's posts. He knew he should care, but he didn't.

"Yo, he's awake."

Cold water splashed in his face, making him gasp. "There you are, sunshine." Reid sounded happy but looked like he wanted to chew nails. "Wake the fuck up."

"R-Reid?"

"That's right."

Cash and Evan stepped into the room.

Smith opened his left eye wider, but his right eye remained sore, so he left it closed. "You look like shit," he rasped to Cash, who sported bruises and limped when he moved.

"You're already on my list, don't add to it."

Evan shook his head. "What is wrong with this family?"

Smith laughed, and not in amusement. "What family?"

"Okay, this self-pity crap? It's done. You're done." Reid threw another glass of water at Smith.

Coughing, Smith shook his head to get rid of the water. "Great. I'm fired. Oo-rah."

"See? I told you. He's a mini-me." Cash sighed. "Smith, you're a huge pain in the ass."

Evan muttered, "Pot calling kettle. Hello."

"I heard that." Cash blew out a breath. "So, we have a couple things to get through. First, the Allen business. You might not want the info, but I do."

"He—"

"Is a piece of our history. So, we're gonna go see what the bitch wants and shut her up. Okay? Then you never have to see her again. You do that for me, I'll fix Erin for you."

"It's too late." Hell, he didn't even know what he was saying.

Evan shook his head. "You are so ridiculous I can't even... Let me recap this for you. Erin is hungover and says she wants to go home. Instead of having a mature conversation and asking her why, you don't talk to her and act like the world is ending for two. Whole. Days."

The rage that he'd thought had gone came back. "What the fuck would you know, with your perfect world and your perfect life?" he spat at Evan. "You have no idea what it's like to have no one."

When Evan would have spoken, Reid grabbed him by the arm and said, "Smith, you have—"

"No one, damn it." The tears and pain welled from deep inside, the hurt so fucking bad. It poured out, a rush of all the badness he'd been born with. "The one person who accepts me almost fucking died." Poor Tilly. She could do so much better than him. "Don't you assholes get it? I am nothing and no one. I have no friends, no mother, no father. No brothers," he said with a sneer, because they didn't know the real him. "You say you want to be close, but you have no idea who I am."

"Who are you?" Cash asked.

"I'm trash. A waste, okay?" he yelled, forced to say it, to finally believe it. Fuck. He almost had Erin, but he'd lost her. Because he'd never really had her. Like all the others. She'd seen and was done. And it hurt. It hurt so much. "I did well in the Corps, you know? Always went first, not afraid to be hurt or die, because it doesn't matter when *you* don't matter. But then it wasn't enough." He remembered thinking that maybe after so much time away, perhaps his mother might have missed him. "I thought if I came home, she'd see me." He laughed, a bitter dry husk of the man he was. "And she did. She saw the real me I never wanted to face."

He looked at them and felt himself crying and had nothing left, not even shame. "I'm a loser, okay? I accept it. Move on."

"Why are you a loser?" Reid asked.

"Are you stupid? She *threw me away*," he roared, so fucking done being trash. "She kept you, asshole. Not me. No one has ever wanted me."

"Erin does," Evan said quietly.

"Shut up. She does not."

"We do," Cash said, and suddenly Smith couldn't look at him, because the humiliation came rushing back, a tidal wave of agony that he'd exposed himself and been found lacking all over again. All this feel-good shit was just pathetic and out of pity.

"Go away."

"Oh my God. This pity party is *ridiculous,*" Evan yelled, surprising them all into silence. Evan didn't yell or argue. Evan got along with everyone.

Reid said slowly, "Evan, I don't think—"

"No, no. *I'm done.*" He leaned right in Smith's face and said in even, distinct words, "The woman who has you drowning in your own tears—and I mean Erin, in case you're confused—has no idea what crawled up your ass and died. You want to know why she wants her space? Because she's on her period."

Smith blinked "What?"

"Yes. She's homesick because apparently when she's feeling bad, her mom would rub her head or stomach or something. And she's too embarrassed to tell you about it, because you always seem to see her when she's a crying mess. You know how I know that, dipshit?"

Reid put a hand on his arm, but Evan yanked it away and poked Smith in the chest. "I. Asked. Her."

Cash blew out a breath. "Oh boy."

Evan wasn't done. "Yes, that's right. I had a fucking conversation with your girlfriend. I went to her apartment and spoke like a mature, civilized person—one in a relationship—might. I didn't mope and moan and make everyone else miserable because I don't know how to have a fucking conversation with a woman!"

"Oh my God. Evan, I want to be you when I grow up!" Cash held up his hand for a high-five.

Evan glared at him. "Shut up." Then he slapped Cash's hand.

Smith didn't understand. "She's not leaving me?"

"Who knows?" Evan shrugged. "She might. She might not. But how the hell would you know? You just assumed when a five-minute conversation would have made this hissy unnecessary."

"But...I don't..." He didn't understand. Everything felt fuzzy, and he started to ache all over.

"It wasn't just Erin, Evan," Reid said quietly. "It's all of if it, isn't it, Smith? Finding out about your mom, our mom, Erin, almost losing Tilly, the mess with Meg over Allen. You've had a rocky few weeks."

"I-I don't know." He closed his eyes. "I feel sick."

"Concussion?" Reid asked, sounding concerned.

"Who the hell knows with this dick?" Cash sighed. "Cut him loose, and we'll take him to the ER. And Evan, no telling Erin about any of this. Our boy needs to grow up, but she doesn't need to see it."

"Um, yeah. Good point," Reid agreed. "Come on. We'll take your SUV, Cash."

"Why mine?"

Evan snorted. "Because Reid and I don't want him puking in ours."

By Thursday, four days after Erin had dealt with the hangover from hell, Erin had no idea what to make of Smith being so distant. She'd needed her space, yes, but he acted as if he couldn't bear to be around her. Perhaps Evan had shared their conversation and made Smith uncomfortable? Heck, she'd embarrassed herself when she'd blurted the truth, but she'd felt comfortable confiding in Evan, for some reason.

She could have found out what bothered Smith but hadn't wanted to intrude.

Oh hell, that was a lie. She *wanted* to intrude, but she'd seen his brothers swing by to get him, and she hadn't wanted to interfere, not when she knew how difficult that relationship was for Smith.

But a girl could only take so much. She'd done a lot of soul searching. She'd even met with Cody again, talking to him bluntly and asking him pointed questions about their relationship.

She'd learned more than she'd imagined.

Yes, Cody had been more to blame than Erin for their failed relationship. But she'd learned what she would give and what she wouldn't in order to have love in her life. She had nothing to prove to anyone here. In Seattle, Erin could become anyone she wanted to be. Shy, daring, quiet, loud. No one had preconceived notions of her, and in a city this size, no one cared what she did, which she found liberating.

She'd talked to her mother, her father, her sister. She'd called friends and talked to them as well. Many of them, Jacinda, Kayla, Anna, were already married and had intriguing insights into things they'd do differently or the same after years with their husbands. But the single ones had an attitude she used to have, that *need* to marry and fit in and have babies. Not Erin. She still wanted to find love. Someday she'd have children.

But for now, she wanted to enjoy being in her mid-twenties, to go after her career. And dang it, to have more of those amazing orgasms and post-sex cuddles. She wanted Smith.

She intended to have him.

She just had to find him first. So she called Jordan and Naomi and even talked to Kenzie, finally triangulating Smith's whereabouts. The avoider was at work and would be returning to his apartment in a few hours. Which gave her enough time to prepare…

WHEN SMITH WALKED INTO HIS APARTMENT TWO AND A HALF hours later, he froze.

Erin waited for him to take a few more steps before sliding behind him to lock the door.

He turned, jumpy as a cat, and blinked at her.

She frowned. "Are those bruises?"

He had a few purple marks on his cheeks and an eye that looked like a bag of skittles had vomited color all over it.

"A few."

"Are you okay?"

He stared at her with an intensity she found unnerving. "Maybe." He looked nervous. "Are you okay?" He glanced at her tummy and she knew Evan had told him about her time of the month. Which fortunately had ended that morning.

Erin flushed. "I'm better now, thanks."

Smith shoved his hands in his pockets, but he moved with a stiffness he didn't normally show.

"You're hurt." She couldn't believe no one had told her. Not that anyone owed her any explanations, but she'd made friends with the girls and, she thought, Evan.

"I got into a fight. I'm not proud of it." He looked embarrassed, and she was dumbfounded.

"I thought you lived to fight."

"Normally." He sighed. "I guess we should sit down and *talk*." He seemed to bite out that last word.

She paused, wanting to read him the riot act for ignoring her but concerned. "Do you need a doctor?"

"No." He gave a sad laugh and carefully sprawled out on the chaise portion of his sectional. "I'm so fucked up it's not funny."

This wasn't going the way she'd thought it might, but as her grandma used to say, in for a penny, in for a pound. "Why have you been avoiding me?"

The million-dollar question.

"Because I'm a pussy."

She sat next to him and frowned. "Not the answer I was looking for."

CHAPTER TWENTY

The guys had told him not to tell her what an idiot—or as Cash had so colorfully called him: fuckhead, cheesedick, absolute moron—he'd been. But Smith didn't like secrets, and he figured Erin had a right to know what she was getting into by being with him.

He forced himself to look at her, taking in her beauty, her selflessness, that fact that just looking at her hurt, because he loved her so damn much.

"I'm not good at relationships." He licked his suddenly dry lips. "Um, could you get me a glass of water?"

She narrowed her eyes. "That depends. Are you breaking up with me?"

"Me?" He didn't know if she was joking or not. "Hell no. But I can see you breaking up with me after I tell you what I tell you."

She didn't look so pleased with him, but she fetched him a glass of water.

"Thanks."

"Talk."

He swallowed half the glass and sighed. "I told you Meg, the woman who raised me, wasn't very nice to me."

"She was horrible. Abusive."

"Yeah, well, she kind of gave me a complex. Like, sometimes I can spiral and think I'm no good, and it affects my relationships."

"O-kay." Erin waited.

"So I, well, I didn't mean to, but—"

"You cheated on me." Erin stood and glared down at him. "Just like Cody. Of all the—"

"I did *not* cheat on you."

"The—the… You didn't?" She sagged back to the couch, looking relieved. "Oh, okay. Sorry. Go on."

He carefully sat up so his feet were on the floor, facing her. "They told me not to tell you. That I would look like a bad bet and you'd run off."

"They have no idea what I will or won't do," Erin said, her spine stiff.

"Yeah, that's what I told them. You do what's right. You're sweet and kind, sexy as hell." He tried not to let the truth hurt. "And you can do so much better than me."

"Uh-huh."

He hadn't expected her to agree with him. "What?"

"I'm listening."

"So, ah, yeah." He ran an unsteady hand through his hair and decided to lay it all on the line. "On Sunday, when you said you needed to go home, I kind of freaked out. I thought you were tired of me. You were nasty, and well…"

"Bitchy."

"I wasn't going to say that," he said quickly, though he'd been thinking it.

"I was hurting and weepy and didn't want you to see me like that again."

"Um, I know that now." He flushed. He'd never discussed a woman's time of the month with her and didn't want to start now. "I wish I'd known then. I'd have tried to help you out. Somehow."

"Oh?"

He shrugged. "I don't know. A massage or something." She wore a sly smile he didn't trust, so he continued, "I got into my head you were done with me, and it crushed me. I had all these bad thoughts, about how I'm a loser and trash and no good." He didn't mean to tear up and tried to hide it, but ever since freaking out with the guys, his emotions had been less than steady. A catharsis long in coming, Evan had said. What the fuck did Evan know?

He blinked hard.

"So you think you're trash, and that I want to date trash?"

"No. Not at all." He hung his head in his hands and subtly wiped his eyes. "I just… I finally found you, someone I care about, who makes me feel so damn good. You're smart and sexy as hell. You could have any guy you wanted. And you wanted me. And we were going to live together, to be together. But you wouldn't move in with me, and it felt like you didn't really want to commit. Then I was still worried about Tilly, because she means more to me than I thought she did. I love her."

Erin smiled. "I love her too." She put a hand on his knee, and he slowly, carefully, lifted her to sit on top of him.

It felt so good to hold her again. He didn't know how long it might last, and he gave her every opportunity to move. But when she didn't, he pulled her in close and pressed his head over her shoulder.

"I love you, Erin." *So much. It will kill me if you leave...*

"WHAT?" ERIN PUSHED BACK SO SHE COULD LOOK INTO HIS EYES, stunned to see them filled with tears. So of course that made hers fill. "No. No, no, no. You don't say it first. *I* say it first."

She wrenched herself out of his arms and started pacing, confused and angry with him for thinking so little of himself. "Okay, this is how it goes."

"You love me?" Hope lightened his eyes, and the bright green seemed to glow with promise.

"Shut up. This is my moment. I've grown. I know what I had with Cody didn't work because he—and I—made mistakes. We talked about it, and—"

"Wait. You talked to Cody?" The old Smith returned, anger pinching his cheeks.

"Yeah, face-to-face. And I had French macarons. Deal with it."

"French what?"

She poked him in the chest, and he winced. "I am growing up. Taking responsibility for my actions. I fell in love with you right away, and I kept trying to convince myself it wasn't real. Why?"

"You love me?" he asked, his voice hoarse.

But she wasn't done. "But who the heck—no, hell—do I owe any explanations? I'm not a lady, I'm a woman. One who wants to have orgasms and live in sin in a one-bedroom apartment making meals for a bossy old woman I love like my grandma. And you. I fell in love with you, a gruff Marine who is so sweet though he tries to hide it. You're strong and sexy and kind, and you hate that anyone figures you out. But I see you."

"Are you sure?"

Suddenly something clicked. She knew why he seemed so unsure. "Yes, Smith Riley Ramsey. I'm sure. I know all your ugly spots, your tickle spots, and I love you. Even though I'm now learning you're pretty neurotic, I *still* love you."

His grin brightened the entire room.

"I had a big night all planned. A fancy dinner, an awesome dessert —not chocolate, by the way—and some hot sex after. But I don't think you can handle that."

"I fought Cash and lost. I was out of it, pretty wacked on adrenaline and emotion. I'm not gonna lie, Erin. I got freaked out for no reason, which Evan was happy to point out," he said drily. "I need some help with communicating. And I'm still messed up from what Meg did to me."

"I wouldn't be with a loser. You remember that."

"I try. But then I think I'm not good enough, and you'll realize that and leave. They all left me, Erin." He sniffed to pull back on the pity party, but a tear left him.

"Stop it," Erin ordered, wiping his eyes, then hers. "I'm a crier by proxy. I see it, I do it."

He couldn't help chuckling. "Sorry."

"You are sorry. Your moms, both of them, sucked ass."

He laughed. "Fighting words."

"Yeah. But I have a great mom. I know how to show love. And you have family now. Brothers, Aunt Jane, who couldn't say enough good stuff about you when we went out, by the way."

"Oh." He flushed.

"Look. I get emotional once a month. It just is. And you and I are new, and this is really our first big argument if you think about it, that's not even an argument. I had no beef with you."

He swallowed, looking too scared to hope. Then Smith shuttered his expression, and the kickass Marine returned. "Well, if you do, I can handle it. Just tell me."

"Have I ever, in the entire time you've known me, ever held back with you? I mean, except for the time of the month thing."

He blinked in astonishment. "Not really."

"Not at all," she said proudly. "With you I've been a hundred percent honest with myself. I wasn't honest with Cody, and I didn't realize it until now. I'm being the real me with you. I want to be a cooking star. I want to have hot sex *and* make love. I want to do sixty-nines and bake you cookies until I find a recipe that has you falling in love with chocolate."

"Ah, not sure that will happen." He held his arms open. "Come here."

She sat on his lap and kissed him, moaning at the perfect connection they shared. "I love you, Smith."

"Love you back, Cupcake." He pressed his forehead to hers, and they both started wiping wet cheeks. "And we never, ever tell anyone about this."

"That you're apparently a closet crier? No. You have an image to maintain." She scooted closer and felt him hard and ready under her bottom. "A big image, am I right?"

He groaned. "And growing bigger. How about we take this into the bedroom, and you be gentle as you take advantage of me?"

"How can I say no to that?"

She said nothing but yes until the sun came up.

On Saturday, Smith knocked at Meg's door as Reid, Cash, Evan, and Erin waited for him. He felt nervous and didn't know why.

Meg opened the door. Staring down at her, he saw the familiar loathing, the disgust. But after talking to Erin and the guys about a lot of shit he'd rather forget, he started to wonder who she felt all that negative energy for. Him...or herself?

"Come on in." She stepped back and shut the door behind him. Her thin face looked thinner, pale and drawn. Her blue eyes, so unhappy, had few lines, because she'd rarely in her life smiled. She wore faded jeans and a blue Marine Corps sweatshirt, one he'd given her many years ago.

He said nothing about it and let no expression cross his face. She studied him hungrily, but he had no idea what she wanted to see.

"What? No kiss for your mother?" she said with a bitter smile.

"I don't have a mother," he responded in kind. "Now where's the letter?"

"You pack up my stuff and move it to this address, and I'll give it to you."

"No. You give me the letter first. I don't trust you. I've been a lot of things in life, but I'm not a liar. I give you my word I'll help you out. And here's the money." A thousand dollars in fifties and twenties he'd withdrawn from the bank. More than he could afford to spare, but he hadn't wanted the others to know about that part. That some pussy-whipped idiot inside him still wanted to help the woman out after all she'd done.

No, not pussy-whipped, her heard Erin's voice deep inside him. *A good, kind, decent man, the one I fell in love with.* Because, as Erin continued to tell him, she was too good to fall in love with a loser. So Smith could never be that. And, well, she had talked him into seeing someone to deal with his self-esteem issues. Though she hadn't had to convince him, not when Evan had practically forced him to see a guy who owed him a few favors. A decent therapist who dealt with vets.

So Smith was on the mend, feeling high with Erin and his new family in his corner.

But Meg had no one.

She took the money, looking surprised he'd brought it. She handed him a thick manila envelope. "He passed away two months ago. But he left this for you right before you got back to the States, actually." She gave him a mean smile. "Too bad he died before you could see him."

"Too bad." He agreed, not happy or sad about the fact. Unlike Cash, Smith had no emotional connection to the man who'd sired them. He knew Cash wanted to think at least Allen had been a decent guy, but Smith knew better.

He opened the sealed envelope and glanced inside to see it contained something from a law firm as well as a personal letter and a photo. So she hadn't made up the letter after all. He'd taken a chance.

"It's real. You can see I never opened it," she snapped.

He nodded. Then he asked what he'd wanted to know for so long. "Why?"

She sneered. "Why? Why what?"

"Why were you so cruel to me? What did I ever do to you?"

"You were born." She looked the way he'd felt when he'd unloaded on Cash and the others. All that toxic emotion came boiling out, and Meg seethed and shouted, her words making a sad kind of sense. "Angela and I fell for the same man—Allen. But he only had eyes for her. She was married. Already had a husband, one who would have married me if Angela hadn't stolen him first.

"She married Charles, and then she stole Allen from me too." Her bitter grief seemed to have frozen her tears, the woman unable to shed them. "She got pregnant with Cash, and I was never sure who the father was. I had no idea she'd carried on her affair with Allen for so long. My husband had died, and Allen and I were in love."

"Why didn't he marry you?"

"Because, you dumb shit, he was married to someone else. Rachel Wilson-Smith, of the hotel magnate Wilsons. He married money, a lot of it. But he loved Angela, was obsessed with her. And she knew it would crush Charles if he knew. So she kept Allen a secret, even from me. But Allen couldn't stay away. We took consolation from each other, each of us mourning lovers we could never have. And then she had you, another mistake."

Once that would have crushed him, but Smith was coming to realize the circumstance of his birth didn't matter.

"She had you here, you know, so Charles and the boys wouldn't find out. I couldn't have a baby, so she gave you to me. A gift." She snorted. "Please. You were hers and his. Not mine. Never mine. And the funny thing is, he never knew. He thought you were his and *mine.*"

Smith had wondered.

"He would visit, help me out with child support in cash, so his wife wouldn't find out. And then he stopped coming. Just stopped, though the checks continued to arrive like clockwork." Her eyes shone. "No more contact with Allen Smith." Meg sighed. "I think maybe he knew you were his and hers. But I could never tell. And your paternity didn't matter in bed. He wanted *me* there, not her. Just me." She no longer sounded angry but dispassionate. Detached from it all.

"Jealousy and infidelity. You should be so proud." Smith shook his head. "The sad thing is, you're all alone now. You have no one."

"I don't need anyone. Never have, never will."

"You know, I feel sorry for you. I never thought I would, but I do."

"Screw you." She looked almost scared.

"I would have loved you and taken care of you. I would have helped you find some peace. We could have found it, together. But you ruined all that." *You almost ruined me.* "I'll move your things for you. I brought a moving van and a team." He paused. "My family. We'll move your things into your new home."

"I'm dying. It's an assisted living facility for the sick. Happy now?"

"Are you?" he asked softly.

Her lips trembled. So bitter. So alone. "I'll be in my room. Move all this, and we're done. I don't want to see you again. Ever."

"You won't," he promised.

It was a somber crew who moved Meg's things. Smith took one last look at her before he left her house, the frail old woman sitting in a rickety chair in her otherwise bare room, staring at a photograph he couldn't make out and didn't want to.

They dropped off her things, setting up her new room with a care he'd have said she didn't deserve. Erin watched him, nodding. Understanding. "This is for you. Not for her."

He did right by Meg at the end. Then he left and didn't look back.

THEY REGROUPED AT CASH'S HOUSE, JOINED BY KENZIE, DANIEL, Naomi, and Jordan. Laughter and music filled the air, the house no longer Angela's but a place full of joy and new beginnings.

Smith and Cash sequestered themselves in a spare room with

some butt-ugly wallpaper full of puke-green vines and tacky little flowers.

Cash saw him looking at it and sighed. "I know. It's a work in progress."

"Good. I thought maybe you liked it this way."

Cash grunted, and while Smith opened the envelope and looked through the handwritten letter, Cash held up his hands. "Well, fucknut? Read it out loud. I'm not a mind reader." Cash gestured to the letter.

Smith took his time, deliberately annoying his older brother.

"I hate you." Cash grinned, not meaning it.

Smith grinned. "Not as much as I hate you, dickbag." Then cleared his throat and read the letter out loud:

Riley,

By the time you read this letter, I'm sure I'll be gone. If I know Meg, she'll make sure we never meet out of spite. And that's okay. Because she's due. If I was more of a man, I'd have searched you out already. Instead, I know what I know of you from your aunt.

I truly loved your mother. I always thought you might be mine, but I could never be sure. And Meg made sure to murky the waters.

She'll tell you things. But you need to know you're so much better than those you come from. I fell in love with Angela the day I met her. Unfortunately, we were both married to other people.

Life is funny sometimes. Your mother didn't want to hurt

Charles. I didn't want to hurt Rachel. No matter what Meg might have told you, it was never about money. Rachel was a gentle soul, and I couldn't bear to hurt her. But my love for Angela—your mother—was so real, so visceral, I couldn't deny it.

The years passed, and we loved from afar. Then she broke it off to make Charles happy.

I was devastated. I used poor Meg, feeling closer to her and her new baby. A child I suspected was my own. And sometimes, I drove by Angela's house and saw her boys, and I wondered...

Riley, I think you have a brother. An older boy named Cash. He's good and strong, and you both look so much like me. You'll know him. But don't disregard Reid either. He's got Angela in him. Not the parts that floated away, but the ones that mattered.

I'm so sorry for all that you've been through. That you never knew the love and belonging you deserved. Be better than me. Don't let weakness stand in the way of true love. Weakness of heart, weakness of character. Because in the end, not being true to yourself hurts you most of all.

I've lived with regret, wishing I could undo the past but doing nothing about it.

And now the lung cancer has taken me. I've killed myself in more ways than one. Be a better man, love with your whole heart, and leave the past in the past.

Know I always loved the thought of you and your brothers as my true family. Like Angela, I lived a fantasy where we lived happily ever after.

I don't have much to leave you, as I can't let Rachel know I strayed. But there are photos of you as children, a secret one we took together, Angela and I, playing pretend.

Leave the past in the past and fly to the future, Son.

And remember, family is what you make of it.

Your father,

Allen

Cash looked out of sorts, frowning and reading the letter over, his hand shaking, so he put the paper down on the bed.

Smith shook out the legal documents, which showed that any tampering with Allen's envelope resulted in Margaret Ramsey forfeiting her rights to the two-thousand-dollar stipend per month she'd been living on. No wonder she'd given him the letter.

He shook his head, feeling glad he'd let her go without malice, without trying to get any kind of revenge. She'd spend the rest of her life alone and unloved, and what could be a better revenge than that? "You get what you give," he murmured.

A peek inside showed an old photograph was all that remained in the envelope, and when he shook it out, he stared in shock.

In the photo, a man who looked like Cash and Smith, wearing older style clothes, stood arm in arm with a beaming Angela Griffith. In front of them, three little boys sat laughing as they played together on a picnic blanket, the verdant green bed of grass beneath them and their short-sleeved shirts hinting at spring or summer weather.

On the back of the photo read *Angela, Allen, Cash, Reid, and Riley. Our happy family.*

Smith took one last look at the envelope and its contents spread over the bed. Then he turned and walked away, leaving the past in the past.

Erin, laughing with the others, saw him return and crossed to kiss him. "Everything okay?"

"Everything's perfect, Cupcake. Because I'm finally looking at my future."

Before he could kiss her again, Cash caught him in a headlock, and the guys piled on.

Erin held up a cup with a smile, and the ladies followed suit while the men wrestled and laughed. "To family."

"To family," they said as one.

And Smith had never felt so free.

THANK YOU FOR READING THE CONCLUSION OF THE VETERAN Movers series! If you haven't read from the beginning, start with Reid and Naomi's story in *The Whole Package*. Keep reading for an excerpt.

"Just get in." When she didn't, Reid glowered. "I can wait all night."

Naomi stared back at him, a little alarmed when he closed the distance between them.

Then he shocked her by pressing her up against the car, full-body contact. The heat of him singed her. Suddenly, instead of feeling annoyed or scared, she wanted him in the worst way. *Whoa, momma.*

Reid ran a finger down her cheek. "I'm not letting you drive home."

His implacable resolve surprised her. "Seriously, Reid. I'm a big girl. I know how to get home without getting mugged."

He didn't move, and she didn't want to think about him pressed so *firmly* against her.

She didn't see herself winning this battle, and though it was ridiculous to think she needed rescuing from herself, she had to admit it felt nice to have someone looking out for her. "If you really need to drive me home, go for it. But you're going to feel stupid tomorrow when all that testosterone in your system wears off." She added in a lower voice, "Won't let me go. Please."

"I'd rather feel stupid than regret not helping you out." He moved back to unlock the car and opened the door for her, then waited for her to settle in. After joining her, he followed her directions home.

Naomi could have been angry about it, but his need to protect softened something inside her. Something she'd need to firm up before dealing with the man again. Reid sat far too close. She could smell alcohol and the faint scent of cologne on him, and it went straight to her head. Hell, maybe she was a little loopy. She really needed to get something to eat.

They arrived at her home in Greenwood, a cute little bungalow she'd refused to sell, even after losing her job with PP&R. She'd worked so hard for her home and had finally gotten the house exactly as she'd wanted it

"You okay?" Reid asked as he parked.

"Yes, fine. You've done your duty. Go home."

"Keys."

Her purse was in his hands before she could grab it back.

"Damn it!"

He had her keys out and had already left the vehicle when she'd thrown open her door, only to have him help her out and up the sidewalk. A domineering yet polite gentleman.

He nodded at the house. "Nice place."

"Thanks," she said, grudgingly, loving the homey two-bedroom Craftsman. Dark purple with white trim and a tidy little porch, the house had plenty of room for her and Rex, should he deign to come home. Probably out catting around like half the men in this town, she thought…cattily.

She snorted. "I suppose you want to come in."

"Just to make sure you're okay."

She rolled her eyes at him, but he ignored her. She heard his car beep, locked up tight, and she glared at him. If he had any intention of staying, she'd disabuse him of that notion right away. She watched him unlock the front door then step back to hold it open for her.

Since Rex didn't greet her right away, she figured he was probably touring the neighborhood. With a little huff, she took the keys from Reid and walked inside. He closed the door behind them while she flicked on a light.

"It's you," he said. "Same blue in here as your office walls."

Huh. He'd noticed. What did that mean? That he had good recall or actually possessed an interest in her? And why did she care?

She nearly tripped again and swore, then kicked off her stupid heels.

"You want some water? I know I'm parched. It's been a long day." Reid stepped past her into her open living room that led by a dining area into her kitchen. She refused to follow him inside and instead massaged her aching toes.

He returned with a glass for her.

"Make yourself at home, why don't you?"

He didn't say anything and handed her the glass. She took a sip and handed it back. "There. Now go home, please. Because of you, I'll have to get someone to take me to my car in the morning." Though if she was feeling industrious, she could walk the short distance to get it herself.

"I'll swing by and pick you up."

His bossy attitude that had somewhat charmed her before now annoyed her. "No, thanks." She watched him drink her water and grew even more steamed. "I'm not some silly little woman needing your help Reid. I'm not drunk or impaired in any way. I'm tired and my feet hurt."

He gave a small smile.

"You find that amusing?"

He set the glass down on a coaster on her side table, and she hated that she couldn't nag him about that either. "You're cute when you're mad."

"And helpless, right?" She felt a little lightheaded, which had nothing to do with exhaustion and everything to do with Reid. Around him, she felt more. Angry, annoyed, aroused. The three As of danger drawing nearer as he smiled at her distress. The bastard.

"Want me to help you, you poor, fragile thing?"

She could do without the smirk. "Yes, please," she said, her voice sugary-sweet, then dragged him closer by the shirtfront, shocking him. "Isn't this what you want? To take advantage of a *helpless* woman?"

"Hell, no." Finally, a bit of his anger. He glared at her. "I'm trying to help you out, here, Naomi. Oh, forget it."

"Oh, so now, because I'm a little aggressive, I'm not good enough for you." She started to lose track of what she was saying, so close to Reid, to that firm chin with a hint of stubble, to that sexy smell of man and cologne, to the sheer breadth of him that seemed much bigger up close. Reid stood inches above her own height, their disparity even greater without her heels.

He tried to pry her hands free but stalled when he looked down into her eyes. "Y-you're mad?" He sounded hoarse, his gaze moving slowly over her face and stilling on her mouth. "Hell," he muttered.

"Yeah, I'm mad. You're a menace, you know that?" Out of control and stirred to an angry passion by the man who refused to know she had her own mind, she yanked him down for an angrier kiss. The touch of his mouth under hers brought everything to a halt. An instant connection turned their burning chemistry into an all-out inferno.

The Whole Package

Don't miss this standalone Valentine's Day romance coming February 4, 2020! Axel Heller and Rena Jackson—will they finally get their happily ever after?

The air grew festive again. Someone plugged the jukebox back in, and the music started. Big J and Earl broke up a fight in the back, and two other bouncers Ray had brought in for the night seemed to be occupied near the corner with someone else.

A large hand wrapped around Rena's arm, and heat filled her from head to toe. She didn't know how she knew, but she could always tell when Axel was close.

In a deep voice, he asked, "Ah, can I talk to you?"

"Sure."

He nodded to the left. "Away from the noise, *bitte*?"

She shrugged, doubting his goodbye would take more than a minute at most. Sadly, she'd given up on Axel as boyfriend material. He had looks, a body she'd had many, *many* naughty dreams about, and a great smile. But she needed a man who could communicate. And that was not him.

"Sure." To the gang now watching her, she said, "I'll be right back." *This won't take long.*

Lara and Hope winked at her. The guys gave Axel the evil eye, though she saw her cousins nodding at him. Oh boy. They'd better not have said anything to encourage him.

She shot them death glares as she let Axel lead her back behind the bar. But he didn't stop there. He continued with her down the hallway into the back supply closet. He turned on the overhead light and closed the door behind them.

"Axel?" Rena might be nervous with another guy in a dark closet, but not Axel. From the first he'd gone out of his way to protect her and all the girls in the bar.

He let go of her arm but didn't back up. "Sorry. I wanted to talk to you without interruption."

"Go ahead."

She swore his cheeks turned pink, which intrigued her. Axel Heller did look like a big old Viking. But like the warriors of old, he had a tan from time spent under the sun. How, she had no idea. Seattle didn't like to let the sun out until closer to April. Axel wasn't pale but a warm, buttery beige. His dirty-blond hair looked like a cascade of tarnished gold, and the beard and mustache he'd grown in the past months made her weak at the knees. She normally liked her men clean-shaven, but he was *rocking* that facial hair.

Her fingers itched to cut his mane back, to better frame the hard planes of his face.

She swallowed loudly, aware her heart thundered. With any luck, he'd mistake her silence as patience and not mesmerized awe.

Axel gave a nervous cough, which made him absolutely adorable. "I am happy for you but sorry to see you go."

"Thanks, Axel." She smiled.

His eyes narrowed on her face, and she felt his intensity like prickles of electricity all up and down her spine. "You have the prettiest smile," he said, his voice deep, quiet.

"Th-thanks." She backed up a step, fighting the absurd impulse to throw herself into his arms and just kiss him already. "Well, I'd better—"

"Do I make you nervous?" He closed the distance between them.

"Nervous?" She gave a *nervous* laugh and wanted to smack herself. "Nah. I'm just… I'd better get back to the party."

"I hear you are going to start dating again."

Stupid J.T. and Del. "So what?"

"So… Maybe you and I could… We could… Well, ah, go out for coffee sometime."

Coffee? Lame. But hey, he was trying. Too little too late. She imagined a year of saying hello over lattes while he tried to find a way to ask to hold her hand. "Axel, I'm just going to be honest with you. I want a real relationship. And I don't think that's with you."

After a pause, he asked, "Why not?"

"Because it's taken you almost a year to ask me out. For coffee."

"*Ja*. I know." His cheeks definitely looked pink. "But I wanted to be good with you. For you to like me and trust me."

"I do like and trust you. But I want a real relationship *now*. Not in another year or two years when you've decided we're good enough friends to try a kiss." She blushed, embarrassed to have to put it out there like that. Then she felt bad for being so blunt. Rena grabbed his hand, all too aware of how much larger he was than her. "Axel, sweetie, I don't mean to hurt your feelings. I just think you and I have two different speeds."

The Kissing Game

ALSO BY MARIE

<u>CONTEMPORARY</u>

WICKED WARRENS

Enjoying the Show

Closing the Deal

Raising the Bar

Making the Grade

Bending the Rules

THE MCCAULEY BROTHERS

The Troublemaker Next Door

How to Handle a Heartbreaker

Ruining Mr. Perfect

What to Do with a Bad Boy

BODY SHOP BAD BOYS

Test Drive

Roadside Assistance

Zero to Sixty

Collision Course

THE DONNIGANS

A Sure Thing

Just the Thing

The Only Thing

*All I Want for Halloween (connected)

THE WORKS

Bodywork

Working Out

Wetwork

VETERANS MOVERS

The Whole Package

Smooth Moves

Handle with Care

Delivered with a Kiss

GOOD TO GO

A Major Attraction

A Major Seduction

A Major Distraction

A Major Connection

BEST REVENGE

Served Cold

Served Hot

Served Sweet

ROMANTIC SUSPENSE

POWERUP!

The Lost Locket

RetroCog

Whispered Words

Fortune's Favor

Flight of Fancy

Silver Tongue

Entranced

Killer Thoughts

WESTLAKE ENTERPRISES

To Hunt a Sainte

Storming His Heart

Love in Electric Blue

PARANORMAL

COUGAR FALLS

Rachel's Totem

In Plain Sight

Foxy Lady

Outfoxed

A Matter of Pride

Right Wolf, Right Time

By the Tail

Prey & Prejudice

ETHEREAL FOES

Dragons' Demon: A Dragon's Dream

Duncan's Descent: A Demon's Desire

Havoc & Hell: A Dragon's Prize

Dragon King: Not So Ordinary

CIRCE'S RECRUITS

Roane

Zack & Ace

Derrick

Hale

DAWN ENDEAVOR

Fallon's Flame

Hayashi's Hero

Julian's Jeopardy

Gunnar's Game

Grayson's Gamble

CIRCE'S RECRUITS 2.0

Gideon

Alex

Elijah

Carter

MARK OF LYCOS

Enemy Red

Wolf Wanted

Jericho Junction

SCIFI

THE INSTINCT

A Civilized Mating

A Barbarian Bonding

A Warrior's Claiming

TALSON TEMPTATIONS

Talon's Wait

Talson's Test

Talson's Net

Talson's Match

LIFE IN THE VRAIL

Lurin's Surrender

Thief of Mardu

Engaging Gren

Seriana Found

CREATIONS

The Perfect Creation

Creation's Control

Creating Chemistry

Caging the Beast

AND MORE (believe it or not)!

ABOUT THE AUTHOR

Caffeine addict, boy referee, and romance aficionado, *New York Times* and *USA Today* bestselling author Marie Harte has over 100 books published with more constantly on the way. She's a confessed bibliophile and devotee of action movies. Whether hiking in Central Oregon, biking around town, or hanging at the local tea shop, she's constantly plotting to give everyone a happily ever after. Visit http://marieharte.com and fall in love.

And to subscribe to Marie's Newsletter, go go her website.

NEWSLETTER